Wreaking Havyk

THE HOUNDS OF ZEUS MC
BOOK 4

BY FAITH GIBSON

Copyright © 2020 by Faith Gibson

Published by: Bramblerose Press LLC

Editor: Candice Royer

First edition: January 2021

Cover design: Jay Aheer, Simply Defined Art

Cover photography: © Wander Aguiar Photography

Cover model: Kaz van der Waard

ISBN: 978-1732864894

DEDICATION

For Nikki. Thank you for everything.

"Now hear another monstrous sight: Beware:
The sharp-beaked hounds of Zeus that never bark"

~ Aeschylus, "Prometheus Bound", 5th century
BC

PROLOGUE

Mercedes

MERCEDES ACCEPTED THE glass of agua fresca her husband poured for her. "*Gracias.*" She removed her plastic sunglasses from atop her head and put them on. She didn't wear expensive shades at the pool since the metal nosepieces tended to get caught in her hair.

"I have business to attend, so I will be away a few days." Juan swirled the ice in his glass before taking a sip. Mercedes turned her head his direction, giving him her full attention. This wasn't anything new. He often went away for days at a time.

"*Te voy a extrañar,*" Mercedes lied with a smile. She never missed him while he was gone. Those were the days she looked forward to most.

Juan reached out his free hand, and she took it. As much as she loathed her husband, Mercedes cherished the moments he was gentle with her because they were few and far between. She hated the man, but she was starved for affection. Blue eyes flashed in her mind, and Mercedes smiled for real. If Juan thought the gesture was for him, all the better.

"*Yo también te voy a extrañar, Papá,*" Mateo said in

1

perfect Spanish. Her son would miss his father, and that hurt Mercedes in ways she tried not to think about too often. The boy loved the man he thought his father was. Then again, Juan had never been anything but wonderful to Mateo. Mercedes didn't understand how one man could have two faces. Be two different types of man. The loving father who sold drugs to other people's children. Did he not care that someone else's child was getting hooked on the product Juan was selling? That he was enabling others to ruin their lives? All so he could live in a lavish home, drive expensive cars, wear thousand-dollar suits? Then she thought back to her own father. The man who raised her had never doted on her the way Juan did Mateo, but never in a million years would Mercedes have thought him capable of being another real-life monster.

"*Y yo te voy a extrañar, Mijo. A ti y a tu Mamá.*"

Mercedes didn't think Juan would truly miss her. Mateo? Yes. But her? Juan didn't spend much time with Mercedes when he was home, so his words didn't ring true. She figured he was paying lip service so their son wouldn't know his papa didn't love his mama.

One of the guards approached, staying several feet away. "Sorry to interrupt, Sir, but there's a phone call for you."

Juan released her hand and stood. His phone calls always took precedence over family time. Juan wrapped his towel around his neck. He ruffled Mateo's hair and told the boy to be good while Juan was gone. Mateo smiled up at his father and promised he would. Without a word to Mercedes, Juan strode into the house with the guard following. Mercedes let out a sigh and leaned her head back, turning it to look at her little boy. Her innocent child who had no idea the world he lived in.

One day, Mijo. One day, I'm taking you away from here so you can live a normal life. One with friends. With family not likely to get you killed someday.

Mateo returned to the pool, and Mercedes enjoyed these moments when it was just her and her son. *And several guards watching them both.* Mercedes did her best to ignore the armed men. After eight years, she should be used to their presence.

Almost an hour had passed when Ana Marie ventured out to the pool. The older woman was more than Mateo's nanny and tutor. She was also Mercedes's only friend in the world. Friend was a stretch because Ana was Juan's employee first.

"Elena is serving lunch in the dining room. If you'd like, I'll take Mateo in and get him dried off."

"That would be perfect. *Gracias,* Ana."

"*De nada.* Come along, Mateo." Ana was like a grandmother to Mateo, and he loved the older woman. Without fuss, he climbed from the pool. Ana wrapped him in his towel, and the two of them made their way inside. Mercedes flipped over onto her stomach. She could enjoy a few moments of solitude before she joined them.

Heavy footsteps sounded on the wooden deck where her chair was situated. Mercedes assumed it was one of the guards. A shadow fell across her body, indicating the person was standing beside her blocking the sun. Hmm. Maybe Juan had come back to tell her goodbye. No one else would come that close. Before she could open her eyes to see who it was, excruciating pain radiated across the back of her head. Mercedes tried to drag in a breath, but even that hurt too badly. Her vision dimmed, and she sank into darkness.

CHAPTER ONE

Hayden

HAYDEN WAS *NOT* hiding out in the paint booth no matter what Kyllian said. Kyllian could suck it. The custom paint job was finished, and Hayden had no reason to be sitting on his ass against the door, but there he was. It was the only place he could be alone. When that door was closed, nobody came in to bother him. If someone needed him, they knew to text. If it was an emergency, they were to call. Otherwise, his time in the booth was his. The jobs he took building bikes outside the MC were high-paying gigs, and the work he did was often meticulous. Like the bike he had to put together and deliver to Texas. Hayden was looking forward to the trip south. Not only would he score a big payday, he would also get to spend time with his older sisters. All six of them.

Between his parents, his four brothers, three mates, and toss in his nieces and nephews, Hayden rarely had a minute to just breathe. Normally, he didn't mind his family, but lately, they'd noticed the change in his behavior, and they were getting worried. They shouldn't be. Hay was just in a funk. He'd get over it. His sisters would see to it. Not Maveryck and Warryck, but his three sets of twin sisters. Hayden hadn't seen his older siblings in several years, and he was looking forward to their brand of smothering. They learned from Rory, but where their mother would try to hug

4

the truth out of him, his sisters just plied Hayden with food and alcohol.

Being around his brothers, each finding their mate, was getting to Hayden. He wanted what they had. A female to come home to at night. One who would ride on the back of his Harley and laugh at his stupid jokes. One who looked at him like he'd hung the moon, yet not expect him to be a hardass biker twenty-four seven. He didn't care if she was a badass in her own right like Natalia or a naïve virgin like Rhiannon. Even someone in the middle like Kerrigan would do. Hayden didn't have a type. Not really. He just wanted someone to love him for him, just the way he was.

Hayden flipped the fan off and opened the door. Thinking of Kyllian must have brought his brother to the club because he was sitting on a stool drinking a beer. "Kayos? What's wrong?"

"Nothing's wrong, dickhead. Can't I visit because I want to?"

"You could, but lately, you don't." Hayden didn't mean to get pissy with his best friend, but lately, Kyllian had been spending all his free time at one BDSM club or another. Hayden didn't think less of him for it, but that wasn't Hay's scene.

"And that right there is why I'm here. I've missed hanging out with you. So, what do you say you get cleaned up, and we go out?"

Now that Hayden was paying attention, Kyllian was dressed nicer than just jeans and boots. Instead of a basic white T-shirt, he had on a maroon button-up with the sleeves rolled up. He wasn't wearing his kutte either.

"I can do that. Where are we going?"

"I was thinking the Rooftop, but if there's somewhere else you'd rather go..."

The Rooftop was a forty-minute drive, but it was one of Hayden's favorite places. It was a two-story club with loud

5

techno music downstairs, but upstairs was more laidback. Then, true to its name, the rooftop bar had a view of the city with soft jazz playing in the background, and the patrons didn't have to yell to be heard.

"I'd like that. Have you eaten? Because I'm starving."

"That's what happens when you hole up in there all night." Kyllian pointed at the door Hayden had just exited. Hayden rolled his eyes, refusing to take the bait.

"Yes, but I finished, so tomorrow I can put the tank on and get the bike ready for delivery."

"I can't wait to see the finished product. It's going to be your best one yet." Kyllian drained his beer and tossed the bottle in the recycling bin.

"I was just thinking that same thing. Not because I did it, but because of the subject." The airbrush design was one of the best he'd ever done, if he did say so himself. The biker who ordered it had requested a rendition of his sister who'd gone missing several years ago at the age of fifteen. Photographs were the hardest to get right, but comparing the artwork on the tank to the picture he had blown up and used as a guide, he'd nailed it. Hayden couldn't imagine what the man was going through. Considering he lived near the Mexican border, Hayden had a feeling the girl had been kidnapped and trafficked.

Hayden had shared the photo with Kyllian when the job first came in. "I took extra time on it because I wanted it to be perfect for the client. I can't imagine losing you or one of the others and never knowing what happened. That shit has to eat away at a person."

"I feel ya. But if that were one of us, we'd tear the world apart looking. Now, come on. Let's get out of here. As to your earlier question, no, I didn't eat. I was waiting on you."

"You want to pick something up to eat and take it to mine, or you want to go somewhere?"

Kyllian rubbed his hand together. "Go somewhere. I

was thinking The Villa."

Hayden grinned. "I should have known. You have on your pasta shirt."

Kyllian frowned. "My fucking what?"

"Your pasta shirt." Hayden flicked his brother's collar. "You wear it every time you eat Italian. I figured it was so the sauce blends in when you inevitably spill it."

Kyllian cuffed Hayden on the back of the head. "Fuck you. I do not."

"Bet. I'll call Rory right now."

"You wanna bet me? Seriously?"

"Fuck yeah, I do. I bet you a new tattoo of my choosing in the location I choose."

"And I bet you a new piercing in the location I fucking choose. Call her."

Hayden pulled out his phone and dialed their mom. "Hey, Baby. Everything okay?" Rory asked when she picked up.

"Hey, Mom. Everything's fine. But I have a question. If I told you Kayos and I were going to eat Italian, what would he be wearing?"

"His maroon button-up."

Hayden cracked up at the same time Kyllian groaned. "I'm never wearing this fucking shirt again."

"Uh oh. Did someone lose a bet?" Rory knew her kids. All eleven of them.

"He sure did." Hayden turned the phone toward his brother and snapped a picture, then sent it to Rory. "Thanks, Mom. Love you."

"I love you both. Enjoy The Villa." Rory's knowing laughter came through the speaker before she disconnected.

"Fuck, are we that predictable?" Kyllian asked, scowling.

"Nah. Well, maybe you are." Hayden jumped out of the way before his brother's fist could connect with Hayden's ribs.

After going home and showering, Hayden dressed in a blue shirt that Lucy said made his eyes pop. Hayden never understood that saying, and when he told her he didn't want it to look like his eyes were popping out of their sockets, his niece had laughed a good three minutes before explaining what it meant. It had been months since he and Kyllian had gone anywhere, and riding the backroads together was like a balm to his soul. He might not have a female to go home to at night, but he had his brother. His best friend. At least for one night.

They didn't look at their menus once they were seated. Dinner was predictable, with Kyllian getting spaghetti with extra meatballs, while Hayden ordered fettuccine with blackened chicken. Neither brother was a big wine drinker, but when they ate at The Villa, they each ordered one glass with dinner. It was something Ryker had taught them when they began training as mercenaries. Their older brother was not only their MC Pres, but he also led the family business. Now that Hayden had joined the fray, all five brothers were trained assassins. Hayden had only been on a few jobs. He had his customizing business to keep him busy, and he could ask top dollar for the work he did. But Hay wanted to help with the mercenary business too. It was what his family did outside of taking down The Ministry – the cult responsible for the apocalypse some thirty years ago.

Ryker tried to talk Hayden out of joining his brothers taking merc work, but Hayden needed to be included. Maybe it was because he was the baby of the family. He'd always looked up to his father and older brothers, and he wanted to be like them from a young age. Ryker finally relented and trained Hayden. In doing so, he taught Hayden how to blend in with any group of people. Part of being a good assassin was studying the mark. Getting close enough to whomever he was supposed to kill without getting caught. Not always looking like a roughneck biker. Little things like knowing which wine to order with dinner. What makeup to use to cover the tattoos when he needed to look like every other male in the room. When a suit and tie was appropriate instead of his normal jeans and a tee. Hell, Hayden even had a couple cardigan sweaters that aided in his boy-next-door persona.

Being Gryphons, they usually took out their marks up close with their claws instead of sitting on a rooftop across the street using a rifle. Hayden learned all about where CCTV cameras were located and how to avoid them. He now knew how to pick locks. He was proud of the work he did customizing bikes and the awards he'd won doing so, but the only time he'd felt prouder of himself was when Ryker gave Hayden his first solo assignment. Building a bike from the floor up was something he was good at, and he felt a sense of accomplishment after each one was handed off. Taking out the scum of the earth? That was a sense of rightness. Being a Gryphon was all about protecting humans, so being a mercenary was a step above being a shifter.

It was after eleven by the time they arrived at The Rooftop. They strolled through the front door after paying the cover charge. The first floor was already filled with bodies dancing and grinding. Kyllian led the way, and even with the tight crowd, people parted like the Red Sea, moving out of his brother's way. Now that Ryker had found love with Rhiannon, Kyllian had taken over the roll as broodiest brother. He was like a chameleon, though. Kyllian had always been serious, but he could change his visage to be whatever he needed in the moment. In that moment, he needed to be a bull, charging through the throngs of dancers and partiers to make it unscathed to the stairway.

If Hayden had been alone, he would have stopped to speak to every female who tried to get their attention no matter how much the synthesized music got on his nerves. He would have stopped, not to get into bed with them all, but because he was a nice guy. Too nice most of the time. It was the one thing that had kept Ryker from training him for so long. He had been afraid Hayden didn't have the stomach for "wet work." Hay had no problem ending the life of a criminal. He did take issue with someone being a dick for no good reason. In ignoring the females, Kyllian wasn't being a dick; he just knew Hayden preferred the quieter atmosphere on the roof, and he didn't waste time getting them up there. As soon as they walked out onto the open floor, Hayden was glad his brother had taken lead. Hayden seriously hated techno music.

"You gonna spend some time with the girls while you're in Texas?" Kyllian asked once they had a drink in hand. "The girls" was how Rory referred to their older sisters, even though all six of them were in their eighties with kids and grandkids of their own.

"Yes. There's no way I'd travel so close and not visit them. I made sure to keep my schedule clear for the next couple weeks. Once I've dropped off the bike, I'm going to hang out with all of them for a while. Figure I could use the down time."

"You want some company?" Kyllian didn't have a job other than being a mercenary.

"Don't you have some willing little kitten to tie up and whip, *Master?*" Hayden whispered his question. He was giving his brother grief about his chosen proclivities, but it wasn't anyone else's business what he did in the bedroom. Or dungeon. Hayden had visited a club with his brother once, but it was enough for him to know that wasn't his kink. Hayden didn't really have a kink. The women he'd gone out with lately had expected him to be a hardass just because he was a biker. They expected rough treatment and bad language. That wasn't him. He wasn't Jax Teller from

10

the old biker show *Sons of Anarchy.*

"*Kitten?*" Kyllian's grin was feral. "I have *all* the kittens lined up. But they can wait until I get back. It's all about the anticipation."

"Won't they just ask someone else to...?" Hayden paused, not wanting to offend his brother. "You know."

Kyllian's face softened. "Some will. Those who don't have a contract are allowed to seek out whomever they choose. Those who do have a contract aren't allowed to play with another Dom without permission. With my schedule as it is, I never have a sub sign up for exclusivity. It isn't fair to them. The one I have now will wait until I'm available."

"Is it rude to ask how you got into that lifestyle?" Hayden had been curious since that night he had gone with Kyllian.

"Not as long as you aren't judging, and I know you aren't. I get it; you're curious. The honest answer is I was flipping through some porn, and it caught my attention, if you get my drift. A Dom had his sub tied to a cross and was flogging her. I know a lot of porn is fake, but you can tell the difference between real emotions if you look and listen hard enough. I wanted to be sure it wasn't a fluke, so I searched out more videos of the same nature. I did some online research into the lifestyle, but I knew there was only one way to be certain, and that was to visit a club. I knew, within ten minutes of walking inside, I wanted that connection. There are different types of Doms." Kyllian stopped talking when two females walked over to where he and Hayden were standing.

"My friend and I were wondering if we could buy you two a drink." Both women were pretty, and Hayden had no problem allowing them to buy a drink. But it had been too long since he and Kyllian had spent quality time together.

"Thank you, but we're good here," he responded before Kyllian could.

11

"Maybe some other time," Kyllian added. When the females walked off, he turned back to Hayden. "As I was saying, there are different types of Doms. What they do and what they want out of a scene varies. I went back several times to get a feel for what called to me the most, and then I approached the Dom I felt was closest to who and what I wanted for myself." Kyllian paused to take a sip of his drink.

"How did you know what to do, though? I mean, as Gryphons, we're pretty intuitive, but I can't imagine striking someone with a whip without a shit-ton of practice." Hayden couldn't imagine striking someone even after practicing. It just wasn't in his nature.

"I first became a sub. To know what it was like to be on the receiving end, I gave myself over to a female Domme. Before she taught me about the various tools she used, she taught me about what it meant to take care of someone. That's what being a Dom is all about. It might look like nothing more than whipping or demanding someone to obey, but it's about taking care of someone else's needs." After ordering another round of drinks, Kyllian explained more about the lifestyle, like Sadism, Daddies and littles, and aftercare. Things Hayden would never have believed to be real outside of porn.

"What happens when you find a mate? Are they going to be okay with you having sex with other women?"

Kyllian leaned his back against the rail and crossed his ankles. "Who says I want a mate? My life is perfect. I have the club and our family. I have a job I love, and I have a sub I see every week unless I'm out of town. She recently got out of a long-term relationship where her partner was more of an asshole than Dom. She is busy with her own profession, so the arrangement we have works well for both of us. So, back to my original question. Do you feel like comp—?" Kyllian's phone beeped with an incoming message. After he read it, he clapped Hayden on the shoulder. "Looks like that doesn't matter. Ryker has a job for me." Kyllian downed his drink. "Sorry to cut our night short."

"No problem. I'm planning on getting up early to finish the bike." Hayden knocked back the rest of his whiskey, and the two brothers headed downstairs. When they reached their Harleys, Hayden grabbed Kyllian's arm. "Be safe out there."

"Always. Have fun in Texas, and give the girls my love." Kyllian hugged Hayden tightly before slapping him on the back. They mounted their bikes and rode back to New Troy side-by-side. Kyllian gave Hayden a two-fingered salute when he turned toward his home. Hayden rode the rest of the way deep in thought. His brother's life was perfect, according to him. Kyllian didn't want a mate, and Hayden wanted nothing more.

His three oldest brothers had found their mates. Not once, but twice. Well, Jenna hadn't been Maveryck's true mate, but she did give him the twins. Now, Mav had Natalia and the boys filling his days with love and laughter. So much laughter. Hayden wanted that. He wanted kids to make him laugh at their silly antics. Wanted to watch them find themselves and grow into teens then adults. Whether they be human or Gryphon, he didn't care. He wanted to be surrounded in his own home by those who meant the most to him.

In the next couple weeks, he would be completely surrounded by his sisters, their kids, and grandkids. It would be chaotic, and it would be fun. The perfect environment Hayden needed to keep his mind off things he didn't have.

CHAPTER TWO

Mercedes

MERCEDES PUSHED HER sunglasses to the top of her head when her son ran over to her chaise, dripping cold water on her heated legs. The droplets were as welcome as his bright smile.

"*Mamá, mírame!*"

Mercedes did watch as her five-year-old performed a lopsided cannonball into the swimming pool. When Mateo bobbed to the surface, he was grinning.

"*Salte del agua.*"

Mercedes jumped at the stern voice ordering Mateo out of the pool. Antonia blocked the sun as she stepped closer. Mateo did as commanded and rushed to stand beside Mercedes's chair, putting Mercedes between his little body and his aunt. The woman lived to make Mercedes's life miserable, but only when Juan wasn't home.

"Juan Carlos has guests coming, so you need to go back to your room and keep the brat away from his father's office." Antonia's English was harsh in her Mexican accent. Antonia never referred to Mateo by his name unless Juan was around.

"No problem there." Mercedes preferred to remain in her end of the villa. She and her son were happiest when it was just the two of them. When the other woman didn't

14

make a move to leave, Mercedes asked, "Was there something else you needed?"

Antonia was leering at Mateo, but he was cowered behind Mercedes's back. She didn't know what happened between her son and the woman when they spent the day with Juan while Mercedes was relegated to her suite, but she figured it wasn't good if the boy hid his face whenever Antonia was around.

"*Mocoso lloron,*" Antonia muttered before turning on her heal and returning inside. Mercedes had also been called a sniveling twit when she first arrived at Juan's estate. She'd been a fifteen-year-old girl taken from a decent home where she had a big brother who thought she'd hung the moon, a mother who loved her. A mother who did her best to keep the peace with a father who was absent most days. When her father, Ricardo, was home, he all but ignored Mercedes, remarking how she'd never be more than her looks, just like her mother. Mercedes spent years wondering why her father wasn't like her friends' dads. Wondering why he didn't have a nine-to-five job.

Mercedes had never truly feared her dad until the day she heard him on the phone making a bargain. Trading Mercedes for a debt. It didn't make sense at first, but soon after he hung up, he grabbed Mercedes and told her to get in the car. Her mother had gone to the grocery store, and her brother, Dominic, had been gone from home a while, only coming home every other Sunday for dinner with the family. Mercedes fought her dad, knowing deep in her heart if she got in the car, she'd never see her mom again. In the end, she was no match for a man who was larger and on a mission. Within an hour, her life as she knew it was changed forever. Her father handed her over to Juan Carlos Alvarez, and the man said Ricardo's debt was wiped clean.

Juan Carlos took Mercedes by the arm and dragged her to a waiting vehicle where a large man held open the door.

15

They were barely seated when the SUV began moving, and Mercedes didn't see her father or the other men left behind. That had been eight years ago.

Mercedes helped her son dry off and wrapped the towel around his body. She pulled on her swimsuit cover and slid her feet into a pair of expensive sandals. Even in the privacy of her secluded oasis, Mercedes was expected to look like a million dollars.

"Mamá, tengo hambre." Mateo dropped the towel as soon as they entered their suite and stood in front of Mercedes with his big, brown eyes. His father's eyes. Mateo was a mixture of both Mercedes and his father, but it was the eyes she loved and hated in equal measure. Where Mateo's were expressive and innocent, Juan's were cold and calculating unless he was looking at her or Mateo.

"You're always hungry, *Mijo."* Juan insisted his son learn to speak Spanish, and Mercedes had learned the language along with him. In the privacy of their suite, she made sure her son knew the English equivalent of the Spanish he was taught. Growing up in south Texas, she had known some Spanish words and phrases but not enough to keep up with the rapid-fire conversations between Juan and whomever he was speaking with. It wasn't until she had been with Juan three years that she understood exactly who he was other than her captor-turned-husband – a big-time drug lord. It was then she realized who her father had been. Ricardo had worked for Juan, and when he couldn't pay the money he owed for the drugs he'd been in charge of, he'd offered Mercedes in exchange. Mercedes had been worth four hundred thousand dollars.

Juan had taken Mercedes to his home and kept her hidden for three years. For thirty-six long months, Mercedes had been transformed into someone Juan paraded around in front of his men. She had been schooled in dinner etiquette so she didn't embarrass him. Her clothes went from jeans

16

and T-shirts to tight dresses showing the curves she developed early on. She learned to walk in five-inch heels and how to apply makeup that transformed her from pretty to sultry. Now, eight years later, she could apply her makeup flawlessly in under ten minutes. Mercedes had always had good hair. Long and thick. Nobody had to teach her how to make it look good except when Juan wanted her to wear it up. A messy bun was not what he thought of as a proper updo. Mercedes became a trophy wife – a term she learned in a fashion magazine.

"*Mamá*," Mateo whined.

"I know, *Papi*; you're hungry." Mercedes picked up her son's towel on her way to the desk, then called to the kitchen and asked for their supper to be brought to their room. Mercedes missed cooking. It was something she had shared with her mom. Every night, Gloria would show Mercedes how to fix elaborate dinners, even if it was only the two of them eating. Gloria had taught her how to wash clothes. How to sew on buttons. How to ice a cake with fondant and make flowers to dress it up. Mercedes's heart hurt whenever she allowed herself to remember her mom, which wasn't often. She'd long ago resigned herself to this life of hers. Hers and her son's. If it wasn't for Mateo, she'd have tried to run. Tried to find a way out of her Mexican hell. If Juan caught her, he'd probably kill her, and she refused to leave Mateo without a mother. Without someone to shield him from Juan and Antonia. Without someone to teach him how to be good when everyone else around them was bad.

To anyone on the outside looking in, Mercedes had a charmed life. She had a handsome husband, a beautiful child, and lived in a sprawling villa, which came equipped with a swimming pool and tennis courts. Mercedes loved to swim, but she hated tennis. She had servants taking care of everything. Juan showered her with fine jewelry. Expensive clothes. He pretended to care for her deeply, and Mercedes was pretty sure that was why Antonia hated her. Because she no longer came first in his life. He might bestow lavish gifts on Mercedes, but he didn't allow her to have the one thing she wanted most in the world – to go home. Juan might have received Mercedes in trade, but the man seemed to genuinely care for her as much as a monster was capable of such feelings. At least he pretended to. Maybe he secretly hated her as much as she did him.

Mercedes got Mateo changed into dry clothes before swapping her bikini for one of the hundreds of dresses in her enormous closet. A closet that was larger than her bedroom back home. *Home.* Mercedes couldn't think of the two-story house back in New El Paso without tearing up, so she pushed it out of her mind. Her home was a sprawling estate across the Mexican border in Nuevo Laredo, where her husband kept her hidden from the world. The door opened, and the devil himself strolled in carrying their supper tray.

"Papa!" Mateo ran to his father and hugged him around his legs. Mercedes stood, as she'd been taught, waiting for Juan to acknowledge her. Juan might care for her, but he was gone over his son. Her role as the wife of a drug lord was to be seen, not heard. To bear his child. To be available whenever he wanted sex. To always look perfect. It was not her role to raise their child. That fell to Juan and the tutor. To Antonia. Mercedes hated her husband and his sister, but she never let them see it. She never let on how badly she loathed her life. Had since the day she'd been traded.

Juan placed the tray on the table before picking Mateo up. He carried on a low conversation in Spanish with his child. Mateo giggled, and even though her son's laughter was the best sound in the world, it cut that this monster was the cause of it. Mercedes might open her legs to him willingly because what other choice did she have? But she didn't suffer illusions of the type of man he was. A drug runner. A gun trafficker. A man who had hundreds in his employ who only cared about money. One who didn't care about the teen girl he married and got pregnant on their wedding night, nor the families they destroyed in recruiting young men and women to haul their product. He did care about the small child who had no clue who and what his father was, but it wasn't enough. Mercedes was no longer that scared, sniveling girl, but neither was she someone who could figure out how to escape the man everyone else thought of as a god. A king. Someone to be admired.

Juan placed Mateo in his chair at the dining table, then turned his attention to Mercedes. He cupped her cheek and pressed a kiss to her red lips. *"Tonight, my love. We celebrate."*

Mercedes knew what that meant. The meeting was a big one, and once it concluded, she would be naked in her husband's bed. He would be celebrating, and she would be pretending. She spent the next three hours enjoying time with her son. She was his mother, but she didn't have access to him twenty-four seven. That had taken time to get used to. It had also taken time and lots of bargaining with Juan to be the one who bathed Mateo. Who read him a book before bed. Who sang him to sleep. It was her favorite time of day.

Mercedes had just finished singing Mateo's favorite song when Ana Maria came into the suite. The older woman watched over Mateo whenever Mercedes was required in Juan's presence.

"El esta listo para ti," the older woman said softly.

But I'm not ready for him. Mercedes would never admit that aloud, not even to the woman who'd become a surrogate mother. Ana Maria had been there when Mercedes arrived as a scared teen, providing a modicum of warmth. She was with Mercedes when she gave birth to Mateo, and she was there for the boy when it was Mercedes's time to perform her wifely duties. As much as

19

she doted on Mercedes, Ana Maria was loyal to Juan Carlos for some reason.

Mercedes checked her hair in the bathroom mirror and applied a fresh coat of lipstick to her already stained lips. She slipped into her stilettos before making her way to the other end of the large house. Mercedes ignored the armed men patrolling the halls as her heels clicked on the marble floors with each step she took toward Juan's suite. Although she went to his bed almost every night, she didn't think of his room as theirs. Her clothes were back in the suite she shared with her son.

When she reached the door, she knocked three times and waited for him to answer.

"Pasa, mi pajarito." Juan began calling her "little bird" after hearing her sing to Mateo. Mercedes pushed open the door, then closed it behind her. She didn't bother locking it because no one would dare enter under any circumstance. She strode across the plush carpet as though she were on a catwalk. Prowling was more like it. Mercedes knew what Juan liked. Knew what made him happy. She'd come to the man a virgin, but as soon as he took her to his bed the first time, Juan instructed her on how to please him. Surprisingly, he'd been gentle with her. He'd been patient as she learned to suck his dick without gagging too much. He'd taken his time in pleasing her as well. Mercedes was under no illusion she was the only one he sought for sex, but she never gave him a reason to be displeased with her performance.

Her fake smile came easier these days. Mercedes had plenty of practice, and if Juan didn't believe she was happy, he never let on.

"Come here." He held out his hand, and she went to him. Juan pulled her to him when she was close enough to touch. Threading one hand through her long hair, he pulled. Not hard enough to be painful but enough to let her know his mood. Things were going to be gentle, and for that, she was grateful. "I had a very good meeting. I won't bore you with the details, but let's say I'm moving up in the world." Juan never talked specifics about his drugs or guns. From previous conversations she'd overheard when he didn't know she was listening, Mercedes had figured out her husband wasn't one of the major players in his world. He didn't have one of the largest cartels. Did moving up mean he had taken over one of them? The man was already rich beyond anything she could imagine.

"I'm happy for you." *Liar.* Then again, the larger the cartel, the more he was on the radar of the authorities. Maybe this was a good thing. Maybe he'd piss someone off and... No. If he pissed someone off, things could go sideways. Another leader could take over Juan's business and everything that came with it, including her and Mateo. Better the devil you know, as her mama used to say. Now Mercedes understood. She had once asked her mother why she didn't leave Ricardo, and that would be her answer right after she exclaimed how the church didn't believe in divorce, citing for better or worse. Having grown up Catholic, Mercedes had read the Bible. All of it. Mercedes argued those vows were nowhere in the Bible. She'd even looked them up on the internet back then.

"I have to go away for a while. I'll have more men on the house while I'm gone, so you and Mateo will be safe."

"Are you taking Antonia with you?"

Juan scowled. *Shit.* "I was planning on it. Do you not want her to go?"

"Yes," Mercedes responded too quickly. *Calm down.* "I was just curious. When do you leave?"

"In the morning. I'm not sure how long I'll be gone, but I'm only a phone call away." Juan stepped around Mercedes and pushed her hair to the side so he could get to her zipper. Slowly, he lowered it, trailing his fingers along her skin as he went. Mercedes shivered, and Juan chuckled low. He thought his touch affected her in a good way.

As he did every time they were alone, Juan lowered the dress inch by inch, his fingers skimming her skin. The man was twenty years her senior, but he had the sexual appetite of someone much younger. At least that's what she'd read in one of her magazines. It was the only outside source of information he allowed her. She could watch certain videos but no television where she had access to the news. The only computer in the house was in his office, and she wasn't allowed to go in there. Even when he left the estate, Mercedes didn't dare step foot into her husband's domain. His men were loyal to him, and they would tell him if she were to trespass.

What started out as gentle lovemaking got rougher as the night went on. By the time he allowed her to sleep, her body ached, and she would have bruises from the tight grip he'd kept on her hips. Red marks would cover her breasts and stomach where he bit and sucked. There would be no bikini for her in the next few days. She would never allow her son to see the marks his father left when he was in one of his moods.

When Mercedes woke the next morning, she was alone. Most nights, he sent her back to her room, but he had been in a good mood the night before. The sheets on Juan's side of the bed were cool. It amazed her how hard she slept knowing she shared a bed with a monster. Then again, said monster did keep her up most of the night. Mercedes slipped from the bed and retreated to the bathroom. She turned the water on in the shower as hot as she could stand it. While it heated, she brushed her teeth. Her birth control was back in her bathroom. It surprised her when Juan presented the pills to her after Mateo was born. She figured he would keep her pregnant so he could have many children, but she never questioned it. She was perfectly

22

happy only having one child to worry about. She hated Juan. Hated he was Mateo's father. But she would never resent having her son in her life. He was the only thing that kept her going.

After bathing, Mercedes grabbed one of the more comfortable dresses she kept in his closet for the walk back to her side of the house. The tight red number she had on the night before would be cleaned and returned to her closet. When she reached her suite, Mercedes bristled when she saw who was in her room.

"What are you doing in here?" Mercedes strode to the sofa where her son was eating a pastry while Antonia was sipping coffee next to him.

"Waiting on your lazy ass to wake up." Antonia stood and ruffled Mateo's hair. What the fuck was going on? Antonia was never nice to Mateo.

"Where's Ana Maria?"

"She had work to do, so I offered to sit with the boy."

"I thought you were going with Juan."

"You shouldn't think. It'll tax your brain."

Bitch. "Well, I'm here now, so you can go." Mercedes sat down next to Mateo who was watching the two women like a tennis match.

"Watch yourself, Mercedes. You wouldn't like me when I'm mad."

"I don't like you anyway," Mercedes said before she could catch herself. Antonia's grin was feral.

"Feeling's mutual, *Perra.*" With that, the woman casually strolled to the door. When she opened it, she turned back to Mateo. "Remember what I said."

"What *did* she say?" Mercedes asked her son when the woman closed the door.

Mateo's eyes watered. *"Que ya no debo hablar ingles."*

"Why aren't you supposed to speak English, *Mijo*? And tell me in English."

"Because it makes *Papá* mad."

Mercedes pulled her son onto her lap and hugged him close. "Oh, *Mijo*. Your *papá* adores you. Has he told you not to speak English?" Mateo shook his head. "Then don't worry about it until *he* tells you otherwise, okay?"

Mercedes didn't know how, but one day, she was going to kill that bitch.

CHAPTER THREE

Hayden

HAYDEN TOOK A couple steps back from the bike and smiled. It was the best work he'd ever done, and that was saying something. It wasn't conceit to make him feel that way. The awards he had stashed around the shop and his home were proof he was one of the best in the country. But damn.

"Holy shit."

Hayden turned toward Ryker who had walked into the shop with Spyder behind him. Ryker circled the bike, and Spyder squatted to get a better look at the paint job.

"I second the sentiment, Havyk. This is unbelievable." Spyder stood and held out his hand for a knuckle bump. "It's amazing."

"I'm proud of you, Havyk. If this wasn't a personal job, I'd tell you to enter it in the East Coast show coming up. You'd definitely win top prize." Ryker squeezed Hayden's shoulder, smiling. It was odd seeing his oldest brother without a scowl on his face and more open with his affection.

"Thank you. I don't think the owner is going to ride it, but even if he does, he could enter it himself in the Southwest show. He'd get the win, but my name would be listed as designer. It'd be a win-win." Hayden walked over to the small refrigerator and grabbed a beer. He deserved it after spending all day working. "Beer?" he asked, holding the bottle out.

Both Hounds took one, and Ryker held his out. "Cheers to the best bike builder in the world." Hayden and Spyder clanked their bottles to Ryker's and chugged.

"What brings you two by?" Hayden tossed his empty in the recycle bin before snagging another full bottle.

"Quinn sent a job over, and I wanted to talk to you about it. It's a big hit, down in Mexico, just across the border. I figured since you're going to be down there anyway when you deliver the bike, you might want to take it. But, like I said, it's a big one, and it's going to be a two-man job. That's why Spyder's here."

"So, Spyder's taking lead and I'm backup?"

"No. If you agree, this will be yours, and he'll be providing support."

"You think I'm ready for something of this caliber?"

"Don't you?" Ryker tossed his bottle in the bin, then crossed his arms over his muscled chest.

"I don't even know what the job is, but yeah, I'm ready." Hayden wasn't joking. He had been on enough solos he felt he was ready for something on a larger scale. Especially if Spyder would be there to guide him. That was the nice thing about working with other Hounds. There was no ego involved. No one-upmanship. Spyder would take a secondary role, and he would follow Hayden's lead. If Hayden needed advice, he would ask. He wasn't too cocky to think he had everything figured out when it came to their mercenary work.

"That's what I wanted to hear." Ryker pulled a set of papers out of his back pocket and handed them over. "Spyder's already looked over the contract, so I'll leave the two of you alone to hash out a plan. I know you're planning on visiting the girls while you're in Texas, and I think you should still do so. It'll make a good cover for the two of you being in the area."

"Thanks, Ryot. I won't let you down."

Ryker gave Hayden a side hug. "I know you won't." Ryker bumped Spyder's knuckles as he strode out of the garage.

Hayden looked over the contract, his heart speeding up the more he read. Fuck, this wasn't big – it was fucking huge. For a split second, Hayden wondered if he could pull it off, even with Spyder's help.

We've got this.

Yeah, we do.

His Gryphon was always there, ready to give him a boost when he doubted himself, which wasn't often.

The rumble of a couple bikes had Hayden looking toward the parking lot of the clubhouse. Mayhem and War pulled in and parked. Two little helmets bobbed and weaved as they climbed from their sidecar attached to Maveryck's bike. Marshall waited for his dad, but Major took off running toward Hayden and Spyder.

"Hey, Hay." Major was furiously working the strap of his helmet while trying to navigate around Hayden's toolbox. Spyder was there to intercept the boy so he didn't hurt himself.

Hayden tried not to laugh at his nephew, but the kid was so fucking cute. "Hey, Little Dude. What's shaking?"

"My dang head. Get this thing off me," Major grumbled. Hayden and Spyder burst out laughing, and Spyder unhooked the chin strap. Major jerked the helmet off his head and shook his blond hair. "Thanks, Spiderman."

"You're welcome, Major Tom."

"My name's not Tom."

"And my name's not man." Spyder ruffled Major's hair earning a big grin. Spyder had taken a liking to the twins when they all went camping, and Major was smitten with

27

Spyder and his long hair. The oldest twin was letting his hair grow out instead of keeping it short like Marshall's.

Marshall walked up to Hayden and held out his little fist for a bump. "'Sup, other Little Dude?"

"Daddo said you're leaving. We came to say bye." Marshall was just as cute as his brother, but he was definitely more laidback.

"And we wanted to see the finished bike before you hauled it off to Texas." Maveryck walked up with War, his own twin, in tow.

"Where're your mates?" Hayden rarely saw his brothers without Kerrigan and Natalia.

War crouched beside the tribute bike, studying the artwork. "We dropped them off at Ryker's. They're hanging out with Rhi and Mac today."

"What's Eli doing with a house full of females?" Hayden asked. Elijah, McKenzie's boyfriend, was still getting used to life outside the cult he was rescued from.

"He rode with Pop to talk to a couple boys who were rescued from The Sanctuary. The brothers are having a tough time being on the outside, and Sutton thought Eli could help them." Maveryck leaned against a toolbox with Marshall tucked against his side. "When are you headed out?"

"I'd planned on leaving first thing in the morning." Hayden turned to Spyder. "That okay with you?"

"Yep. As soon as Ryot showed me the contract, I went home and did laundry."

"Contract?" War asked as he stood and joined the rest of the Hounds.

"Yeah. Cartel crossing over from Nuevo Laredo. The leader's expanding, and his new product is the live version," Hayden explained cryptically so the younger twins didn't know he was talking about human trafficking.

"Isn't that a bit above your expertise?" War asked.

Hayden bristled. He knew his brother had his best interest at heart, but it still pissed him off. "No, it's not. This is a two-man job, and Spyder's going with."

Warryck turned to Spyder who held his hand up. "Save it, War. I've got Havyk's back."

"What's wrong with Hay's back?" Major asked. The little boy walked around behind Hayden and looked him over. "I don't see nothin'."

Hay turned around and grabbed Major, picking him up like a sack of potatoes. "It means he's my buddy and will watch out for me."

"Oh. He's got your six. Why didn't he say that?" Major asked, hanging over Hayden's shoulder, slapping Hay's back like he was playing the drums.

"Where'd you learn that?" Hayden asked, setting the boy on his feet.

"From Lollipop when me and Marsh went to the doctor for a shot. I told her I didn't want to get shot at, and she said not to worry. She had my six. The stupid doctor still shot me."

Maveryck rolled his eyes. "The doctor gave you a shot; he didn't shoot you. Big difference, kiddo."

"Nuh uh. It hurt like shiitake."

Hayden and the other Hounds laughed at the boy trying to stay out of trouble. Major was a sponge, and he repeated everything his dad said until Rory threatened to wash his mouth out with soap. Natalia was teaching the boys creative words so they didn't get in trouble.

"Shiitakes are gross. They're squishy and taste like dirt," Marshall said. "I like dirt. Playing in it. Not eating it. Rhi Rhi lets me help her."

Rhiannon, Ryker's mate, was a pagan with a special gift. She was in tune with nature and loved spending her spare time growing all types of plants and herbs.

After Maveryck took his turn gushing over the tribute

bike, he corralled the twins. "All right. We'll get out of your hair. Tell the girls we said hello and we love them." He hugged Hayden, then he and Spyder knocked forearms. The younger twins gave their uncle and Spyder fist bumps and took off out the door like their asses were on fire. Their father and War followed at a slower pace.

"I want one," Spyder muttered, watching the boys go.

"I hear you. Those two are something else. Now, let's sit down and talk about this contract." Hayden was younger and less experienced, and he felt it best to have some type of plan in place before hitting Texas. He and Spyder spent a couple hours going over everything they knew, and they tossed about ideas of things that could potentially go wrong considering who their mark was. It would take quite a bit of recon before they could approach the drug lord. After Spyder left for home and some sleep, Hayden memorized the photos of the mark and the guards he kept with him anytime he left his compound. There was no photo of the wife.

Hayden stopped and picked up Spyder at his home early the next morning so Spyder's bike would be safe in his garage. They left New Troy and headed south, settling in for a long drive. Fifteen hours later, Hayden pulled off a busy exit and navigated to the hotel they were staying in that night. They were at the halfway mark between New Troy and New Victoria. Poppy and Holly, the older twins, lived three hours out from New Laredo where Hayden's customer was. He and Spyder had switched out driving several hours ago, but Hay was still ready to be out of the SUV. As he did every time they stopped, Hayden opened the trailer door and checked on the bike. Spyder didn't give him shit for doing so because he understood what this bike meant to both Hayden and the customer. It wasn't just an investment of time and money; it was in honor of someone Dominic had lost - his younger sister. Being the baby,

30

Hayden didn't know what it was like to love a younger sibling, but he did know how he would feel if he lost any one of his older brothers or sisters in such a traumatic way. Disappearing never to be heard from again.

Spyder had his arms stretched high overhead, twisting at his waist. The pops of his spine cracking were loud in the late night. "I'm hungry." Spyder looked around and pointed across the street to a popular chain restaurant. "If you want to check us in, I'll head over there and grab some grub."

"Sounds good. Just get me a couple double cheeseburgers and a large fry."

Hayden locked the trailer, satisfied the bike hadn't shifted during the drive, grabbed their duffels, then went inside and got their door cards. He texted Spyder the number after letting himself in the room. Since they were just there to sleep a few hours, Hayden hadn't sprung for a suite. They could manage with two double beds for one night.

Spyder knocked, and Hayden let him in. Spyder divvied up the food, and they sat on their beds, leaning against the headboards to eat. Hayden hadn't spent a lot of one-on-one time with the other Hound, but they'd talked quite a bit on the drive down. Jude "Spyder" Sterling wasn't as tall as Hay and his brothers, but he was built. And he had attitude for days. The male was funny, confident, and had plenty of stories to tell, keeping the conversation flowing all day. The male had already lived a full life, even without having found a mate. Hayden had admitted he was ready to settle down and have a few kids.

After they ate, they both settled in for a few hours' sleep. Being Gryphons, they didn't require much, but Hayden liked feeling refreshed. He liked how his mind could settle for a few hours without thinking. Because when he was awake, all he focused on was how lonely he was. It hadn't really hit him until his brothers began finding mates

31

again. The three of them had been lucky early on. Younger than Hayden was now. Hayden prayed that once he found his mate, Zeus allowed her a long life, and Hayden wouldn't endure the same heartache as his brothers.

The next day was the same as the one before with a long drive. By the time they rolled into New Victoria, Hayden was ready to shift into his Eagle and spread his wings. He knew that wasn't a probability, not when he had to deliver the bike, then spend time with his sisters while he and Spyder prepared for the job they were on. The plan was to find their mark and follow him for at least a week. Find out what his schedule was. Who he had surrounding him. Hayden had no problem taking someone out, but there had been two names on the contract. Husband and wife. Hayden had never killed a woman, and he wasn't sure he had it in him to do so now. Not unless he was one hundred percent sure she was as guilty as her husband. If she was? Maybe Spyder could take the female.

Poppy's house was the biggest and had a couple spare rooms where he and Spyder would be staying. He loved all his sisters equally, so he didn't care who they stayed with, but Poppy's made the most sense logistically. When they pulled down the long driveway leading to the Spanish-style structure, Hayden smiled. It had been a while since he'd been to Texas, and he was looking forward to spending time with his sisters, their kids, and *their* kids. And there were a lot of them.

"Damn, this is nice," Spyder said from the passenger seat.

"It is. All the girls have a nice spread, but this is my favorite."

The circular driveway curved around in front of a courtyard where Poppy stood waiting for them alongside her mate, Daniel. Poppy's smile was so much like Rory's, as were most of her other features. With the exception of Ryker

32

and Kyllian taking after Sutton, the rest of the siblings took after their mother with their blonde hair and striking blue eyes.

"If I didn't know better, I'd swear that was Rory." Spyder stared out the windshield at Poppy.

"If they all didn't have different haircuts, you'd probably get really confused. All six twins are the spitting image of our mom. There are subtle differences you'll see when they're all together. The genes are strong, but at least their kids managed to get some of their dads' genes, so you won't have twenty clones you're calling the wrong name."

"Thank Zeus for that."

Poppy was there with open arms as soon as Hay exited the SUV. "Oh, I've missed you," she breathed against his ear. He could hear the smile in her voice, and his heart warmed. Growing up with four older brothers had been great, but Hayden couldn't say he would have minded having his sisters around. The six of them were strong, independent females, the same as Rory, but they were softer and tended to dote on Hayden since he was the baby. He had nieces and nephews older than him. Even some of the grandkids were his age, so he truly felt like the baby of the family. He didn't hate it most of the time.

"Poppy, Daniel, this is Jude Sterling. Spyder, my oldest sister, Poppy and her mate, Daniel." Poppy released Hayden and shook hands with Spyder who had already greeted Daniel.

"It's a pleasure to meet you, Poppy, and please forgive me if I stare. You look so much like Rory, but I should know that since I've already met Holly."

"I'll take that as a compliment. Now, come on in. I figured the two of you would be hungry, so I have a late snack prepared."

"Snack, my ass." Daniel pretended to cough into his hand, but his words were clear. Poppy backhanded his chest, but she was grinning.

After dropping their bags into the rooms they'd be sleeping in, Hayden and Spyder wound their way through the long hallways to the open dining room. All the girls learned their cooking skills from their mom, so by late snack, Poppy meant a big spread of cold fried chicken, shredded smoked pork, and all the side dishes one would imagine being served with both.

Spyder groaned when he saw all the food. "This looks amazing. Thank you."

"You're welcome. I have tea, sodas, and beer in the fridge."

"Tea," Hayden and Spyder said in unison. They both loved the sugary drink, and unless they made it at home or had it at Rory's, they didn't find it up north.

When they were settled around the table with plates overloaded with food, Poppy talked while the two of them ate. She filled Hayden in on all the latest gossip, which Hayden knew most of since Rory tended to share. Spyder asked questions when appropriate, seeming eager to learn more about the Lazlo clan he had yet to meet. Daniel was quiet for the most part, sitting next to his mate with his arm around her shoulder, his fingers brushing her skin. The two of them had been mates for over sixty years, and they were still as in love as they were in the beginning. Hayden wanted that. Wanted to gush over his own kids and grandkids.

When their bellies were full, Poppy told them to go relax with Daniel while she cleaned up the leftovers. As with all the girls, they knew about the mercenary business, but none of them were interested in the details. Daniel, who had served in the military with Sutton and was one of his best friends, was eager to hear more. Being Gryphons and never aging past their forties, the two males had both opted out at the same time before their higher ups got suspicious.

Daniel, like Sutton, was over one hundred, but he had known Poppy was the one for him from early on. The male had been honorable and kept to himself, never even looking at another female until Poppy was old enough to date. Hayden couldn't imagine what that would be like. Didn't want to think about it. He prayed when he found his mate, she would be of legal age and ready for a relationship.

"Tell me about this job," Daniel urged when the three males sat in the living room. Hayden loved the wide-open space in the middle of their home. Whereas the kitchen was where everyone usually gathered at his parents' home, here at his sister's place, the well-used living area had two large sofas facing each other with several oversized chairs between. There was no coffee table. Instead, smaller end tables were nestled between all the seats.

Hayden and Spyder took one of the sofas, and Daniel sat across from them. The male had been in law enforcement for several years after retiring from the military, but when he found out about the Lazlos' mercenary business, he left the police force and opened a private investigation business so there wouldn't be a conflict of interest. He'd seen too many evil men and women slip through the judicial cracks over the years, and he appreciated the work the Lazlo family did. Daniel was a Hound of Zeus in the Gryphon sense, but he wasn't part of the MC. Still, he helped any way he could.

Daniel was aware of the drug lord, but he hadn't heard the man was moving into the human trafficking arena. Having several grandchildren the same ages of those who were being taken lit a fire inside the male, and he offered his services to Hayden and Spyder in whatever capacity they needed him. They spent another hour visiting with Poppy and Daniel before heading upstairs to get some sleep.

Chapter Four

Hayden

AFTER A BIG breakfast, Hayden and Spyder left Poppy's home to meet up with Dominic to deliver the tricked-out Harley. When they pulled into the lot of the Norse Gods MC compound, a large number of bikers were waiting on them. In that moment, Hayden became Havyk, having already adorned his own kutte, showing off the Hounds of Zeus rocker. The Hounds were well-known throughout the country as being one of the largest MCs, and as such, were well-respected. Like the Hounds, the Norse Gods was a club that did good. They were primarily made up of ex-military who wanted to make their little piece of the world a better place and show that not all bikers were gangbangers who passed around women like they were property. It was the main reason Hayden had taken the commission.

Dominic "Iceman" Rodriguez was a tall, imposing Latino. His patch indicated he was the club's VP. Havyk held out his hand, and Iceman gripped his forearm, pulling Havyk to his chest, and slapped him on the back.

"I have to admit I'm a little nervous." Iceman ran a hand through his dark hair, staring at the closed trailer. "I know from your reputation the bike's going to be sick, but..." The male swallowed hard, then shook his head. "Let's see what you did." Havyk expected the man to be emotional when he saw the photo of his sister on the tank, but for him to have this reaction before laying eyes on the bike was telling. Dominic Rodriguez was still reeling from losing his sibling.

Spyder opened the doors to the trailer and locked them in place before lowering the ramp. Havyk unhooked the bike and carefully backed it out until it was on solid ground. The other members of the Norse Gods waited while Iceman inspected it, probably giving him time to get his emotions under control. According to Dominic, the club had chipped in to have the motorcycle commissioned for him. The man squatted next to it and reached out his fingers toward the gas tank, but he pulled them back before actually touching it. A sob escaped, and he clamped his hand over his mouth as tears streaked down his ruddy cheeks. Only then did someone else move in, and Havyk glanced at the patch on the man's kutte. Kodiak was the president of the club, and his name fit the bear of a man who knelt beside his second-in-command.

"Fuck, Brother. It's like looking at her," Kodiak whispered. He glanced up at Havyk, tears threatening his own eyes. "That's..." He shook his head. "Talented doesn't do you justice, Havyk. That right there is beyond anything we ever imagined. Thank you." Kodiak put his arm around Iceman, and the two of them stared at the image of Sadie Rodriguez.

Havyk and Spyder stood off to the side while the rest of the club came forward to examine his work. He was always proud of every bike he built, but seeing the emotions from all these rough men gripped at his soul. It was obvious Sadie meant something to all of them.

A few minutes later, one of the bikers appeared with a bottle of tequila. He handed it to Kodiak, who turned and faced the group. "Family is the most important thing there is, whether that be by blood or by choice. Sadie is Iceman's blood, but she's our little sister through him. No matter where she is, Sadie lives on in our hearts, and now on this beautiful tribute. To Sadie." Kodiak took a swig and passed the bottle to Iceman. He knocked back a hefty swallow, then whispered, "To Sadie." The bottle was shared between everyone, including Havyk and Spyder. When Spyder handed the near-empty container to Iceman, he finished it off.

Kodiak slung his beefy arm around his comrade's shoulders, but spoke to Hayden. "Are you headed straight home, or are you staying a while?"

"I actually have family here, so we'll be staying and visiting a couple weeks."

"In that case, we'd be honored if you would join us for a ride. We have some prospects who have agreed to loaning you their bikes for a day."

Havyk knew what a big deal that was. A male's bike was as personal as a wife or girlfriend. One didn't share their ride with just anyone. "It would be our honor to ride with the Norse Gods."

"Perfect. I'll call you in a couple days and set it up."

"We look forward to it." Havyk and Spyder said their goodbyes knowing Dominic needed some time to get his emotions under control after having seen the tribute bike.

Once they were in the SUV, Spyder sighed heavily. "That right there is why we need to put down Alvarez and all the bastards like him who think taking and selling people is okay. Fucking greedy sons of bitches. And for what? These assholes have more money than they can spend in several lifetimes. It's not like they're doing good with it. Don't get me wrong. I like knowing I can pay my bills and buy nice things as much as the next guy, but I'm not going to make my living off someone else's back."

"You're preaching to the choir, Brother. It's why Sutton got into the merc game in the first place. To take out those who think they're above it all. But people have been greedy since the beginning of time. If everyone was good, Zeus wouldn't have felt the need for Hounds, and the other gods wouldn't have created Gargoyles." Hayden was curious about the Norse Gods' pres. "What did you think about Kodiak?"

"You get a vibe from him too?" Spyder tapped his fingers against his thighs. "I thought it was just me."

"Nope. My Gryphon was antsy the whole time we were there. I doubt Kodiak's a Gryphon or else he'd be riding with the Hounds. Could be a Gargoyle and not aware of us."

"Or he could be something else altogether. Fuck, man. If there are two types of shifters, who's to say there aren't more? I mean, his nickname is Kodiak, and he looks like a fucking bear. Wouldn't that be something?"

Hayden laughed. "Yeah, but wouldn't he live in Alaska? That's where all the Kodiak bears are."

"Maybe he did at one point but had to move around like the rest of us. And I'm impressed you know that little fact."

"I actually paid attention in school. Science and art were my favorite subjects."

"I can see that. Me and art didn't get along unless I was looking at it. Hell, I can't draw a decent stick figure. No, give me literature, and I was a happy little Gryphon. I'd get so lost in books the teachers would have to drag me out of the library."

"You don't consider your rope work art?" Hayden knew Spyder was into the lifestyle, and when he'd joined Spyder and Hawk at the club, Spyder had given a Shibari demo.

"I guess I never thought of it like that, but I can see where you'd think of it as art. To me, it's more about giving the person being wrapped up something they need. Being in the ropes is like being held in a warm embrace."

"You've let someone do that to you?"

"That's part of the learning process. At least that's how I was trained. The Master I learned from said you need to know firsthand what your sub is experiencing. With ropes, it can be a pleasant experience, or you can cut off circulation or manipulate your sub's body the wrong way. Same as with other types of BDSM, like impact implements. Without having the proper training, a Dom could do a lot of damage."

"Impact implements?"

"Yeah, like floggers, paddles, canes, and whips. There are a lot more examples, but those are four of the most popular from what I've seen. Personally, I'm not into that type of play."

"You probably think I'm boring since I didn't find any of it enticing." Hayden had been excited about seeing the inside of the club, but nothing had turned him on. Even the naked female hanging on the St. Andrews cross being spanked hadn't got his dick hard. He couldn't concentrate on the woman's body for fear she was being harmed. He understood it was something she wanted. Craved even. But Hayden didn't get it.

"Vanilla, yes. Boring? Never. Look at what you just gave that male back there. Havyk, you have a gift. One you should be proud of. Who cares if you aren't into a different sexual lifestyle? I promise when you find your mate, she's going to match you perfectly. I know the last few dates haven't gone the way you wanted, but be patient. The right female will come along, and you're going to rock her world just the way you are."

"Thanks. Right now, I'm ready to focus on the job."

Mercedes

BY THE TIME Juan returned from his trip almost a week later, Mercedes was going stir crazy. She rarely left her suite when he was away. She didn't trust his men, nor did she want to run into Antonia if she happened not to have gone with Juan. Mateo was always a good child, never complaining. The boy didn't know any different. Mateo wasn't holed up in their suite for days on end. He left the room with Ana Marie to go for his tutoring. Mercedes thought he was too young to spend so much time learning, but Juan insisted his education begin early on, and what Juan wanted, Juan got.

Mercedes always waited until Mateo was out of the suite to take her shower. She spent as much time with her son as possible. She stood in front of the mirror combing the tangles out of her hair and dancing to a tune in her head. She had always loved to dance, and surprisingly, Juan enjoyed it as well. On the few occasions he took her out, the two of them lit up the dance floor together. Those were the few times in recent memory she was truly happy.

The bedroom door opened, and Mercedes clutched her robe until her husband stood in the doorway. She hated always being on guard, but such was her existence.

"*Hola. Como te fue en tu viaje?*" Mercedes couldn't care less how his trip was, but she pretended to be interested. Mercedes kept her eyes on her husband as she continued detangling her long tresses.

"Successful." Juan's gaze traveled down her body and back up. Anticipating his return, she'd opted for one of the silk robes he preferred over the comfy, thicker ones she wore when it was just her and Mateo. "I have invested in a new business venture. One which requires my presence over the border. While I was away, I secured a second estate. You and Mateo will come with me, and we will be staying there for the next few months."

Mercedes kept her face neutral. If she showed too much excitement at the prospect of being back in the States, he would either leave her in Mexico, or he'd punish her. "I'm happy for you," she said as sincerely as possible. "Will Ana Marie be coming with us?"

"If that is what you wish."

"It is. Mateo loves her." And Mercedes trusted the older woman with her son. She was the only one Mercedes felt comfortable taking over care of the boy.

"Then I will have her pack her things as well as yours. We leave tomorrow." Juan closed the distance between them and took the comb from Mercedes, placing it on the counter. He tugged at the tie securing her robe, and the panels fell open, exposing her body to her husband's hungry eyes.

"*Te extrañe, Pajarito,*" he whispered.

But I didn't miss you.

Juan placed one hand on her hip and the other slid into her damp hair, gripping it so he could tilt her head to the side. Leaning in, he ran his nose up the column of her neck, inhaling deeply. The body wash as well as shampoo and conditioner she used were ones he had chosen. All her toiletries were the best money could buy. A far cry from the ones she'd used back home. Her makeup was also expensive brands. This she knew from the fashion magazines her husband allowed her to read. Mercedes had been taken eight years ago, but she worked hard to remember everything about her life before her father handed her over to Juan Carlos. She never wanted to forget the life she had with her mother.

Her husband nipped her earlobe before releasing her. "I

42

have much to see to today or else I would take you right here." Juan bent and caught her nipple in his mouth, laving it, then sucking hard. Mercedes's bud hardened automatically, betraying her heart and mind. She hated her husband. Hated his touch. But her body was in tune with the way Juan played it. He was the only man she'd ever been with, but when she was alone, she dared to imagine someone who would care for her gently. Touch her with tenderness. Ask what she needed instead of taking what he wanted.

Juan bit down on the tip, and Mercedes cried out while remembering to keep her hands to herself. She'd learned the hard way that trying to push her husband away resulted in bruises. The sting from his teeth did nothing for her. She wasn't into pain, and that one bite quelled any passion her body had longed for moments earlier. Thankfully, Juan stepped back without assaulting her further.

"Later." And with that one threatening word, he was gone. Mercedes hated when her husband was excited. It was like his endorphins were on steroids and they made him crazy. When Juan was crazy, he took it out on her body. He was rough on a good night, but when he was in one of his moods? Mercedes sighed and closed her robe. There was no use dwelling on the inevitable. Instead, she allowed herself to dream of moving to a new house, one closer to the family she'd been taken from. *Taken, right.* Mercedes prayed her mom had never given up on trying to find her. Unless her father had told Gloria the truth, she'd still be looking. Mercedes knew if something ever happened to Mateo, she'd never give up. Not until she had proof… Nope. Not going there. Nothing was going to happen to her son. Not as long as she was alive.

The rest of the day was a blur of packing. Ana Marie helped gather all of Mateo's things. Clothes, toys, everything the child owned. When Juan said they were moving, Mercedes didn't realize it was more of a permanent move than just the few months he'd mentioned. Mercedes didn't understand how a Mexican could simply purchase a home in the States without being a citizen, but she wasn't knowledgeable in things of that nature. She'd not finished her education after being taken, and what she had learned in her first two years of high school left a lot to be desired. Juan had made the exchange from her father in Texas, so it was possible he had the necessary documentation to live both places.

Large clothing boxes had been brought to her suite, and Mercedes busied herself transferring her dresses over from the closet. The myriad shoes were then placed in the original boxes they came in before being stored into larger containers. She assisted Ana Marie instead of sitting and watching. She was brought up to be useful, and that was one lesson she tried to hang onto as long as Juan or Antonia weren't around to witness. By the time night fell, Mercedes's excitement over moving to the States was replaced with dread. She had hoped to have dinner with Juan in the dining room. When she and Mateo joined the man, his mood lightened, and he focused on their son. Mercedes had dressed for the occasion, but when their dinner had been brought to her suite instead, her own mood fell. When Ana Marie knocked on her door at half past nine, Mercedes had already gotten Mateo into his pajamas and in bed. She was sitting on the edge of the sofa, and the older woman nodded.

As Mercedes passed Ana on the way to the door, the woman placed her palm on Mercedes's cheek, but she didn't say anything. Her eyes gave way to the emotions she couldn't speak aloud. Mercedes squared her shoulders and mentally prepared herself for the night ahead.

Mercedes knew she was in trouble the second she opened the door. Juan was standing in the middle of the room, his chest bare and his belt unfastened, hanging loose. It did no good to beg. She was sure he liked when she cowered, and Mercedes wouldn't give him the satisfaction. Instead, she lowered the side zipper on her dress and let the garment slide to the floor. As she stepped out of the bunched material, Mercedes unhooked her bra and slid the straps down her arms before dropping it next to the dress. Standing in only a pair of heels, she waited. Juan licked his lips as he removed the belt from his slacks. She didn't lower her eyes the way he preferred. No, Mercedes stared at him as he doubled the belt, then slapped it against his palm.

Better his palm than my ass. But that was the kind of night she was in for. A painful one.

"*Colocate en posición.*"

When he told her to "take her position," she knew what was coming. Mercedes didn't hesitate to walk over to the bed and lean forward, spreading her arms above her head. She pressed her cheek to the soft duvet, grabbing it in both fists, and only then did she close her eyes. After the first strike, she knew the ride to their new home was going to be painful. Her husband was rarely a gentle lover, but nights like this one proved how much of a monster he was. He lashed out so many times she lost count. Then, without giving her time to recover, he shoved into her, and a cry left her throat. All Mercedes could do was endure the dry fucking. The one time her body didn't betray her by being ready for Juan was after he whipped her. He didn't care. He took her hard, grabbing her hair and pulling. Mercedes cried out again against her will. The only good thing about nights like this was the sex was over quickly.

As soon as Juan found his release, he didn't linger. He pulled out, leaving her spread over the mattress. She remained where she was until he gave her permission to move. It didn't take long.

"*Vuelve a tu cuarto,*" Juan said, commanding her to go

back to her room.

Mercedes was thankful for the reprieve. She would rather lick her wounds in the privacy of her suite than endure lying next to her husband and pretend she was okay. Mercedes was far from okay. She dressed as quickly as possible and left without looking back. Antonia was leaning against the wall outside the door to Juan's suite. She glared at Mercedes but didn't say anything. Mercedes mentally rolled her eyes. One day, she was going to figure out why Antonia hated her so much. If she didn't know better, Mercedes would think her sister-in-law was jealous.

Ignoring Juan's guards on the walk to the other side of the estate, Mercedes held her head high and did her best not to hiss at the sting of her tight dress rubbing against her ass. She held the tears at bay until she entered her room and closed the door. Ana Marie looked up from the sofa where she was flipping through one of the fashion magazines.

"El baño esta listo para ti."

"Gracias." She hated that the older woman knew enough about Mercedes's sex life to have the bathroom ready with the special lotions that would ease some of the pain. Mercedes had never questioned how Ana Marie knew Mercedes needed the medicated creams, but she was thankful the woman had delivered them to her room one night and told her they might help. They did take away some of the sting, but they did nothing for the emotional scars that were left long after the whelps faded.

Mercedes didn't bother with a shower. She couldn't stand the spray hitting her abused skin. Instead, she removed her dress, applied the cream, then bathed as best she could at the sink. Mercedes never went to sleep with her husband's release or scent on her body if she could help it. When she exited the bathroom, Ana Marie gave her a small smile before leaving Mercedes alone. Instead of getting into her bed, Mercedes went to Mateo's room and climbed in beside her son, letting the little boy's soft snores ease her mind enough that she could fall asleep. Eventually.

CHAPTER FIVE

Hayden

THE INFORMATION QUINN had on Juan Carlos Alvarez kept coming in. Since Hayden was new at the merc game, he asked Spyder about it. "Does this happen often?"

"No. We're given a target, then left to do the recon afterwards. Whoever put the hit out on Alvarez wants to make sure we get the man."

"And his wife. I'm going to tell you straight away I'm not ready to swipe my claws on the female. Not until I have solid proof she's a partner in her husband's crimes."

"You think women can't be as ruthless as men? Because they can. I've seen some evil females in my years." Spyder held a copy of the latest intel in his hands, but Hayden didn't think the male was reading over them. He wondered if Spyder was recalling someone from his past.

"No, I know they can. Just look at Cassandra and what she did to Natalia and Ryker. I'm just saying, this is a young mother. I don't want to leave a small child an orphan unless I know without a shadow of a doubt the woman is a monster."

One of Poppy's grandsons, Jericho – a.k.a. Joker – had offered for Hayden and Spyder to stay with him instead of with Poppy since his house was closer to New Laredo. Like them, he was a Gryphon as well as a Hound in the MC, and their club had eyes and ears all over the Southwest. Jericho also offered his help in this particular job. "Word on the street is Alvarez has crossed the border. He 'bought' an estate in New Laredo, which means he overthrew the previous owner, thus inheriting all his assets. I would say I'm sad about that, but Hector Ramirez was a known human trafficker, so good riddance."

"Maybe I'm way off base here, but I just can't imagine a young mother being okay with buying and selling other humans." Hayden couldn't imagine how anyone was okay with it, but then he knew there were some truly vile people in the world. Thus the need for mercenaries and assassins.

Spyder tossed the papers onto the coffee table. "Maybe she's not okay with it but goes along with her husband since he puts her up in million-dollar homes and lavishes her with expensive gifts. She could claim blissful ignorance."

"Or," Hayden countered, "she could be another victim. She's only twenty-three with a five-year-old son."

Spyder stood and stretched his arms overhead. "Whoever took out the contract has a beef with her, though." When Hayden opened his mouth to argue, Spyder held his hands up. "I'm not saying we take her out immediately. We have a lot of ground to cover in finding the best way to get close to her husband. In doing so, we'll watch the woman. If we don't find enough evidence of wrongdoing on her part, we'll figure something out then."

"How will that go over with your handler? If you don't complete the contract on both husband and wife, will you still get paid?" Jericho asked.

Hayden rolled the documents in his hand. "It's our responsibility to find out as much as we can about our marks. With Alvarez, it's cut and dried since he's a known drug lord. We would rather not get paid than take out an innocent."

"But won't whoever put out the contract get pissed? Put

49

out another contract?"

"It's possible, but if we do find out she's innocent, I'll do whatever I can to protect her," Hayden vowed.

Spyder crossed his arms over his chest. "Why are you so invested in this woman you've never met?"

Hayden knew that question was coming, and he didn't have a good answer, so he went with the truth. "Call it a gut feeling." He ran a hand through his hair and blew out a breath. "I just…"

"I'm not saying you're wrong, Havyk. I've been where you are. One of the first jobs I went out on had me second-guessing everything. I was supposed to take out a schoolteacher. She was single, early thirties. The woman didn't even have so much as a parking ticket. Allegedly, she was a pedophile. I watched her for days. Yes, she had kids over to her home for tutoring, but I was able to see into her house through the front windows. The parents remained in their cars at the curb while their kids went inside. Not once did she do anything remotely inappropriate. She sat on one side of the table with the student opposite. When their time was up, she walked the kid to the door. Yes, sometimes they would hug her, but it was purely innocent. No lingering touches in places hands shouldn't have been. When I was ready to call Ryot and tell him I wasn't doing the hit, I saw something."

"Please don't tell me she molested a student," Hayden said.

"Quite the opposite. The student went after *her*. He was older. Had driven himself to her house. She stood in the doorway without asking the teen inside, but he pushed past her. Instead of remaining in the house across the street where I was watching from, I rushed over there. The kid was yelling at her that she ruined his life, and he was going to make her pay. I listened long enough to get an idea of what was going on, then I knocked on the door, and when she opened it, I pretended to be her boyfriend. Long story short, the teen had a crush on her, and when she refused to tutor him after he made advances toward her, he failed his algebra class. The kid was a star linebacker, but the coach had a strict no-fail policy. On the night when scouts were sitting in the stands, the kid had been benched. He blamed her, told his dad she molested him. The dad, having money, put a hit out on the woman. It didn't take long to get to the bottom of everything, but when I did, the dad was arrested, and the teen... Let's just say he was convinced to tell the truth."

Jericho reached out to give Spyder a knuckle bump. "How did you explain your presence at the door to the teacher?"

"I told her I heard their fight as I was walking down the sidewalk. Then I had her go into the other room to call the cops. While she was doing that, I had a little chat with the teen. By the time the police showed up, the kid was subdued and willing to spill his guts. The teacher was so thankful I stopped the teen from hurting her she asked me to stay for supper." Spyder wiggled his eyebrows, and Hayden groaned while Jericho laughed. "I told you all that to say I understand. My gut told me she was innocent, and I was right. If I hadn't watched her as long as I did, I would have taken out an innocent."

Hayden was glad his fellow Hound understood. There was no proof Mercedes Alvarez was innocent, but until he had evidence that she was guilty, he wouldn't kill the woman. He wasn't sure he could kill her even if he knew she was in on her husband's activities. "Let's go over what we have so far, starting with where the new house is located."

Being at Jericho's instead of Poppy's allowed them privacy to discuss the case without being interrupted for a few hours. When the three of them decided to break for

51

lunch, Hayden decided to visit one of his sisters knowing he would get a wonderful meal. Jericho headed to the clubhouse, and Spyder opted to drive by the Alvarez compound. When Hayden reached Iris's home an hour later, he grinned when he saw all the cars. He should have known word would get out he was close by. The six sisters lived within a few hours of each other, with most of their offspring living all around the southwest. He figured it was better to get the visits over with before he got too deep into the job.

All six twins had Gryphons for mates, which meant all their kids were shifters as well. Some of Hayden's nieces and nephews had found human mates, so their kids were a mixture of both. Hayden couldn't remember which ones were shifters since there were so many of them, but it didn't matter in the long run. They were all family, Gryphons or not.

By the time he made it back to Jericho's house, Hayden's belly and his heart were full. He loved his brothers, but there was something about being surrounded by his sisters that reminded him of Rory. The girls doted on Hayden, and he soaked up the attention.

Spyder was kicked back on the sofa, bare feet resting on the coffee table. "How'd it go?"

"It's like having six of Rory taking care of you all at once." Hayden presented two cloth bags full of leftover containers. "They wouldn't let me leave empty-handed. They also made me promise to bring you next time."

Spyder jumped to his feet, rubbing his hands together. "I smell something spicy."

"You're not wrong. There's a little bit of everything in here, including your favorite – tamales."

"Please tell me Holly made her famous pork and peach ones." Spyder's face was as hopeful as a kid waiting for candy on Halloween.

Hayden grinned. "Maybe. Wait. How do you know about those?"

"This isn't my first trip to Texas, my friend. Now, give me." Spyder took the bags from Hayden and went into the kitchen where he unloaded all the containers.

"There better be some chili rellenos left," Jericho said as he came in the back door. "Aunt Holly called me and said I better hurry home if I wanted to eat."

Spyder pushed a container toward the large Hound. "They're all yours. But these babies are all mine," he said, guarding the dish of tamales.

Jericho grabbed two plates from the cabinet and passed one over to Spyder. The two of them dug into all the food Hayden brought from his sister's. He snagged three beers from the fridge and passed them out before leaning against the counter, watching the two males chow down. He didn't begrudge them their lack of conversation. Just a few hours prior, he had been the one stuffing his face.

When Spyder was finished devouring the food, Hayden asked, "What did you learn about the compound?"

"It's heavily guarded. There were eight men patrolling the outside, and from what I could tell, at least that many more are on the inside."

Jericho rinsed his empty container in the sink, then put it in the dishwasher. "When I went to the clubhouse, I had a talk with the Hounds who were there. We've always kept our eyes on Ramirez, and now that he's no longer in play, Alvarez has our attention. A couple of the males have mates who like to dance. Alvarez has been spotted at a couple of the nightclubs holding court in the VIP sections. Not only are there guards with him but also a woman. Could be the wife."

"That could be our in. It would be easier to watch the man out in a crowded nightclub than trying to infiltrate a heavily guarded estate." Spyder did a little Salsa move. "I could be up for some dancing."

Hayden wasn't much of a dancer, but Spyder was right about the logistics. "I didn't pack clothes for clubbing. Looks like I'm going shopping."

"Yes!" Spyder grabbed Hayden's hands and tried to do a snazzy dance move, but Hayden just stood there.

"You know I can't dance, right?"

"I'll teach you, *mi amigo*. Just follow my lead."

"Do you think this is necessary?"

"A sultry dance is always necessary. You want to blend in, not stick out like a wallflower. Tell him, Joker."

"I have to agree." Jericho moved Hayden out of the way and took Spyder's hands. "Watch and learn, Uncle."

"Wait." Spyder pulled his phone out of his back pocket, and soon, Latin music was playing. He set the phone on the counter and retook Jericho's hands. Hayden stared in amazement as the two males gracefully moved back and forth in perfect sync.

"The hips don't lie," Spyder told Hayden, grinning.

"They really don't," Hayden muttered. He studied their moves, trying to emulate what they were doing.

"No, like this." Spyder stood behind Hayden and gripped Hayden's waist.

"You don't have to exaggerate the moves the way Spyder does." Jericho demonstrated what Spyder was attempting to show Hayden, and after a couple minutes, Hayden got into the rhythm.

"That's it. Now try it with a partner." Jericho took Hayden's hands and placed them on his shoulders before Jericho clutched Hayden's hips. "You'll need to lead since you're the male, so feel how I guide you with my hands." Hayden was too busy concentrating on getting the steps down to feel self-conscious about dancing with his great-nephew.

"You're a natural." Spyder danced beside them,

popping his hips with his arms stretched out as though he had a partner.

"Naturally awkward." Hayden fumbled several times, but he thought he was doing pretty well for his first lesson.

When the song ended, Jericho stepped back. "We'll keep practicing, and by the time we hit the clubs, you'll have all the ladies swooning. This is going to be fun."

Hayden had to admit he was enjoying himself. Then again, he was with family. They wouldn't make fun of him. "Are you sure I can't just dance like I normally do?"

Spyder arched an eyebrow. "When do you *normally* dance?"

"Uh, never."

"Exactly. Trust me; it's easier to blend in on a crowded dance floor than sitting at the bar staring. It's also a lot more fun. Who knows? You might find the love of your life amidst all the ladies begging for your attention."

"I'm not here for love. I'm here for a job."

"Truth. But there're no rules saying you can't enjoy yourself. "

"Like you did with the waitress?"

Spyder gave a full-body shiver. "Yeah, no. She only pretended to be a kinky minx. Turns out she wanted a bad boy in name only. When it came time for spankings, she turned into a vanilla chihuahua. She had a lotta bark, but she literally turned in circles to keep me from getting my hands on her ass. *C'est la vie.*"

"Yet you spent a week with her," Hayden reminded the male.

Spyder shrugged. "I had to hide somewhere. Now, enough about that. Let's go shopping."

"Mind if I tag along?" Jericho was already walking toward the door. "I want to hear more about the vanilla chihuahua."

Hayden almost felt bad for Spyder. If anyone

understood about females wanting to be with a bad boy, it was Hayden. He should hook Spyder up with the last woman Hayden had taken on a date. *She* would probably have loved a spanking.

"I FEEL LIKE you're trying to make me look like the 'Staying Alive' version of John Travolta." The pants Spyder insisted Hayden try on were so tight he couldn't breathe. "And who wears white pants?" He turned to look at his ass. The seams of his briefs were clearly visible.

"What's 'Staying Alive'?" Jericho asked from his own dressing room.

"A fantastic disco movie from the 1970s," Spyder answered before breaking into a Bee Gees song, his falsetto strangely on key. When his voice moved, Hayden opened the door and stuck his head out to see Spyder strutting down the carpeted floor in step to the song. Instead of white pants, the shorter Hound was wearing black slacks. He had topped those with a lavender shirt he'd left unbuttoned halfway down his chest.

"All you need are a few gold chains, and you'll have the local pimps beating your ass," Hayden teased.

"Don't hate me because I'm beautiful." Spyder flipped his long hair over his shoulder before turning and strutting back toward Hayden. "Let's see what you got." Spyder pushed the door open before Hayden could stop him. "Yeah, those don't work. Your ass is too thick."

"Did you just say I'm fat?" Hayden placed his hands on his hips, glaring.

"Are you kidding me? I'd kill to have a bubble butt like yours. Hang on." Spyder disappeared back into the store, and Hayden turned to look at his ass. He couldn't help if all of him was muscular.

"Bubble butt, my ass," he grumbled. Jericho burst out laughing from just outside the door. Hayden eyed his nephew, who was wearing gray pants with a pale blue shirt. "Why do the two of you look normal while I look like a gigolo?"

"Here. Try these." Spyder thrust several pairs of darker pants at him. "I brought the next two sizes up."

Hayden closed the door in their faces, then struggled to get the tight, white pants down his legs. He let out a sigh when he was no longer constrained. His dick thanked him for the reprieve. Hayden chose a charcoal pair, fastening them with no trouble. "Now that's more like it." He admired them in the mirror, twisting to look at his bubb—

"Fuck you, Spyder," he mumbled.

"What was that?" Spyder opened the door without knocking. "Those are too loose. Try the next size down."

"What? No. These are perfect."

"Dude, you want to show off your assets."

"My assets like the way these fit. And why are you so interested in my assets anyway?"

Spyder waved his arm down Hayden's body. "I'm secure enough in my malehood to admire a nice form."

"Fine, just close the fucking door." Hayden begrudgingly tried on the smaller size, and he had to admit they did make his ass look good. They weren't so tight he would split them if he moved the wrong way.

"They look great, don't they?" Spyder asked, his voice smug.

"Nobody likes a know-it-all." Hayden separated all the clothes from ones he wanted to those he didn't. Back home, he had a couple pairs of suit pants, but none that fit the way these did. He rarely wore them because most of the time he was in jeans. The jobs he'd been on so far didn't require him dressing up to fit in, but he had to admit he was looking

57

forward to going to the club to scope out Alvarez. And yeah, maybe dancing with a pretty *señorita* or two.

When they returned to Jericho's, Hayden tossed all their purchases in the washing machine so they wouldn't have that stale, just-bought smell. While he waited, he asked the males to help him some more with his dancing. Hayden would never admit he was enjoying himself, but he loved art in all its forms, and he considered the elaborate moves they were doing to be just that.

Jericho called several of the Hounds and asked them to join the trio on their first night out. There was no guarantee Alvarez would be at the club, but it would give Hayden a chance to practice his new skills.

CHAPTER SIX

Mercedes

MERCEDES WAS AMAZED at how much the new house mirrored the one they'd left behind in Mexico. The layout was practically the same with his and hers suites on the opposite ends. The furnishings were opulent if less gaudy. She wasn't dumb. Mercedes knew someone had lived there recently, and she wondered what happened to the family, but she wasn't about to ask Juan. When she said her prayers that night, she would include them, whoever they were. There was a large swimming pool just outside a sunroom, but there were no tennis courts. The landscaping surrounding the property was lush, even this late in the year.

Mateo was happy to see his own playroom, which his father informed the boy would double as his classroom. Mateo's face lit up, but Mercedes's heart broke for whatever child or children the room had belonged to. Antonia and two guards followed the three of them on their tour as though Juan wasn't capable of walking through the house unaided. Mercedes should be used to their presence after all this time, but she hated having shadows.

Juan had them eat supper together in the large dining room as a family – just the three of them. Mercedes preferred when it was just her and Mateo in their suite, but

Juan was in a good mood. Much different than the night before when he'd striped her ass. After they finished eating, Juan, along with Antonia and a couple guards who had been waiting outside the dining room, escorted Mercedes and Mateo to their wing of the house. When they reached Mercedes's suite, Mateo ran ahead. Mercedes made to follow, but Juan paused at the doorway, grasping her hand. "We'll be going out tonight." Antonia beamed behind her brother, until he wound a strand of Mercedes's hair round his finger. "You'll be coming with me."

Mercedes wanted so badly to laugh at the shock on her sister-in-law's face, but she knew she'd catch hell later if she did. Instead, she turned to Juan and gave him her most sincere smile. "Really? Oh, thank you, Juan." Mercedes threw her arms around his neck and kissed him on the cheek. "You know how much I love to dance," she whispered in his ear. When Juan nuzzled Mercedes's neck, she didn't miss the daggers Antonia glared her way. Seriously, what was the woman's problem? Juan was Mercedes's husband. Did Antonia expect him to never allow her to leave the house? She probably wished it were that way. Mercedes leaned back and cupped her husband's cheek, pretending to be appreciative. "Would you like me to wear red or black?"

"Black. I don't want you looking too sexy. Be ready by nine." Juan kissed her forehead before walking away. If he were any other man, the gesture would have been sweet. Mercedes entered her room and checked the time. She only had a couple hours until she would have to get ready, so Mercedes spent all that time with Mateo. The little boy had already settled into his new environment. Mercedes wished she could do the same, but thoughts of who previously walked those same halls haunted her. Had Juan sent them away with nothing? He had to have since the home was filled with everything except for clothes and toiletries.

Mercedes had plugged in the hot rollers earlier, so while her hair set, she meticulously applied her makeup. Juan seemed to appreciate when she went for what the magazine writers deemed a smoky look, so she chose the darker colors. Thirty minutes later, she was dressed and ready to go. Since he was taking her dancing, Mercedes opted for a pair of platform pumps. The shoes had a five-inch heel, but they allowed her to move gracefully without the tightness of her stilettos. If she ever got away from her husband, Mercedes was going barefoot the rest of her life. Or maybe she'd find a nice pair of cowboy boots. She really missed those and blue jeans.

Ana Marie was already seated in the living area, so the knock on the door didn't bode well. Juan would've walked in with no warning. Mercedes grabbed the small purse which matched her shoes and strode to the door. She caught Ana's eye, and the woman smiled.

"Te ves hermosa come siempre. Diviertete."

Mercedes would never call herself stunning, but she appreciated the sentiment. As for having fun? She would. Somehow Mercedes would enjoy the evening, even if Antonia attempted to ruin the night. Instead of her sister-in-law waiting in the hallway, it was one of the older male guards. Tomás looked to be in his forties, but he was no less intimidating than the younger men Juan employed. He was also one of the only men who didn't give Mercedes a once-over every time she came out of her room dressed to go out. Maybe it was because he was old enough to be her father. Whatever the reason, she appreciated it.

They walked in companionable silence through the quiet house and out the front door where three SUVs were waiting. Tomás opened the back door of the vehicle in the middle, closing it once Mercedes was safely inside. Juan was focused on his phone, so Mercedes enjoyed the silence. They were fifteen minutes into the drive downtown before he looked up. Juan eyed her appearance, then looked out the side window. His moods were ever shifting, and Mercedes prayed whatever new project he was working on was going well. She knew it was shitty and selfish to think that way. He wasn't a good man, but when his business dealings stressed him, he took his frustrations out on her. If it weren't for the miracle ointment she used on her backside, Mercedes wouldn't be sitting comfortably on the leather seat, no matter how soft it was.

When they rolled up to the curb outside the club, Mercedes waited for Tomás to open her door. She slid from the vehicle, and while she waited for Juan to join her, Mercedes looked around. The club was quieter than those back home. The music was barely loud enough to hear from outside. There was a line of people waiting to get in. Every head was turned their way, and Mercedes chanced looking at a few faces, but Juan wrapped his arm around her shoulder directing her to the front door. Antonia was a couple steps behind, dressed similarly to Mercedes. Had the woman worn black just because Juan insisted, or had she done it to try and outshine Mercedes? Antonia was beautiful when she wasn't glaring, and she turned just as many heads as Mercedes did if not more.

Three guards preceded them, and three more flanked their walk through the busy downstairs area. The dance floor was crowded, and Mercedes wished to join in the throng. She would have to wait until Juan had several drinks in him. He pretended he didn't care for dancing, but once he was out on the floor, he ate up the attention. Mercedes just loved to dance.

The elevator was crowded with all nine of them shoving in, but the ride was short. Mercedes would have gladly walked up one flight of stairs. It wasn't like they were hiking five miles for goodness' sake. The area where Juan led them was like other VIP sections they had visited before, overlooking the floor below. The revelers couldn't see them if they were seated, so Juan took a spot by the railing, insisting she stand beside him. Antonia stood on his other side. Mercedes wondered what strangers thought of her husband and his two women. To anyone who didn't know the man, it probably appeared as though both Mercedes and Antonia were his companions. He liked to flaunt his wealth as well as his young wife. Mercedes thought it was tacky, a man his age married to someone so young. If she ever found someone else, he was going to be young and sweet. And honestly, Mercedes didn't care if the man had a lot of money. As long as he loved her and her son, that was all she needed. *Like Juan would ever let her take Mateo away from him.*

Juan stood watching the crowd as though he were a king looking out over his kingdom. Maybe he was. Her husband was well known back home. Had he already secured his place in New Laredo? She had so many questions about why they had moved, but she knew better than to ask. He made it clear early on that his business wasn't any of hers. All she had to do was whatever he told her while looking pretty. Those had been his words to her when she was seventeen and her curiosity got the better of her. In those early days, she prayed her brother would somehow figure out what happened, but the more time went by, she gave up on someone saving her. Mercedes vowed to save herself and her son. Somehow.

Movement below caught Mercedes's attention. Several men moved through the club, some with women, some not. Those who were single had caught the eye of every female and a few men in their vicinity. Mercedes was enthralled, but she was careful to keep her gaze averted lest Juan catch her looking. Tomás presented a tray of drinks, and Mercedes grabbed her champagne, thanking the man. While her back was to Juan, she glanced down to where the group had snagged a high-top table. One of the men, a blond, caught her eye, but before she could get a good look, Juan wrapped his arm around her waist, pulling her into his side.

For the next hour, Mercedes sipped champagne and pretended to enjoy herself. She swayed to the music, letting it and the alcohol mute her worries for a little while. Antonia remained plastered to Juan's side the whole time, though her eyes seemed to be set on the same table Mercedes had been sneaking peeks at.

"Dance with me," Antonia suggested to Juan. Mercedes couldn't see his face or hear his answer when he leaned in and spoke to his sister, but whatever he said to her did not make the woman happy. She chugged her drink, then slammed the empty glass down on the table so hard Mercedes was afraid it would break. With a glare at Mercedes, Antonia brushed by the guard standing at the top of the steps and headed downstairs.

"I don't think she likes me very much."

"She's jealous," Juan replied. Mercedes looked up at her husband, certain she had misheard. "I want to dance with my stunning wife, not my sister. Are you ready?" Juan held out his hand, and Mercedes took it. Instead of getting back on the elevator, Juan escorted Mercedes down the stairs, one slow step at a time. It was more for his benefit than hers. Juan was making his entrance, allowing his admirers to get a good glimpse of the man with the beautiful young woman on his arm. Mercedes knew she was nothing more than a shiny bauble Juan dangled to make everyone else jealous. It was times like these when she wanted to duck her head and hide her face. She didn't want anyone to believe she was with Juan of her own volition. But she had a part to play, and if she didn't play it well, she would suffer. This she learned early on too. So, with a fake smile on her face, she allowed herself to be led downstairs.

As though they knew he was someone important, the

crowd parted, allowing the two of them to walk to the center of the floor. Antonia had snagged one of the men from the table Mercedes had been watching. She was grateful it wasn't the blond. Why, she couldn't figure out. There was something about the man that Mercedes couldn't stop thinking about. When Juan gripped her waist a little too tightly, she turned her attention to her husband and kept it there. Mercedes allowed the music to wash over her, and soon she was lost in the rhythm. Other than spending time with Mateo, dancing was when she was happiest.

Hayden

THERE WAS SOMETHING familiar about Mercedes Alvarez. Hayden couldn't believe their luck in finding the drug lord in the first club they entered. When Jericho tuned Hayden and Spyder into that fact, it was all Hayden could do not to stare. He had tried to catch Mercedes's eye from the moment he'd stood by the open table, but other than a few glances his way, the woman had kept her face hidden. When he and the others first arrived, Hayden had seen Juan Carlos standing by the rail in the VIP section with two gorgeous women beside him. Hayden didn't know which one was the wife until the taller of the two had made her way downstairs and approached their table. She had eyed each of the single men, but it was Spyder who spoke to her.

"Hello, darlin'. I'm Jay," Spyder said, giving a fake name. "And you are?"

"You may call me Antonia." The gorgeous brunette's accent was thick as she looked Spyder over.

"Well, Antonia. Would you care to dance?" Spyder held out his hand, and she took it. Spyder drew the woman onto the dance floor and proceeded to garner not only her attention, but that of everyone around them. After a few beats, it was apparent the male had been holding back in Jericho's kitchen. Even Hayden was enthralled by the way his friend commanded the room. That was until all heads turned toward the stairs.

Juan Carlos, with the younger of the two women – and the prettier – waltzed down the steps. His wife's hand was wrapped around his arm. Hayden studied her closely. Mercedes in her tall shoes was still shorter than her husband. She was thicker than Antonia, but Mercedes's curves were not a detraction. If anything, they had Hayden's dick chubbing behind his slacks. The crowd parted, allowing the couple to reach the middle of the floor, and when Mercedes glanced at Hayden, it was as though time stopped. Their eyes locked until she turned away to focus on her husband.

Did that just happen?

It sure did. You need to get her away from him.

Hayden's Gryphon wasn't usually the pushy sort, but it was vibrating beneath the surface. Hayden pushed back.

We're here to observe, not cause a scene.

Speaking of causing a scene, the Alvarezes could have won a competition the way they moved together. It was apparent this wasn't their first time wowing a crowd. The other dancers were satisfied watching. Everyone, that is, except Antonia. She pulled Spyder toward the other couple and proceeded to try and outshine them. Spyder kept up with her, and they were stunning together, but they couldn't hold a candle to Juan Carlos and Mercedes. Hayden couldn't take his eyes off Alvarez's wife. How could someone so young marry a man twice her age unless it was for money? He knew there were plenty of gold diggers in the world, but this woman could have anyone she wanted, so why had she latched on to an older criminal?

Maybe she didn't have a choice.

Hayden prayed his shifter was right, because if it wasn't? That meant Mercedes wasn't a good person. He studied her face as best he could with her twirling around quickly. More often than not, her back was to Hayden, allowing him a good look at the way her black dress hugged her body. Hayden reached for his beer to help cool himself only to find it empty. He needed another drink desperately, but he didn't dare move from his spot at the table. Not while he had an unobstructed view.

Jericho nudged him, holding up his own empty bottle. Hayden nodded, and his nephew wound his way through the crowd to get to the closest bar. As the song came to a close, Juan Carlos dipped Mercedes, and the other dancers shouted and cheered before rejoining the floor. The couple remained where they were, but during the next song, they kept their movements to the small area around them instead of using the whole floor. Spyder and Antonia ended up next to the couple, and Hayden didn't miss the way Antonia's focus was on Juan Carlos and Mercedes. Spyder didn't miss it either if his frown was any indication. Still, the male remained where he was with his hands on his partner's hips.

When it was apparent she wasn't going to catch the other couple's attention, Antonia dragged Spyder off the floor toward the back of the club. Spyder glanced over at Hayden and winked. Hayden grinned, shaking his head. Maybe Antonia wanted a spanking. No. That woman would be the one doling out any kinky punishment to be had. Jericho returned a few minutes later with their drinks and sidled up next to Hayden.

"Where's Spyder?"

"Antonia dragged him toward the bathrooms." Hayden

downed half his stout in one go, then wiped his mouth with the back of his hand.

"I guess we now know which one is the wife."

"I guess so."

A couple women approached Hayden and Jericho to dance. He knew it was the perfect opportunity to get closer to Mercedes. *And Juan Carlos.* He wasn't there to stare at the woman wishing he were the one dancing with her, even though it was the truth. He didn't understand his infatuation with a possible criminal, but something in his gut was telling him she was innocent. Knowing he wasn't skilled didn't stop him from following Jericho and the females. Right as they reached the dance floor, Alvarez grabbed his wife's hand to lead her away from the crowd. Forgetting the female he'd been walking with, Hayden changed course to put himself closer to the couple. He kept his eyes averted as Juan passed, but Hayden looked directly at Mercedes. Two things happened in that moment. Her eyes met his, and Hayden could have sworn they were begging him to help her. He didn't have time to think if he was seeing things that weren't there because also in that moment, he noticed a mole above her lip. The same mole in the same spot he had painted on Dominic's bike.

"Sadie?"

Mercedes either didn't hear him, or she wasn't the biker's missing sister.

We have to help her.

I can't just grab the woman and haul her out of the club.

Yes, you can.

Jericho approached with the two women in tow. "Hayden? What are you doing?"

Hayden grabbed Jericho's arm. "We need to find Spyder." Hayden left Jericho apologizing to the two confused females and took off toward the back of the club. Pushing his way through those coming from the restrooms,

Hayden didn't see Spyder, but he did see Antonia, who was having a heated discussion with one of Alvarez's guards.

"You don't talk to me that way. I'll tell my brother and—"

"Mr. Alvarez is the one who sent me to retrieve you, so yes, I'll talk to you any way I please. You have a job to do, and it doesn't include swapping spit with some gringo."

Antonia tried to slap the guard, but he caught her hand and twisted her arm behind her back. They had drawn a crowd, but nobody seemed ready to jump in and defend the female. If Hayden wasn't after the man who employed these two, he might have been inclined. Since he didn't want to draw any attention to himself, he turned and walked the other way. By the time he reached the table, Spyder was already there.

"We need to go. Now." Hayden was thrumming with excitement. He chanced a look up into the VIP section, but Mercedes wasn't standing by the rail. Neither was her husband. Had they left? It didn't matter. What did matter was getting out of there and talking to Dominic.

Jericho tried to get Hayden's attention while walking through the club, but he ignored him until they were outside, away from anyone who might work for Alvarez. He was silent until they reached the SUV. Once they were seated and closed in, he let out a deep breath. Hayden had jumped in the back seat, so he leaned forward. "You know the tribute bike I did?"

"Yeah, for the Norse Gods biker." Hayden had shown Jericho photos of the finished job.

"Sadie, the girl in the photo? I'm pretty sure she's Mercedes Alvarez."

"What?" Spyder turned sideways in the passenger seat. "Havyk, how sure is pretty sure?"

"Ninety-five percent? I mean, she's older, but she has the same golden eyes and the mole above her lip."

"Do you know anything about the time she disappeared?" Jericho asked.

"Not really. Dominic didn't elaborate other than to say one day his mother called crying because both Sadie and their father disappeared."

"Wait. What's the father's name?" Jericho asked.

"I don't know, but Dominic's last name is Rodriguez."

"Fuck me. I remember hearing about that on the news. The dad was found with a bullet to the forehead, and they put out an amber alert on the girl. Dollars to donuts the dad was involved in something he shouldn't have been, and Sadie was collateral damage. If she ended up with Alvarez, I'd bet the dad was working for Alvarez or one of his enemies. Hay, if Mercedes is Sadie, I think your gut was right."

"Playing devil's advocate here." Spyder looked at Hayden. "Don't get pissed, but did the woman on the dance floor look traumatized to you? Did she look like someone who had been kidnapped after a drug deal gone bad? Or did she look like a happily married woman?"

"Appearances can be deceiving. I swear when the two of them passed by me, she was pleading with her eyes."

"Or maybe she was warning you not to stare at the wife of Juan Carlos Alvarez."

"Men were staring at her the whole time the two of them were dancing. If he didn't want others looking at his wife, he wouldn't parade her around the way he did."

"I just said don't get pissed." Spyder pulled his long hair back and secured it with a tie he kept around his wrist. "I get what you're saying. But eight years is a long time, and she has a child with the man. What if she has Stockholm Syndrome and genuinely cares for the bastard?"

"Or what if she doesn't and has been stuck with the bastard all this time?" Hayden leaned back against the seat. "I need to call Ryot. This job just went sideways."

CHAPTER SEVEN

Mercedes

TENSION WAS HIGH on the ride home. Juan's mood changed the second they stepped back into the VIP area. At first, she thought he might have noticed the moment her eyes met the blond man's, but Juan's back had been to her when he was leading her off the dance floor. If one of the guards noticed, he could have said something, but her fear was assuaged when Juan shouted at the guards to find his sister. Well, not immediately. Mercedes was afraid her husband was waiting for a report. That Antonia had possibly been watching Mercedes and was going to tell Juan what she saw. As soon as Antonia reappeared, Juan said, "Let's go." He didn't yell. Mercedes almost wished he would have. When her husband's voice was low and cold, things were worse.

As soon as they were inside the front door, Juan gripped Mercedes's chin. "Go to your room. I'll see you in the morning." He didn't kiss her, which was odd. He never missed an opportunity to show the men who worked for him who Mercedes belonged to. His eyes were blazing with anger, and she prayed that anger wasn't directed at her. She was almost to the doorway when Juan said, "Where the fuck were you?"

Mercedes didn't have to turn around to see who he was pissed at. It was evident when Antonia responded in

71

Spanish.

"I was dancing, same as you."

"I don't pay you to dance. I pay you to do as I say, and what were your orders?"

"To play shadow to the bitch." A loud smack echoed, followed by Antonia cursing her brother.

Mercedes continued down the corridor that led to her suite. There was no way she would get caught listening in, but she did stop long enough to take off her heels. The way the house was designed with its high ceilings, voices carried as did the tapping of her shoes on the marble floor.

"You will watch your fucking mouth. Just because I took you in doesn't mean I have to keep you around. Get out of my sight before I do something you'll regret."

Mercedes hurried off at that point since Antonia's room was on the same wing as Mercedes's suite. She had just closed the door when the sound of the other woman's heels echoed loudly down the hallway. Mercedes leaned against the door and shut her eyes. When Antonia's footsteps halted on the other side of the wall, Mercedes held her breath and waited. What seemed like an eternity later, the footsteps continued back the other way, and soon after, a door slammed.

"Mercedes?" Shit. She had completely forgotten about Ana Marie. "*Estas bien?*"

Was she okay? Mercedes pushed off the door and approached the woman. "*Si. Como estuvo Mateo?*"

It was a foolish question because rarely did her son wake after he was down for the night.

"*Un perfecto Angelito. Vas a estar en la noche?*" Of course she would ask if Mercedes were in for the night. Whenever Juan took Mercedes dancing, he normally required her to continue their evening in his suite.

"*Si. Gracias.*"

"*Buenas noches.*"

72

"Buenas noches, Ana."

Mercedes waited half an hour before taking her dress off or washing her face. Juan could change his mind and demand she come to him. No matter the time of day or the amount of notice he gave, her husband expected her to look put together. When the thirty minutes passed, she went about her nightly routine. While she did so, Mercedes went back over the whole evening, starting with the blond. She had never been drawn to another man when she was out on the town. Had never allowed herself to look anyone's way, but there was something about the man that called to her. Maybe it was her desperation to get away from Juan, but she could have sworn the man called her Sadie. That was a name she hadn't heard in eight years. She chalked it up to hope, hearing her old nickname. She didn't fail to notice he had approached the dance floor with a woman before switching directions. Mercedes's direction. The moment their eyes met didn't last long – just a couple seconds – but it was long enough to catch the deep shade of blue as well as the intensity with which he stared at her.

Mercedes sighed as she took stock of herself in the mirror. All makeup was gone, and she picked up the jar of cream that was both restorative and soothing. Not that she had any blemishes or lines which needed restoring. By using the cream, she hoped to keep her skin clear and wrinkle-free for as long as possible. When she was first abducted, she had pimples like most girls her age. Back then, she was merely a prisoner in Juan's large home, not an object for him to play with. She hadn't been free to roam the house without a guard at her side. She was still a prisoner, but at least now she and Mateo could walk about freely. There were guards stationed at every door, so there was no going outside without someone being aware.

Thinking back to the argument between Juan and Antonia, Mercedes cringed knowing she was a job to her sister-in-law. Mercedes always assumed Antonia followed Mercedes just because she wanted to piss her off. To let her know Antonia had the upper hand. But to find out Juan ordered his sister to watch over her? *That* pissed Mercedes off. Now she understood why the woman followed her every time she went to the restroom when they were at a club. Juan paid her to. It wasn't like Mercedes could escape with Tomás parked outside the restroom door waiting on her. Thinking back, tonight had been the first time Antonia had left Mercedes's side when they were out. It all made sense now. As much as anything in Mercedes's life did.

All this thinking was giving Mercedes a headache, so she did her best to put it out of her mind. She popped a couple pain relievers, then padded into Mateo's room. The sight of her son always put her in a better mood, but tonight, it made her feel worse. Her innocent little boy was being raised by a monster, and if she didn't find a way to get him away from Juan, Mateo would more than likely follow in his father's footsteps one day. Knowing she wasn't going to be able to sleep well, Mercedes went to her own bed instead of lying down with her son.

Mercedes picked up one of the magazines she kept on her nightstand hoping the articles and photos would take her mind off everything. It didn't. Her thoughts kept going back to the stranger and the way he stared at Mercedes. It wasn't as though he was the only man to ever look her way, but he was the only one to *see* her. Something about his gaze had been different. Mercedes had long given up hope anyone would come save her, but as she put the magazine aside and slid down to rest her head on the pillow, she allowed herself to imagine the blond storming into the house and rescuing her and Mateo.

Hayden

WHILE HAYDEN DREW a picture of Mercedes Alvarez, Spyder scoured the web for a photo of the woman. There hadn't been a picture included in the information Quinn sent with the job. It had been too late when they got back to Jericho's to contact the handler, but it hadn't been too late to contact Lucy. Hayden's niece kept late hours. She also had access to computer equipment he didn't, so he sent her a copy of the photo of teenaged Sadie and asked that Lucy produce a time-lapsed image, progressing the girl eight years. Since Spyder was striking out on finding any information on the woman, Hayden also asked Lucy to do some digging. His niece responded, reminding him she was in New Atlanta with Jonas Montague and not at the lab, but she would get on it, asking the Gargoyles' computer expert for help. Hayden assumed Lucy was referring to Henry Palamo since Julian Stone's mate had given birth to their first child and was taking some time away from his job. Hayden didn't care who helped as long as someone did.

After his discussion with Lucy, Hayden did the one thing he was good at – he drew. He asked Jericho for some paper, and Hayden sat down with a regular lead pencil and began sketching the woman's face from memory. Her image was imbedded in his brain. From the almond shape of her amber eyes, to her full lips, to the curve of her cheekbones, and that mole. He knew having a beauty mark wasn't enough to prove Mercedes and Sadie were one and the same, but the placement was identical. As was the unique color of her eyes. When he finished, he scanned the picture to his phone, then printed out a copy.

"Holy shit, Uncle. I knew you were good, but that's like looking at the woman." Jericho handed the paper he had retrieved from the printer over to Hayden.

Spyder stood from the computer and looked over Hayden's shoulder. "This is why he wins awards. Havyk could do anything he wanted in the art world and would be successful. We're lucky he likes working with bikes. Why don't you print off a copy of the photo of young Sadie so we can compare?"

Hayden pulled up the picture Dominic had given him to do the tribute and sent it to the printer. Jericho grabbed it when it was ready, then placed it beside the drawing of Mercedes. "I'm willing to bet my Harley this is the same person."

Hayden wouldn't take the bet because he already knew in his heart they were looking at Dominic's sister all grown up. "Regardless of her identity, we have to first figure out if she's innocent. If it turns out she isn't and we take her out, that will only cause Dominic more heartache. Do we want to tell him we found Sadie only to have to kill her? I don't want to start a war with his MC."

"You think if he knew she was part of her husband's criminal world he would care?" Jericho sat down across from Hayden. "If that was one of my sisters, I wouldn't give a shit what she was caught up in. I'd want to know she was alive. I would also do anything in my power to get her away from her drug-lord husband. People can change, you know."

"They can. But what if sweet Sadie changed into something worse?" Spyder held up his hand. "Again, playing devil's advocate. We all know people do things they don't want to in order to survive. What if she went along with Alvarez in the beginning because she had no other choice, only to find she didn't care what they did or who they hurt as long as she and her son were safe? If I ever have a child, I'll move heaven and earth to ensure he or she is safe."

Hayden pushed his chair back and stood. "And I'm saying the look she gave me wasn't one of a woman content. She didn't look at me like she knew I was one of the many men in the club who wanted to be her husband. Who wanted to be the one with a beauty like her on their arm. She wasn't smiling or smirking. Mercedes Alvarez wasn't happy."

"And you got that from a two-second glance?" Spyder asked.

"Yes, I did. You know as well as I do that Gryphons have a sixth sense about others, and mine was telling me to grab her and run. And that was before I noticed the mole. Before it dawned on me she was possibly Sadie Rodriguez."

"Let's take a step back." Jericho pulled both sheets of paper across the table and studied them. "Let's assume Mercedes is Sadie and she's innocent. What would your handler want you to do in this situation?"

"She would want us to get Sadie and her son somewhere safe before taking out Juan Carlos." Hayden stretched his head side to side, popping his neck.

"And if we find out she isn't innocent? Would your handler be okay with you letting her live?"

Hayden couldn't answer that. He had never met Quinn Shepherd. Ryker was in charge of the mercenary jobs they took, and he was the only one who'd ever met Quinn and her father. "I honestly don't know. I doubt she would get paid for the job if we didn't follow through, but we also don't know who put the hit out on Alvarez or why. If it's a rival drug lord, he or she wouldn't care if Sadie is innocent."

Jericho turned sideways in his seat so he could see Hayden where he stood by the window. "If it's a rival drug lord, they'd probably do the job themselves. Alvarez did that very thing with Ramirez, and now he's living in the other man's home. I can't help but wonder what happened to Ramirez's family. Did Alvarez off them too? Or did he pay them to disappear?"

"Let's hope it's the latter." Hayden had never given much thought to the workings of a drug cartel. Most of his family's dealing had been with the cults. "If it isn't a rival who put the hit out, then who? Spyder, did you get anything from Antonia while the two of you were cozied up on the dance floor?"

"Other than a hard-on? No." When Hayden growled at the male, Spyder laced his fingers behind his head, grinning. "What? She's a gorgeous female who was rubbing all over me. But no. She wasn't interested in making small talk. I was hoping to do a little interrogation when she dragged me to the back of the club, but before I could start asking questions, one of Alvarez's guards showed up, so I made a hasty retreat."

"Yeah, I overheard part of that conversation. It was intense. He said Antonia was there to do a job, not swap spit with some *gringo*."

"I have been called worse, but we never got to the swapping of spit. As for the job, I would say she's responsible for watching Mercedes. The whole time we were dancing, she rarely took her eyes off the other woman."

"Maybe she was watching Juan," Jericho said.

Spyder waved a hand down his body. "Why would she have her eyes on that old man when she could look at me instead?"

Hayden always enjoyed Spyder's playfulness, but in that moment, he ignored the question and returned to the table, leaning his forearms on the back of a chair. "When Antonia and the guard were arguing, she said she was going to tell her brother about the way the guard was talking to her, and the guard said Mr. Alvarez was the one who sent the guard after her. There was nothing in the information Quinn sent about Juan Carlos having a sibling." Hayden's phone pinged with a text. When he opened the message, it was from Henry. The male had managed to do the age progression photo. "I was right." Hayden turned the phone around so the other two males could see it. The drawing he'd done earlier was almost identical to the image on his screen.

Jericho turned and propped his arms on the table. "I still think you should tell Dominic his sister's alive. He has a right to know."

"You think he's going to be happy when we tell him how we found her and why?"

Hayden knew what Spyder was getting at, but he also knew in his gut the woman wasn't like her husband. "No, and I doubt he's going to be happy to find out his sister's married to Juan Carlos Alvarez and they have a son together. I say we get the proof we need she's innocent, then tell him."

"And how do we do that? I've never gone up against someone like Alvarez. I'm used to going after the crazies in the Ministry. They aren't heavily guarded," Jericho asked.

"Some of them are. The compound Ryker's mate escaped from was being supplied with enough rifles to start a small army, thus the need for Spyder to hunker down with his waitress."

"Not my waitress." Spyder stood and stretched his arms over his head, then twisted at his waist. "I say we figure out how to take down Alvarez, then when the smoke clears, we talk to Mercedes and use our Gryphon voice on her to get the truth. It's the only way to know for certain she's honest about her part in her husband's dealings."

"It helps that he's moved to New Laredo. Crossing over the border to get to him was going to be a hassle. How about if we use our Eagles to watch the estate and establish patterns of both Alvarez as well as the guards. I don't want to try and take him out in a club or somewhere equally as crowded. If Maveryck can take out Natalia's mob family, I don't see why we can't do the same thing here."

"Natalia's cousin didn't have as many guards as Alvarez does, but I agree we should attempt to go after him at home. You want to go do a flyover tonight?"

Hayden pushed away from the chair. "Absolutely. My Gryphon is antsy anyway. Jericho, you coming with?"

"Like you even have to ask. Let me grab my pouch." Hayden and Spyder had left their bags in the SUV. Being able to carry their clothes while in Eagle form was much better than worrying about being left naked should they needed to shift quickly. Jericho returned from his bedroom, and the three males piled into the SUV.

The estate Alvarez had seized from Ramirez sat on approximately five acres with a Spanish-style house nestled in the middle. From the air, Hayden counted six guards stationed around the perimeter. The home was a sprawling single-story structure with a courtyard in the front and a large pool in the back. There was a massive patio separating the pool from the house. The half of the patio closest to the building was covered and contained sofas and chairs surrounding what appeared to be a gas firepit. The open area was lined with chaise lounges and a couple tables with four chairs each. Umbrellas in bright colors were currently closed. Hayden could imagine Sadie resting on one of the chaises while her son splashed in the water.

No thinking of a bikini-clad female. Focus.

Shit, his Gryphon was right. He had to first figure out how to get inside the house and take down Alvarez and rescue Sadie. Then he could think about other things. Things he shouldn't be considering since he didn't know what kind of woman Mercedes Alvarez was deep down.

Being in their Eagles gave the males plenty of time to scope the house, but after an hour, Spyder got their attention, and the three of them retreated to where they'd parked. After shifting back, they got dressed.

"With the house being one story, it's going to be hard to get inside without being seen." Spyder shook his long hair out before securing it in a low ponytail. "Not impossible, but we need to watch during the day as well. I can't imagine those six males remain in one place more than a few hours at a time. They have to take breaks, so we need to figure out their schedule."

Jericho bent down to tie his boots. "We also don't know how many are inside. We do know that Alvarez leaves the house often at night since my guys have seen him at the clubs more than a few nights over the past couple weeks. As far as I know, this was the first time he took Mercedes with him. If we can catch him gone, it's possible we could get Mercedes and the boy out of the house first."

Hayden liked that plan. "That'll piss him off, and a pissed-off male is liable to make mistakes. We're going to need somewhere safe to take her if we manage to rescue her, though."

"Rescue?" Spyder narrowed his eyes. "Careful, Havyk. I know your gut is telling you she's innocent, but we don't know that. I don't want you getting your hopes up or letting your guard down where she's concerned. We have to play this smart as well as safe."

Hayden knew Spyder was right, but that didn't mean he would treat the female harshly if or when they got her away from Alvarez. Nor would he allow Spyder to treat her that way either. Instead of arguing, he settled on a partial truth. "I'll be careful, but until we have proof she's guilty, I'm going to assume she's innocent. I hope you'll do the same."

CHAPTER EIGHT

Mercedes

THE TEMPTATION TO hide out in her suite was great, but Juan insisted Mercedes and Mateo join him for breakfast. That wasn't unusual. What was odd was the fact that Antonia wasn't present. The female rarely left them alone, and Mercedes wondered if it had to do with the argument from the night before. If Juan was pissed, he didn't show it. Her husband was more chipper than usual.

"I have some calls to make, so give me an hour, then I'll join you two by the pool."

"We'll be waiting." Mercedes had hoped to swim alone with Mateo, so she didn't rush away from the table. She had long ago gotten used to leaving the dirty plates for someone else to clean up. When she first came to live with Juan, she'd tried to help out, but he informed her that wasn't necessary. She was there as his "guest", not to work. She didn't want Mateo to grow up never learning responsibility, so she at least had him put his toys away in his room every night.

Mercedes and Mateo had been outside over an hour when Juan finally joined them. Instead of sitting next to Mercedes, Juan joined their son in the pool. He might be a bad man, but he did love his child. Mateo loved his father too. That was one thing that made Mercedes miserable. Knowing if she ever got the opportunity, she would be taking Mateo from a parent he adored. But the boy was too young to understand the kind of father he had. The things his papa did to make money.

She kept hoping work would call Juan away, but he continued to play with their son. Since she didn't have to keep an eye on Mateo while he was swimming, Mercedes flipped over to her stomach so she could get some sun on her back. It was also so she didn't have to look at her husband. Before she closed her eyes, Mercedes noticed Antonia standing inside the door, watching. The other woman's eyes were trained on Juan and Mateo. Sure, she was a guard, but Mercedes thought it odd just how closely she watched her brother. Juan's words from the night before came back to her. *"Just because I took you in doesn't mean I have to keep you around."*

Mercedes knew nothing about Juan's family other than both parents were deceased. With her being married to the man under the circumstances she'd come to be with him, Mateo would never know grandparents. Her mother had no idea she was a grandmother. Hell, she didn't know Mercedes was alive and well. Dominic had no idea she was living practically down the road. If he was still in the area. She had no doubt he would take her in if she were to get away from Juan because that's what family did. Or should do. Was Antonia grateful to her own brother for getting her out of a bad situation? Was it gratitude which made her watch him so closely? And why did she dislike Mercedes so much? Mercedes had been a kid when Juan kidnapped her. The other woman hadn't been so blatant in her hatred until Juan married Mercedes. And when Mateo came along? It was as though Antonia thought Mercedes got pregnant on purpose.

If Mercedes thought telling her sister-in-law the truth would help, she would. But Mercedes would never utter a harsh word about Juan to the woman because she had no doubt Antonia would turn around and tell Juan. That would accomplish nothing good. Not for Mercedes anyway.

Instead of thinking about things she couldn't change, Mercedes let her mind wander to the stranger from the club. She had often allowed herself fantasies of being rescued by a handsome, faceless man, but now she had a face to go with her fantasies. Eyes the color of a cloudless sky filled her daydreams. She hadn't been able to check him out thoroughly, but in her fantasy, the man had a hot body under his tight pants. She had caught a glimpse of ink on his chest. Mercedes imagined tracing tattoos with her fingertips. Or her tongue. She let herself believe sex with someone like him would be enjoyable. That he would take his time making love to her instead of using her for his own pleasure, which with Juan was more often than not rough.

Mercedes really should stop reading articles in her magazines. The words of other women made her wish for things she couldn't have. Gave her ideas of having a life completely different than the one she was living. Sure, she had all the things money could buy, but those weren't the things she craved. Mercedes wanted love. Friendship. Freedom. Things she would probably never have.

A shadow fell across her body taking the sun's heat. She opened her eyes and turned her head to find Juan standing beside her chair. He was drying off. Mercedes flipped over, not wanting to be in such a defenseless position. Not that she could defend herself from her husband, but she liked to be able to see his face. To gauge his moods. In that moment, he appeared as happy as she'd ever seen. When he took the chair next to hers, he waved his hand in the air. One of the guards approached with a tray of drinks. Whiskey for him and *agua de fresa* for her and Mateo. The strawberry-flavored water was Mateo's favorite, and Mercedes drank it without fuss. She'd rather have a soda, but those weren't allowed in the house.

"Mateo, *ven a tomar algo*." Juan held up the plastic cup. He offered the boy a dry towel when Mateo approached his father's chair. Mateo didn't have to be told what to do. He wrapped the smaller towel around his body before taking the drink. Mateo had his own smaller lounge chair, and he carefully climbed onto it so he didn't spill his juice. Mercedes accepted the glass her husband had filled for her.

"*Gracias.*" She removed her plastic sunglasses from atop her head and put them on. She didn't wear the expensive shades at the pool since the metal nosepieces tended to get caught in her hair.

"I have business to attend, so I will be away a few days." Juan swirled the ice in his glass before taking a sip. Mercedes turned her head his direction, giving him her full attention. This wasn't anything new. He often went away for days at a time.

"*Te voy a extrañar,*" Mercedes lied with a smile. She never missed him while he was gone. Those were the days she looked forward to most.

Juan reached out his free hand, and she took it. As much as she disliked her husband, Mercedes cherished the moments he was gentle with her because they were few and far between. She hated the man, but she was starved for affection. Blue eyes flashed in her mind, and Mercedes smiled for real. If Juan thought the gesture was for him, all the better.

"*Yo tam in te voy a extrañar, Papá.*" Mateo would miss his father, and that hurt Mercedes in ways she tried not to think about too often. The boy loved the man he thought his father was. Then again, Juan had never been anything but wonderful to Mateo. Mercedes didn't understand how one man could have two faces. Be two different types of man. The loving father who sold drugs to other people's children. Did he not care that someone else's child was getting hooked on the product Juan was selling? That he was

85

enabling others to ruin their lives? All so he could live in a lavish home, drive expensive cars, wear thousand-dollar suits? Then she thought back to her own father. The man who raised her had given her away to pay a debt. He had never doted on her the way Juan did Mateo, but never in a million years would Mercedes have thought him capable of trading her to save his own hide.

"Y yo te voy a extrañar, mijo. A ti y a tu Mamá."

Mercedes didn't think Juan would truly miss her. Mateo? Yes. But her? Juan didn't spend much time with Mercedes when he was home, so his words didn't ring true. She figured he was paying lip service so their son wouldn't know his *papá* didn't love his *mamá*.

One of the guards approached, staying several feet away. "Sorry to interrupt, Sir, but there's a phone call for you."

Juan released her hand and stood. His phone calls always took precedence over family time. Juan wrapped his towel around his neck. He ruffled Mateo's hair and told the boy to be good while Juan was gone. Mateo smiled up at his father and promised he would. Without a word to Mercedes, Juan strode into the house with the guard following. Mercedes let out a sigh and leaned her head back, turning it to look at her little boy. Her innocent child who had no idea the world he lived in.

One day, Mijo. One day, I'm taking you away from here so you can live a normal life. One with friends. With family not likely to get you killed someday.

Hayden

"ALVAREZ IS ON the move," Jericho said after disconnecting his phone. "He, along with several guards, left the estate and drove to a small airfield where he boarded a jet. If you want to grab Mercedes, I'd say now is the best time. She and the boy are out by the pool." Jericho had called some of his cousins who were part of the Hounds of Zeus MC Laredo chapter to watch the house overnight.

Hayden knew Jericho was right, but they didn't have a solid plan. "We don't know how many guards Alvarez left behind. We need some sort of distraction to get them out of the house. And then we still won't know if Mercedes is alone."

"I've been thinking about that." Spyder pulled a T-shirt over his head as he walked into the living room barefoot. "We need to purchase some guns."

"And where are we going to get said guns?" Hayden had already taken his turn in the shower and was dressed and ready to go.

"From Alvarez. That's our in. We'll ask some of the other Hounds to ride with us. We'll roll up to the gate and tell the guards we want a meeting with the boss. While we're doing that, you and Jericho can come in from the sky and shift close enough to get dressed behind the trees before hauling ass across the lawn."

"What happens if we don't get her and the boy out?" Hayden thought the plan had merit, but he liked to think things through completely before going in half-cocked.

"We go back later. I doubt they let us in the gate in the first place since Alvarez isn't home. It'll give you time to scope things out from the back of the house. I'll use my Gryphon voice on them to buy you some time."

"What if they recognize you from the club?" Jericho asked.

"I'll tell them I was there to meet with their boss, but something came up before that happened. It's logical."

Hayden was cautiously optimistic. MCs were known to run guns as a way to make money. The only problem he had was wondering if he would be able to convince Sadie to come with them. They didn't know if she wanted to get away from her husband. After Hayden went to bed the night before, he went back over the brief moment their eyes met and began doubting himself and what he'd seen. Yes, she had once been Sadie Rodriguez, but she had been Mercedes Alvarez for a lot of years. What if she had grown accustomed to the lifestyle her husband offered? What if she actually loved the man? The what ifs kept him awake a couple hours before his Gryphon groused at him to shut that shit down.

"Havyk? You with us?" Spyder sat down on the coffee table in front of him.

"Yes, just thinking." Hayden twisted the thick, silver ring on his right hand.

"About?"

"Sadie. What if she's happy?"

"Doesn't matter if she's happy or miserable. The job we accepted is to take them both out. If we get Mercedes away from the house and find out she isn't innocent, we'll decide what to do with her then. Having her and the kid away from the estate gives us leverage over Alvarez. You need to remember that first and foremost, this is not a rescue mission. This is us fulfilling the contract you took from Quinn. Getting the female means getting information that'll help us take out a drug lord. That's the mission."

Fuck. "You're right. Let's do this." Hayden stood and strode to the window, looking out at nothing. He waited for Jericho to call Devil, the Pres of the club, and for Spyder to put his boots on while getting his head in the game. Just because he wanted Mercedes to be the Sadie her brother remembered didn't mean she would be. Hayden and Spyder climbed into the SUV and followed Jericho on his bike to the clubhouse. Devon "Devil" Ellis was one of Hayden's nephews. He was also Jericho's dad.

"Havyk, good to see you. You too, Spyder."

"Looking good, Devil." Havyk gave the older Hound a back-pounding hug. When they broke apart, Devon held out his fist, which Spyder bumped with his own.

"Joker told me about the contract. What can we do to help?"

Hayden gestured for Spyder to fill the male in since he'd come up with the plan.

"Sounds easy enough. I'd suggest not taking too many Hounds with you though. I've been around men like Alvarez a long time. You don't want to appear too threatening."

"Since he left town, we don't expect to talk to him at all today. We merely want to cause a distraction long enough for Havyk to get the female and kid out of the house. I figure I'd use my Gryphon voice on the men and have them call for backup to get as many guards out of the house as possible. It'll also give us a chance to ask about security in the house. If they have cameras, we need someone to hack in and disrupt the feed so Alvarez doesn't see Havyk or Joker in or around the house."

Devon scratched his beard. "I might know someone who's willing to help. Samson owes me a favor."

After Devon got hold of his friend, they moved out. Spyder, Devil, and two other Hounds – Samson, the hacker Devon had called, and Storm – waited until Hayden and Jericho were in place to approach the gate. Jericho parked in the same location as the night before, and now he and Hayden were ready to shift. Hayden texted Spyder with the go-ahead, then he and his nephew stripped, placed their clothes in their bags, then shifted into their Eagles. Gryphons had the ability to alter their size when in Eagle form. If they were merely scouting, they appeared no larger than a regular eagle so as not to draw attention, which was now the case.

Everything was quiet when they reached the trees lining the property. Too quiet. If Sadie and her son were in the pool, there would have been some noise. The sounds of splashing or talking or something. The boy was nowhere to be seen, and Sadie was lying on a chaise lounge. Except...

Hayden shifted and took off running, not bothering with clothes. Jericho was right behind him.

"Havyk, wait!"

Hayden didn't care that he was naked. Or that he was risking his life being out in the open. Sadie was lying at an odd angle, and when he reached her, he saw why. The female was bleeding, and crimson was spreading beneath her head onto the beige cushion.

"Fuck!" Hayden had dropped his pouch when he shifted, and he didn't have his phone.

"Hay, we need to get the fuck out of here." Jericho was crouched beside him, alert to their surroundings. At least one of them was.

Hayden checked Sadie's pulse. It was steady. Not taking time to think things through, he lifted her into his arms and took off running toward the edge of the property with Jericho on his heels. No one came after them. No shouts to stop or gunfire to slow them. Hayden had a bad feeling about the whole situation.

"What the fuck is going on?" Jericho handed Hayden a beach towel he'd grabbed before he opened his bag and began dressing.

Hayden was frozen with Sadie nestled against his chest.

She's ours.

No, she's not. She's a married woman.

She's fucking ours!

Hayden didn't move until Jericho held out his arms. "Give her to me, and get dressed. We need to get out of here."

Reluctantly, Hayden handed her over and pulled on his own clothes. As soon as he was dressed, he took the female from Jericho. "Let's go." His phone vibrated, but Hayden ignored it until they reached the SUV. Once he was seated in the back with Sadie across his lap and the towel beneath her head, he checked the message.

Spyder: *Call me*

Jericho hadn't moved. "Drive, Joker. She needs the hospital. Drive!" Jericho turned over the ignition and eased out of their hiding spot. Only when he reached asphalt did he speed up, heading toward town. Hayden hit Spyder's contact info and pressed send.

"We've got a shitshow out here, Havyk. You and Joker need to stand down until—"

"Sadie was hurt. We're on our way to the hospital."

"Fuck! It's a fucking bloodbath here. All the guards are down, Antonia was hit, but it was just a crease, and the kid is gone. Antonia's lost her fucking mind, yelling about someone taking the kid. Other than her, the only ones still standing are the nanny and the cook. Both females are shaken but otherwise okay." Devil was talking in the background, and Spyder said, "Hang on."

"Havyk?"

"Devil. I have Sadie. She's losing blood from a head wound."

"Take her to my house, and I'll call Theo."

"Devil, she needs—"

"Hayden, listen to me. If you take her to the hospital, they're going to call Alvarez. Theo will take care of her."

He knew his nephew was right, but Hayden wasn't thinking clearly. "Joker, your dad said to take Sadie to his house so Theo can look at her."

"Good. Yeah. Uncle Theo's a damn good doctor."

"Spyder and the rest of us are getting the hell out of

91

here once Samson makes sure the security feed is wiped. The nanny already called the cops."

"Don't you need to stick around? Fuck, Devil. Now you all can be identified."

"No. We used our Gryphon voice on everyone left alive. We'll meet you back at my place as soon as we can."

Devil disconnected, and Hayden blew out a breath. "Hang on, Sadie." He brushed the female's hair off her pale face. Gone was the smoky makeup she'd worn at the club, but she was no less stunning. Without the heavy eyeshadow and mascara, Hayden could better see the resemblance to the photo of her fifteen-year-old self. More than once he had to push back against his Gryphon. It was demanding Sadie was theirs. It was also determined to shift and go back to the house for the boy.

The boy's not there. You heard Spyder.

He could be hiding.

Antonia said someone took him. We need to focus on Sadie, then we'll find her son.

If he hadn't been studying her face, Hayden would have missed the fluttering of her lashes. For a few seconds, unfocused amber eyes gazed up at him before her lids closed once more.

When they arrived at Devon's home, several of Hayden's nephews were waiting. Theodore, another of Poppy's sons, opened the back door as soon as Jericho had the vehicle in park. Theo helped Hayden with Sadie, but as soon as his feet were on the ground, Hayden cradled her to his chest once again. He didn't understand why he felt so possessive of the female. Okay, he did. His shifter had claimed the woman, but she was married and possibly a criminal. The Gryphon growled in his head at that thought.

Once inside, Theo had Hayden take Sadie to a bedroom that had already been prepped. As gently as possible, he laid her on her stomach. The need to cover her bikini-clad body was strong. Jericho must have felt Hayden's rising unease because he grabbed a blanket and put it over Sadie from the waist down before stepping back out of the way.

Theo was thorough in his inspection. "Looks like she was hit with a blunt object, possibly the butt of a pistol. The cut is pretty deep, and she'll need staples. I'm sure she has a concussion, but I won't know if there's further damage until I get a scan. I'm going to clean the wound and dress it. After she wakes up and talks, we'll get her to my clinic."

"Thank you, Theo." Hayden sat on the opposite side of the bed, holding Sadie's hand. *Please be innocent.*

Chapter Nine

Sadie

SO, THIS WAS Hell. Mercedes always thought she'd end up in heaven when she died. At least a version of it. Maybe not the one with streets of gold and pearly gates she'd heard about when she was younger, but floating away on clouds or possibly dancing to her favorite Latin tune. Instead, her head felt like it had been split in two. The pain was excruciating. The torment part of Hell was right. But she didn't feel any flames licking at her skin. Now that she was paying attention, whatever she was lying on felt more like that fluffy cloud she'd envisioned. *Not a cloud.* A bed. Mercedes wasn't dead, so what the hell happened? Had she fallen at the pool and hit her head on the concrete? And where was Mateo? Oh god, her son. She'd left Mateo to fend for himself!

"Mateo?" she tried to call, but her voice came out sounding like a frog croaking.

"Shh. Try to relax." Mercedes didn't know the voice, but it was definitely masculine. She eased her eyes open and shut them quickly against the harsh light. "Hang on. Let me dim the lights." The bed dipped and rose as whoever was there stood. The bed dipped again when the man sat. A callous hand gripped hers gently. "You're safe, Sadie. I promise I won't hurt you, but whenever you're ready, I need you to open your eyes so we can talk."

Sadie? How did this man know her old nickname? She squinted to test the lighting and found the room was no longer bright. What she did find was the blond from the club. Only he looked different. Gone was the man who had dressed to impress, and in his place was someone more rugged like her brother, the biker. The man sported a tight, black T-shirt that showed off a whole lot of tattoos. She had gotten a peek at them underneath his dress shirt at the club. When he didn't move, she looked up at his face.

"Who..." Mercedes cleared her throat. "Who are you, and where am I? Where's my son?" *Oh, god.* "Mateo? Mateo!" Mercedes tried to get out of the bed, but strong arms held her down. "Let me go! Mateo!"

The door flew open, and another man she'd seen at the club was standing there. This one was shorter, and his hair was longer, but he was no less threatening. "Do you want me to get Theo?"

"No. I've got her. She just woke up, so give us a few minutes before you send him in."

The man narrowed his eyes at her before backing out of the room.

"Sadie, do you remember what happened?" the man asked as he rose and stood beside the bed.

"H-how do you know that name?"

The blond glanced away and took a deep breath. When he turned back, he told her, "I was sent to find you. You *and* your husband." The man paused again. "Are you aware of your husband's business dealings?"

Mercedes's chest felt funny, and there was a buzzing in her already-throbbing head. She started to nod, then thought better of it. "A little."

"Tell me what you know." The man's face was blank. There was no smile. No frown. Just cold indifference. She didn't blame him. If he knew about Juan Carlos, he probably thought the worst of her too.

"He sells drugs."

"What else?" He fisted his hands and released them before crossing his arms over his chest and taking a step back.

"That's all I know for sure. I only know that much because I overheard the guards talking outside my suite one day."

"Do you help him in any capacity?"

"No. God, no." Her eyes burned, but she blinked to keep from crying. "He kidnapped me when I was fifteen. I've been a prisoner ever since."

"But you're married to the man." The man's face changed then to a scowl.

"I had no choice. He said if I didn't marry him, he would kill my family."

"Are you aware of the reason Juan Carlos moved from Mexico to the States?"

"He said he invested in a new business venture, but I figured he was talking about more drugs."

"Do you take drugs? Does he?"

"I've never done drugs a day in my life. I have no idea if he does or not. I don't see him that often." Mercedes clenched the blanket covering her legs. "Where's my son?" The buzzing stopped, but the pain didn't subside. She couldn't stop the tears from streaming down her face.

The man's demeanor changed, and his eyes softened. "Do you remember anything about what happened? How you came to be harmed?"

Closing her eyes, Mercedes thought back. The last thing she remembered was Mateo going inside with Ana Marie. The woman had come to collect them both, saying it was time to eat lunch. Mercedes thought that was odd considering they usually ate by the pool, but she didn't argue. Mercedes never argued. "I was outside when Ana

96

Marie came for Mateo. Instead of eating outside, she was going to get him dried off to sit inside at the table. They went into the house, and I decided to stay outside for a few more minutes. I..." *Footsteps. Mercedes opened her eyes when the shadow fell across her body, then pain. Blinding pain.* "I was lying on my stomach. I heard footsteps, and someone was standing behind me. They hit me on the head. That's all I remember. Please. Please tell me Mateo's okay."

Mercedes reached up and swiped at her cheeks. She leaned back, and the pain worsened. She automatically raised her hand, but before she could touch the back of her head, the man grabbed her wrist.

"You have five staples where you were attacked. The doctor says you have a concussion, but we won't know if it's worse than that until he can take you in for a scan. As for Mateo, he's missing." Mercedes gasped, and the man tightened his hold on her hand. "There was an attack on the house. All the guards are dead. The nanny and housekeeper weren't harmed, and Antonia was shot but not fatally. She was yelling about Mateo being taken. That's all we know."

"But how do you know all that? Why were you there?" Mercedes leaned back against the pillow, turning her head away from the worst of the pain.

"Like I said, I was sent to find you."

"Who sent you? Who are you?"

The blond sat beside her hip, still grasping her hand. "My name is Hayden. You are at my... cousin's home. Another one of my cousins is a doctor. He's the one who tended your wound and will look after you until you're better."

A knock on the door sounded before it was opened, and a different man than the one before came in. This one was carrying a black satchel.

"Sadie, this is the doctor I was telling you about." Hayden released her hand to stand, but before he could, she grabbed his arm.

Sadie. It had been so long since anyone called her that, and it felt good. She preferred it. Always had. It would take a while to get used to hearing it or thinking of herself as the person she had been back before she'd been given to Juan.

"Please don't leave." She had no idea who this man truly was besides the one she'd dreamed of being the knight who saved her. Maybe he was her savior. Or maybe he was someone who knew her husband and was just as bad as Juan. She didn't get the same evil vibe from him though. Especially when he called her Sadie.

"I won't. I'm going to step out of the way so he can talk to you." Hayden looked at the other man and nodded.

The doctor sat beside her. With his dark hair and eyes, he looked nothing like Hayden. They didn't have to have the same coloring to be related. She knew that, but Hayden had hesitated when he said they were cousins. The doctor – Theo – introduced himself before telling her what he was doing. He apologized before shining the bright light in her eyes. Sadie couldn't help but squeeze them shut against the pain.

"Sorry about that. Are you hungry? Do you feel like eating?"

"No. I just want my son." Sadie's eyes welled up again. Her poor little boy. At least she'd been a teenager when she'd been taken away from everything she knew. Mateo was so young and helpless. *Please, God. Please keep him safe. Please don't let anyone hurt him. I'm begging.*

"We're going to do everything within our power to find Mateo and bring him home. In the meantime, you need to keep up your strength. Will you please try to eat something?" Hayden asked.

"I doubt I can keep anything down."

Theo gripped her hand and squeezed before letting go. "Let's try some soup. My sister-in-law has some broth warming on the stove. Also, I can either give you a shot for the pain, or if you think you can manage pills, I have those as well."

Sadie didn't know these people. They seemed nice enough. If they were going to hurt her, they wouldn't have stapled her head back together, nor would they be offering to feed her. "A shot will work quicker, right?" The doctor nodded, and she made her choice. "I'd prefer that then."

Theo produced a vial of medicine and a syringe out of the black bag. While he was doing that, a woman entered the room carrying some clothes.

"I thought you might be more comfortable wearing something besides a swimsuit." Her smile was genuine. "I'm Nora. I brought a variety of things so you can choose what suits you best."

Theo prepped Sadie's arm with a cotton swab, then plunged the needle into her skin. She didn't wince, because the little prick of pain was nothing compared to what was going on in her head.

"There. That'll take a few minutes to kick in, but once it does, you might get a little drowsy. Hayden and I are going to step out of the room so you can change clothes. Nora will help you if that's okay."

Sadie didn't want Hayden to leave. "I'll just slip something on over my swimsuit for now, but thank you for the offer. I will take you up on the soup, though." That would get Nora out of the room. Not that Sadie didn't appreciate the woman's kindness, but she didn't want Hayden to go anywhere.

Nora smiled again. "I'll be right back." She waited for Theo to stand, and together, they left the bedroom.

Hayden moved closer to the bed and picked up the items the woman had brought. "Let's see. We have sweats and shorts, a T-shirt, or a sundress. Which do you prefer?"

Mercedes would have been expected to wear the dress

had she been at home, but it had been so long since Sadie had even seen a pair of sweatpants, she chose those and the tee. Hayden helped slide the large shirt over her head, mindful of the staples. When she held out her hand for the pants, the man blushed before turning his back. Sadie thought it was adorable and further solidified her belief he was one of the good guys.

Sadie pushed the blanket off her legs and eased them over the side of the bed. When she went to stand, she became dizzy. Sadie reached for the dresser to steady herself, but Hayden was there to help her.

"Easy. Hold onto the dresser." Hayden took the pants and knelt at her feet, sliding the sweats over her legs. As he pulled them up, he rose to his feet, his fingers skimming her skin as he did. Sadie lifted the T-shirt when Hayden reached her hips. He pulled the drawstring tighter and tied it off. His fingers lingered at her waist, then he jerked back as though he'd been burned.

"Thank you." Sadie avoided his gaze as she sat on the bed and scooted back against the headboard. The door opened, and Nora entered carrying a tray.

"I need to make a phone call. I'll be back in just a few minutes." Hayden didn't look at Sadie before exiting the room.

Nora brought the tray over and placed it across Sadie's lap. "It's not too hot, so don't worry about burning yourself. I brought crackers and some tea. If you'd rather have something else to drink, just let me know."

"This is perfect. Thank you."

"You're welcome. Mind if I sit with you? Just in case you get sick and need help?"

"I don't mind. Thank you for your kindness." Sadie meant it. Other than Ana Marie, no one was nice to her. Nora looked to be in her late thirties, but her demeanor came across as older for some reason.

"You're welcome." Nora opened her mouth, then closed it. Taking a seat on the side of the bed, careful not to disturb the tray, Nora turned toward Sadie. "I just want you to know you're in good hands with Hayden. He's going to do everything he can to find your son."

Sadie chewed, then swallowed the bite of cracker she'd nibbled. "I appreciate you saying that, but if he does find Mateo before Juan does, my husband won't stop until he has Mateo back. I'm not sure Hayden's aware of what he's up against."

"He's well aware." Nora patted Sadie's leg. "But Hayden's family – our family – this is what they do. You don't need to worry about him. Just concentrate on getting better."

"What exactly is it the family does?"

"They take down the bad guys."

Hayden

HAYDEN STEPPED OUT into the hall and leaned against the wall, closing his eyes. *She's innocent.* But still married. Why did she have to be married?

She won't be once you take out the husband.

You think she'll want us when she knows we kill Alvarez?

Yes. You heard her. He forced her into the marriage.

His Gryphon had a point. But Hayden was getting ahead of himself. Just because he felt the connection didn't mean Sadie did. If she did happen to feel something for him, that didn't mean much considering her son was missing. She would eventually be reunited with her family, and they lived in south Texas. Hayden's life was in New York. *If* Sadie felt something for Hayden, it was probably gratitude. Well, it would be when he found Mateo and brought him back to his mom. Hayden wanted a mate so badly he was probably latching onto her for the wrong reasons.

None of that mattered. What did matter was finding Mateo, then taking out Alvarez. Hayden had a job to do. Pushing away from the wall, he strode into the living room where Spyder, Jericho, and Devon were watching something on a laptop. Samson and Storm were nowhere to be seen.

"Well?" Spyder paused the video when he noticed Hayden.

"She's innocent. I voiced her, and she knows nothing about Alvarez's business other than he sells drugs. He forced her into the marriage, saying if she didn't, he'd kill her family."

"You need to watch this." Jericho pointed at the computer. Hayden stepped up behind Spyder, and the male rewound the video.

The scene was like something from a movie. Several masked gunmen opened fire on Alvarez's guards. Guards who hadn't known the intruders were in the house by the way they were ambushed. Antonia was the only one who got a shot off, so maybe that's why she hadn't been killed. The female fell to the floor, clutching the wound in her side. Spyder rewound the video again, clicking the screen to a different view. This one showed one of the guards – or gunmen, it was hard to tell which since they were all dressed the same – enter the kitchen before the chaos began. He opened a door and stepped in. When he reappeared, he was carrying a child who appeared to be sleeping. Then the male rushed out of the back door.

"Do we have video from the outside?"

"Samson's working on that now. I'm going to rewind

102

and play it slowly. Pay attention to this part." Spyder slid the cursor backward and started the video at the point Antonia came onto the screen. Hayden leaned forward for a better look even though he didn't need to with his Eagle eyes.

"She has a clear shot, so why doesn't she hit the guy? And why doesn't the male kill her? He also had a clear shot. Are you thinking inside job?"

Spyder paused the video. "Sure looks that way. It's odd that neither Antonia nor Mercedes were killed."

Hayden put a couple steps between him and Spyder. "You can't possibly think Sadie was in on it. No way would she put her son through being abducted for... No. She didn't have any part in whatever that was."

Spyder stood and rounded on Hayden. "I'm looking at the clues on that video from every angle. It's part of the job. A job you seem to have forgotten about."

The other males in the room took a step closer to them both, but Hayden held up his hands. He knew his family had his back, but he didn't want them getting in the middle of whatever this was between him and his fellow Hound. "I haven't forgotten anything. Now that I know Sadie is innocent, the parameters of the job have changed."

"Is she innocent though? Yes, you voiced her, but did you ask all the right questions? Now that you've seen the video, you need to find out if she's involved. Maybe she hired someone to knock her out and take the boy somewhere safe to get him away from his father."

"No. You weren't in there when she asked about Mateo. You didn't see how distraught she was."

"Maybe she's a good actress. You don't know this female, yet you're thinking with your dick and not your brain."

Hayden lunged at Spyder, but Devon and Jericho stepped between them. "Stop, Uncle." Devon placed his palm on Hayden's chest. "And you," Devon pointed at Spyder. "What is your problem with Sadie?"

Spyder sneered. "*Mercedes* is a target as much as her husband. Someone wants them both taken out. Why? If she's so innocent, why take out a contract on the female? I'm asking the hard questions here. The ones that have to be asked and answered. That video is proof that things aren't what they seem. Maybe the two women are in on it together. Maybe Alvarez is a worse bastard than even we realize, and the two of them concocted a way to get the boy out of the house. The gunmen come in, shoot all the guards, leave the women alive, then they disappear to wherever the boy is being kept. It's not a coincidence the hit happened a few hours after Alvarez got on a plane. Somebody knew he was going to be gone. Knew his schedule. We don't have all the facts. Havyk, I know you think Mercedes is special because she's Dominic's sister, but you have to think logically."

"Wasn't it you who said to trust my instincts? Or was your little story about the teacher all bullshit?" Hayden sliced his hand through the air. "I'll go back in there and voice her again just to prove you're wrong."

"I want to be there when you do."

Hayden glared at the Hound. "Fine. Let's go." Hayden stalked back down the hall to the bedroom. He paused at the door and regained his composure. When he entered the room, he stopped a few steps in. Sadie was in Nora's arms, crying. "What happened?"

Nora's eyes were sad. "She's worried about her son."

"Mercedes, we need to ask you about the attack on the house." Spyder shouldered past Hayden and stopped at the foot of the bed. Hayden wanted to punch the male, but he also knew whatever Spyder asked, the answer would prove she had nothing to do with her son's abduction.

Sadie pulled away from Nora and wiped at her face. "What about it?"

Hayden expected Spyder to puff out his chest and glare at the female. Instead, he softened his gaze and sat on the foot of the bed. "Tell me about your relationship with Antonia." Spyder's Gryphon voice was strong.

"I don't have a relationship with her. We just live in the same house. I avoid her if possible because the woman hates me for some reason. Me *and* Mateo."

"Why would she hate you?"

"I-I think she's jealous. From the first day Juan brought me to live with him, she let me know she didn't want me there. It got worse when I had my son. She calls Mateo names. He's scared of her."

"And you? Does she call you names too?"

"Yes. Only she doesn't do it where Juan can hear. At least she never did until..." Sadie looked across the room, her eyes unfocused.

"Until?"

"When we came home from the club, she and Juan got into an argument. He was mad at her for going off and dancing with you instead of staying where I was. She called me a bitch, and Juan slapped her."

"Do you think your husband loves you?"

"He loves Mateo."

"But does he love you?" Spyder asked again.

Sadie returned her focus to Spyder. "Maybe. Sometimes he acts like he does, but I honestly don't know."

"Did you have anything to do with the attack on the house?"

Nora gasped, and Hayden held his breath.

Sadie fisted her hands, and her body shook. "No! My little boy is out there with killers. What kind of mother would I be if I arranged something like that? Not one who loves her son."

"Do you think Antonia is capable of having your son kidnapped?"

105

Sadie tried to blink away the tears but failed. "Yes."

"Thank you, Sadie." Spyder released his voice, and the pressure in the room eased.

"Satisfied?" Hayden kept his voice low so only Spyder could hear him.

"Yes." Spyder didn't apologize. Instead, he left the room without another word.

Hayden turned to Sadie. "How are you feeling?"

"Sad. Angry. Frustrated."

"I meant your head. Did the medicine help at all?"

Sadie's eyes were red and puffy, but she was still the most beautiful creature Hayden had ever seen.

"I guess. What's going to happen to me?"

"What do you mean?"

"By now, Juan knows that Mateo and I are missing. Once he returns, he's going to tear this town apart until he at least gets Mateo back."

"Do you want to go back to your husband?"

"No, but if he finds Mateo, then I don't have a choice. I won't let my son be raised by that monster alone."

"And if we find Mateo first? Do you want to take your son and return home?"

Sadie shook her head. "No, but what choice do I have? He's a powerful man, and I'm nothing. I have no education, no job, no money. I don't have a driver's license. I don't even have my birth certificate. I..." Sadie closed her eyes, and more tears fell. "None of that matters without Mateo. He's my world, and without him, it's not worth living."

CHAPTER TEN

Antonia

ANTONIA HAD FAILED. "Please, I need to stay here until my brother gets home." She didn't want to go to the hospital. Not with the police in the house. She needed to call Juan and tell him what happened. Antonia didn't want him coming home blindsided. None of the guards had lived through the attack on the estate. Mateo had been taken, and Mercedes... Antonia didn't know where the girl was or if she was alive. She had mentioned her sister-in-law to the detective hoping to get some information. So far, nobody was mentioning the other woman.

She had already given her statement while the EMTs were checking her over and the cops were questioning Ana Marie and Elena. Antonia couldn't hear what the women were saying. Not that it mattered. The gunmen had worn masks, and she had no doubt the guns they used wouldn't be registered. This was a professional hit. They wouldn't be dumb enough to leave evidence behind.

"Ma'am, this is a crime scene. Your brother won't be allowed back in the house, at least not until it's been processed. You already said he was out of town, so CSU should be finished by the time he returns." Detective Adam Hague was a no-nonsense kind of man, and he wasn't backing down. If the situation were different, Antonia would find the man attractive. As it were, she found him annoying. He motioned for the EMTs to continue pushing the gurney she was strapped to out the door and into the ambulance.

He was going to kill her. Juan Carlos was going to finish the job the gunmen started.

Hayden

HAYDEN'S HEART BROKE for Sadie. He couldn't imagine what she was going through, not knowing where Mateo was. He wanted to stay with her and offer comfort, but he couldn't do his job sitting there holding her hand. With Juan Carlos out of town, Hayden wasn't worried about the hit. No, he wanted to focus on finding Mateo. And to do that, he needed outside help. Samson had hacked the security feed at the estate and provided the video. Hayden needed to find out if the Hound's level of expertise went further. If not, he would call Lucy.

"Sadie, do you have any idea who would have attacked your home and taken Mateo?"

"Not really. I mean, you know who Juan is and what he does. I'm sure he's made a lot of enemies. Maybe the family that used to live in the house Juan took over? I don't know who the house belonged to or what Juan did to make that happen. If the former owner had a wife and kids, maybe they paid someone to get back at Juan for taking away their home."

"It belonged to Hector Ramirez. Is he the only one you know your husband has gone after lately?"

"Juan doesn't share anything with me. Maybe you could ask Antonia. She travels with Juan sometimes. Joins him for his meetings."

"And you don't know who these meetings are with?"

"No. Whenever someone comes to the house, Mateo and I aren't allowed outside our suite."

"You mentioned that before. You don't share a room with your husband?" Hayden had been curious as to why Sadie and the boy had their own rooms.

"No. He calls for me whenever he wants..." Sadie looked away. She pulled her legs to her chest and clasped her hands around her shins. "Once he's done with me, he sends me back to my room," she whispered.

What a motherfucker. Alvarez used his wife for sex. If Hayden was right, the drug lord married Sadie, had her produce an heir, and kept her secluded until he wanted to fuck her or take her out to a club and show her off. Hayden wasn't knowledgeable about the laws in Mexico, but in the States, he was pretty sure wives were exempt from testifying against their husbands should they ever go to court. Hayden was going to make sure Alvarez never made it that far.

"Knock, knock," Theo announced before he entered the room. "Sadie, I'd like to take you to my clinic to run some tests. Do you feel up to a ride? Nora will come with us."

Sadie turned to Hayden. "Will you come with me?"

"Wouldn't you rather I focus on finding Mateo?" Hayden wanted nothing more than to go with her. To keep her within his sights, but he trusted his family.

Sadie bit her bottom lip, staring at him. After a few seconds, she relented. "Yeah. Do you really think you can?"

"I promise I'll never stop looking until he's found." Hayden didn't promise to bring the child back to her alive. He couldn't, because the boy had been taken by some evil people. Hayden had no doubt once Juan Carlos found out

109

his son was missing, he'd be just as diligent in finding the child. If Juan got to Mateo first, Hayden would do the job he'd been hired for, then Mateo could be reunited with Sadie.

Hayden helped Sadie to Theo's car after Nora found her a pair of flip-flops. He insisted she lie down in the back seat. He told her it was so she would be comfortable, but it was so she wouldn't be seen. Theo promised to keep her safe before sliding into the driver's seat.

Nora patted Hayden on the chest. "We'll protect her with our lives. You focus on finding the boy."

Hayden thanked his nephew's mate, then stood in the driveway watching the car until it was out of sight.

Spyder, Jericho, and Devon were waiting for him on the porch. "Let's get busy." Hayden strode past them into the house. Once they were seated, Hayden turned to Devon. "How good of a hacker is Samson?"

"Not Lucy level of good." When Hayden's eyebrows rose, Devon shrugged. "What? Rory talks. She's proud of all her grandkids, but Lucy holds a special place in her heart. It might be because she wasn't raised in the family like the rest of us."

"Okay, so not as good as Lucy, but can he get into the CCTV footage close to the Alvarez compound? Hack into Alvarez's phone? Things like that?"

"I'm not sure. What are you thinking?"

"First, I want to see if there are any visible signs of who was in the area at the time of the attack. Two or three vehicles traveling together. There were several gunmen, and I doubt they all rode in one vehicle. If we can find the cars, we can see who owns them. See who took Mateo. I also want to know if Antonia has her own bank accounts. Were any large withdrawals made? If it were Alvarez, I'd say he paid in cash, but if his sister is the one who ordered the hits, she probably wouldn't have that kind of money lying around."

Jericho unsnapped then snapped the black cuff on his wrist. "You think Antonia would take out her brother's men? Why?"

"Sadie said the woman hates her and Mateo. What better way to eliminate them than hire someone to come in while Juan Carlos was away?"

"But she was shot," Jericho said.

"But not fatally, which would make it appear she was another victim."

"What about Alvarez?" Spyder asked.

Hayden narrowed his eyes. "You mean the hit?"

"Yes. We still have to take him out."

"I'm aware." Hayden's patience was thread-thin and ready to snap. He admired Jude. Knew he was a good male and a better mercenary, but Ryker trusted Hayden's judgment, or he wouldn't have offered him the job. "I haven't forgotten, and I'd appreciate it if you stop reminding me. That shit's getting old. I know what the fucking job is, but I won't let a small child remain out there with motherfuckers like the ones who associate with Alvarez. With Juan Carlos out of town, we can't get to him anyway, but I have a proposal for you."

"What's that?"

"You take over the hit on Alvarez. Focus on taking him down while I search for the child."

"Fuck." Spyder reached back and rubbed at his neck. He stared at Hayden who glared back. "No. We do this together. I'm sorry I keep reminding you, but I get it now."

"Get what?" Hayden wasn't ready to accept his apology.

"Mercedes – Sadie. You think she's your mate. I've seen this enough times to know how this is going to go down, so I'll back off. It's going to take all of us to get to Alvarez."

"I don't think... She's not..." Hayden was lying. He did

think that, but it didn't matter. "Sadie's married. And even if we take out her husband, she's got a family waiting on her. A mom and brother who've been waiting eight years for a reunion, or at the least, some closure. They have a grandchild and nephew they're going to want to get to know. I plan to make that happen. I'm going to give Sadie her life back. Do I feel a connection? Yes. But I won't sacrifice her happiness for mine. Devon, get Samson on the phone. Find out if he's willing to help. If not, I need to call Lucy."

"He's willing. He took a laptop from Alvarez's office while Spyder, Storm, and I were voicing the females. He also has a phone Storm took from Antonia. I'll go call and see if he's found anything." Devon left the room to make the call, and Hayden stood, walking over to the front window and looking out at the various plants growing in the brutal Texas heat. He could picture Rhiannon out there talking to them, drawing from their energy.

Jericho came and stood beside him. "Lindy is a nurse over at the hospital. I can call and see if she's on duty. If she is, I'll have her check on Antonia." Lindy was one of Laurel's granddaughters. Hayden had lost count of how many great nieces and nephews he had, most still living in the surrounding area.

"No. I don't want anyone who isn't a Hound involved. If Antonia had something to do with the attack, she's just as evil as her brother. I don't want Lindy on the other female's radar."

"Samson is already digging into Alvarez." Devon waved his phone as he walked back into the room. "He hasn't found much on the computer, but right now he's focused on the phone we took from Antonia. So far, there's nothing suspicious like emails or texts regarding the hit, but she did keep Alvarez's schedule on it. The trip he's on was to meet with someone named Benning in California."

"She would have used a burner phone. One her brother didn't know about. Devon, did you ask Samson about checking cameras?"

"I did, but he doesn't have the necessary equipment. I was going to suggest calling Lucy."

"I'll do that now. Spyder, can you forward that video to my phone? I want Lucy to take a look at it."

"On it." Spyder returned to the table and tapped a few keys. Hayden's phone pinged. He then forwarded the video to his niece before stepping outside to call her.

"Hey, Hay," Lucy answered.

"You sound like Major," he joked.

"That kid. If my child turns out to be half as special, I'll be lucky."

"Something you want to tell me?" Hayden would love to have another niece or nephew to dote on back home. He had countless in Texas, but with him not living there, he wasn't as close to them as he was Maveryck's twins and Lucy.

"Not yet. Doesn't mean we aren't trying. Now, I know you didn't call to talk about kids. I got your video. What am I looking at here?"

"Actually, it is about a child. That time-progression picture I asked you for? That was the boy's mother. I'm on a job, and the marks are the woman and her drug lord husband. Turns out, the woman is an innocent. We found out the male flew out of town, so we went in to see about getting the female out of the house. When we arrived, what you're seeing on the video had just happened. Sadie was outside by the pool, and someone had knocked her out. The men who hit the house left all the females alive, but they got away with the son. I have a Hound down here doing some digging, but he doesn't have the skills or equipment you and Henry do."

"What do you need from us?"

113

"I'm sending you the address of the house. See if you can find any vehicles in the area around the time of the hit that look suspicious. At least two coming and going in the same area."

"Got it. Do I need to wipe the security feed at the house?"

"Samson said he took care of that, but if you could hack into the feed and double check, I'd appreciate it. Also, if you would, see if you can get feed from the back of the house. Someone took off with the boy."

"I'm on it. I can't imagine what the mother is going through." Lucy sniffled, and it reminded Hayden what a good heart his niece had. She didn't know Sadie, but she felt for the woman.

"She's shaken, that's for sure. She was forced into a marriage with the mark at a young age. She's lived as a prisoner in his home for eight years. I'm going to do my best to find the boy and reunite them."

"And I'll do everything I can to help you. Let me get busy."

"Thanks, Lucy." Hayden disconnected and pocketed his phone, then sank down into one of the cushioned patio chairs on Devon's back deck. He closed his eyes and tried to clear his mind, but Sadie's face was front and center. Hayden knew he'd been given this particular job for a reason. He'd been put in Sadie's path, and he thanked Zeus for it. If Spyder had taken the job without backup, the male might have taken out Sadie and Juan Carlos without first figuring out that Sadie was innocent.

You're being a little harsh.

Am I? He's being a dick.

He's being thorough.

Who's fucking side are you on? You're the one demanding Sadie is ours.

She is, but I'm also realistic where Spyder is concerned.

114

Don't get your hopes up about Sadie.

One of us has to.

Hayden would let his Gryphon do the hoping, because he couldn't do it. Yes, he wanted a mate. A family. But he couldn't count on it being Sadie. The female had too much going on in her life to go from being married to a drug lord to falling in love with the male who was going to take out her husband. She had a child to think about. Hayden would find Mateo, reunite him with his mother, and whatever happened afterward, he would accept. Just because all his siblings except Kyllian had found their mate early in life didn't mean Hayden would. And according to Kyllian, he didn't want a mate. He was happy with his current lifestyle.

The back door opened, but Hayden didn't have to look to know it was Spyder. The male took the chair next to Hayden and stretched his legs out, crossing his ankles. "Did you get in touch with Lucy?"

"Yes. She's going to do the things Samson doesn't have the ability or resources to."

"Good. She's something else."

"She really is." Hayden ran a hand down his face and opened his eyes.

"I'm sorry." Spyder threaded his fingers together and set them on his flat stomach. "I know you're capable, and I'm being a dick." Hayden wanted to agree, but he kept quiet. When he didn't respond, Spyder turned and looked at him. "Nothing to say?"

Hayden sighed. "I accept your apology."

Spyder smirked. "Not going to argue about me being a dick?"

"What's there to argue about?" Hayden grinned at the male, glad they were back on even footing. "Let's talk business. Alvarez is in California, so even if he left straightaway to come back home, he won't be allowed in his house because it's a crime scene. And when he does come

115

back, the police are going to question him."

"True, but his child is missing. I think the need to find his kid is going to overrule any trepidation he has about talking to cops."

"So you think he'll come back right away?" Hayden stood and walked over to the railing. He turned and leaned against it, crossing his arms over his chest. He hadn't given much thought to Alvarez beyond what the man meant to Sadie. Or didn't mean to her. Finding out the man had forced her into marriage had pissed Hayden off. Now he wanted to take his claws to the drug lord and give Sadie her life back, if that were possible.

"Probably. It would look suspicious if he didn't. I doubt there was anything in the house pointing to the fact that he's a drug lord. If the police had something on him, they'd have arrested him the minute he set foot in New Laredo."

"If we can get to him as soon as he returns, the police might believe his death is related to the hit on his home."

"Maybe, but the cops are also going to be keeping a closer watch on him, and Alvarez is going to be more guarded than before. Right now, as far as he knows, both his wife and child were taken by the same person or group of people."

"Fuck. The attack made our job harder, didn't it?" Hayden rubbed his chin.

"Probably, but not impossible. Like you said, when we take him out – because we will – the cops will think the two hits are related. It would be aces if we could find those responsible, take the guns they used to kill the guards at the house, and use one of them to take Alvarez out. That would link the two attacks. But that would mean prolonging the hit."

"It would, but if we find those responsible, we also find Mateo. Yes, I want to finish the job, but I really want to find the boy. I keep thinking about Major and Marshall. What if it were one of them who'd been taken? They're so little. Mateo's only a year older than the twins, and he has to be scared out of his mind. If..." Hayden closed his eyes and prayed to Zeus the boy wasn't being harmed.

"He's alive. We have to believe that."

"You're right, because I won't accept the alternative. But I'm telling you now, if something does happen to the boy? I'll burn the world down until every one of the fuckers who took him are nothing but ash."

CHAPTER ELEVEN

Sadie

SADIE'S HEAD HURT. The shot Theo had given her earlier worked for a bit, but now she was in pain again from crying. She couldn't stop the tears. Didn't a body eventually run out of them? Her baby was out there. Taken by men who had killed all the guards, and he had to be frightened.

"The scan looks clear. You have a concussion, but with a bit of rest, it will go away. Let's get you back to the house so you can lie down." Theo held out a hand to help her stand, but Sadie sat mutely.

"Sadie?"

A sob broke from her chest, and she covered her face with her hands. Sadie didn't want to rest. She wanted to tear the city apart until she found Mateo. She wanted to call her mom and her brother. Wanted them to know she was alive. Wanted to tell them all about her precious little boy.

Nora sat next to Sadie and wrapped a strong yet gentle arm around her. "I can't imagine what you're going through. If anyone had taken Jericho or one of his sisters when they were little, I'd have lost my mind. The only good thing about this is you have our family on your side. They won't stop until your son is found."

Sadie rested against the other woman, soaking up the comfort. Wait. Jericho? Sadie leaned away from the woman, squinting. "Jericho can't be your son, unless you had him when you were ten."

"I'm older than I appear. Good genes run in our family. But yes, Jericho is mine. Now come on. Let's get back to the house so Hayden can see you're okay."

"He said someone sent him to find me. Do you know who?" Sadie stood from the seat she'd been waiting in and allowed Nora to guide her to the back door. Theo had explained he had parked in the back where no one would see them. With someone after Juan, they couldn't be too cautious.

"I don't. All I know is things have gone sideways, but Hayden and the family are good at what they do. He'll figure all this out."

When they reached the back door, Theo told the women to wait. He took a look around outside and unlocked the car, then motioned for them to hurry. Sadie climbed into the back seat and once again stretched out so she couldn't be seen. Her mind wouldn't still. Who had sent Hayden to find her? Had it been her mother? Had she somehow found out what happened to Sadie all those years ago? No, that couldn't be right. If Hayden was sent to rescue Sadie, he would have gotten Mateo too. Wouldn't he? No, he said Mateo had already been taken by the time he showed up. Someone killed the guards but left the women alive. But Antonia was a guard too, so why hadn't she been killed?

The one called Spyder had asked about Antonia. Was she responsible? She hated Sadie, but why would she have been shot if she were in on the attack? Thinking was making her head throb, but Sadie couldn't turn her brain off. She needed to talk to the cops. Find out what they were doing to find her son. Since Juan was out of town, shouldn't she be at home in case a ransom call came in? Not that she had access to her husband's money, but she could stall until Juan got back.

Sadie sat up, ignoring the dizziness. "I need to go to the police. What if whoever took Mateo did it for ransom? Someone needs to be at home in case they call."

"Please lie back down, Sadie. Let's get you back to the house, and then you and Hayden can discuss going to the police."

"But why does he get to decide what I do? I don't know him. I don't know you either. For all I know, you all could..." Sadie didn't finish her statement. A glance passed between Theo and Nora, but neither one said anything. What if they were in on whatever happened? Yes, they were being nice, but did that mean they were good people?

"Sadie, I promise you we are on your side. You don't know us, that's true, but you can trust us. Hayden gets a say because he was the one sent to find you. In our family, we search and rescue victims. Reunite them with family or get them out of bad situations. I promise you can trust him. Trust us. Now, please, lie back down." Nora's voice was kind, and when she spoke, Sadie's head felt funny. The same as it had when Spyder had questioned her. The concussion must be worse than they thought.

Sadie did as Nora requested and lay down across the seat. A sense of peace washed over her. She still worried about Mateo, but she no longer doubted Hayden and his family. Sadie wasn't sure why. Just because Nora told her to trust them didn't mean the woman was telling the truth, but something inside Sadie shifted from doubt to trust. Closing her eyes, she allowed herself to believe Hayden was good and that he was going to find Mateo.

"We're here," Nora said quietly.

Sadie sat up gingerly. Her door opened, and Hayden was there. He held out a hand, and she placed her smaller one in his calloused grip. The big man was gentle with her, putting a strong arm around her waist as he walked her to the door. His hold wasn't possessive the way Juan's was whenever he held her the same way. No, this was a caring gesture, and it made Sadie want to cry. Again.

"Theo said you can have more pain relievers. Do you want to lie down in the bedroom? Or do you want to sit in the living room. It will be quieter in the bedroom."

"We need to talk, so I'd rather stay in the living room." Sadie thought it was better to be around more people than being alone with Hayden. She was already thinking of him as her personal savior, and she couldn't let herself believe the fairy tale her heart was spinning. The sooner she remembered she was a job to the man the better.

Hayden led Sadie to the sofa where he settled her with a large cushion at her back. He removed the borrowed flip-flops and covered her legs with a soft blanket. Instead of taking one of the chairs, Hayden sat next to her legs and clasped his hands on his thighs.

"You said someone sent you after me. Was it my mother?" Hayden wouldn't meet her eyes. Instead, he pinched the bridge of his nose and rubbed. "Or was it someone bad? Is that why you won't look at me?"

Hayden did look at her then. "Sadie, your husband is a bad man. He's not only a drug dealer, but now he's added human trafficking to his resume."

"What? No. That's… Oh, God." Bile rose in Sadie's throat, and she clamped a hand over her mouth.

"Do you need a garbage can?" Hayden placed his hand on her knee.

"No, just give me a minute." Sadie inhaled through her mouth several times until she got the urge to vomit under control.

"I'm okay. Please, tell me the truth."

Hayden left his hand on her leg, his thumb rubbing circles over the sweatpants. "My family, we rescue people for a living. We go out and find those who have been taken and held against their will. Have you heard of The

121

Ministry?"

Sadie had heard that name a long time ago, but being secluded in Juan's home for the last eight years, she only read what was in fashion magazines, and those articles were only about makeup, clothes, and dating advice. She told him as much, then added, "I wasn't allowed to watch any sort of live television, but that name sounds familiar."

"The Ministry is a worldwide cult. They claim responsibility for the apocalypse."

"Okay, yeah. I remember hearing about them in school."

"Part of what our family does is find their compounds and remove the leaders from power. Anyone who is there and wishes to get out, we help them start over. We offer a place to live while getting them counseling. Not all compounds we come across are part of The Ministry. Sometimes they're just a group of people wishing to live a simpler life. If they aren't harming anyone, if everyone is there of their own free will, we leave those groups in peace. It's the ones who are gearing up for world domination we target. That's part of what my family does. Another job we have is tracking down people the government and law enforcement haven't been able to catch or hold for whatever reason. People like Juan. We go after the worst criminals in the world. Drug lords. Pedophiles. Human traffickers. We use our specialized skills in hunting them and getting them off the street for good."

"And someone hired you to go after Juan?"

"Yes."

"And they wanted you to rescue me and Mateo?"

Hayden's hand tightened around her knee briefly before he removed it. "Not exactly. Whoever took out the contract did so on both you and Juan. I'm sorry, Sadie."

"Me? But I haven't done anything wrong." Sadie's eyes filled with tears when she realized what he was saying.

"Someone wants me dead? Then why didn't they kill me when they attacked the house?"

"It's possible the two aren't related. Whoever took out the contract wanted both you and Juan taken out. If those men who hit your house wanted you dead, they would have succeeded. Instead, they left all the women alive."

"Ana Marie! I need to call her. She has to be just as worried as I am about Mateo."

"Who's Ana Marie?"

"Mateo's nanny. Well, she's more than that, but that's her title. She's also his tutor and my friend."

"Do you have many friends?"

Sadie closed her eyes, and a lone tear leaked out. "She's the only one." Hayden squeezed her knee again, and when she looked at him, his thumb went back to stroking her leg.

"I'm sorry, Sadie. Sorry you've been so secluded these last eight years. I can't imagine what you've gone through. And as worried as the woman probably is, I think it's better that no one know where you are. If or when Juan comes back to town, he's going to question her, the cook, and his sister. If you don't call her, she can honestly say she has no idea where you are."

"You said if or when. Do you think he might not come back?"

"Several men were murdered in his home. The police are going to have questions. Someone like Juan Carlos isn't going to appreciate being interrogated. It's more than likely he's going to hire his own crew to try and find your son."

"But how's he going to know Mateo's missing?"

"You don't think Antonia's called him by now?"

Sadie pulled the leg closest to the couch toward her chest and wrapped her arms around her knee. The blanket fell away, pooling over her other leg. The one Hayden had yet to stop touching. She leaned her head against the pillow and sighed. "I have no idea. For all I know she could be the one who took out the contract. I've lived with the woman for eight years and know nothing about her."

Hayden's phone rang, and he rose from the sofa to answer it. "Try to relax. I need to take this. Hey, Luce," Hayden said as he walked out of the living room at the same time Nora padded toward the sofa.

"Are you hungry?"

"I don't think I can eat right now."

"Okay, but if you change your mind, just let me know. I brought you some pain relievers and water. I also have juice if you prefer that."

"Water's fine. Thank you." Sadie leaned up and took the pills. When she handed the glass back to the other woman, Sadie's curiosity got the better of her. "Who's Luce?"

"Lucy. Hayden's niece, so that makes her Devon's cousin. She's really good with computers."

"Is she like a prodigy or something? I mean, Hayden doesn't look that old."

"Lucy's in her early twenties, so not as much a prodigy as just really skilled. Hayden is the youngest of all the siblings. He's twenty-eight, I think?" Nora looked across the room, her mouth moving silently. "Yes, twenty-eight. He has four older brothers and six older sisters. All the sisters are twins, and one of them – Poppy – is Devon's mom. Two of the brothers are also twins, and one of them – Maveryck – has a set of twin sons who are four. I haven't met them yet, but I've seen pictures."

"Wow, that's a lot of siblings. I have an older brother. He was in a motorcycle club when my dad handed me over to Juan. I have no idea if he's still alive. Him or my mom."

"What about your dad?"

"I'm pretty sure he's dead. After he gave me to Juan, I heard a gunshot as we were driving away."

"Oh, honey. I'm so sorry." Nora clasped Sadie's hand.

124

"I'm not. He traded me to Juan because he didn't have the money he was supposed to pay. I was worth almost half a million, so I guess that's better than like twenty thousand."

Nora pushed Sadie's hair away from her face. "You're such a strong young woman. I'm glad Hayden found you."

Sadie looked around to make sure they were alone. "Did you know he was supposed to kill me?" she whispered.

Nora's green eyes were sad when she nodded. "Yes. I'm sorry about that too. There are some messed-up, evil people in this world."

"Like Juan. Hayden told me Juan is trafficking humans. How can someone do that? How can someone think another person's life is worth nothing more than a dollar amount? Men like him and my father..." Sadie swallowed hard. "I'm not sorry my father's dead, if he is, and I wouldn't be sad if Hayden killed Juan. He took me away from my mom, my home, my friends. He kept me hidden from the world for years. Threatened to kill my family if I didn't marry him. I was just a kid. He..." Sadie blew out a breath. "Sorry. I don't know why I'm telling you all this."

"Probably because you've been holding it in a long time. If he kept you hidden, you probably didn't have anyone to talk to."

"Just Ana Marie, and although she's always been nice, kind of like a mother figure, she still works for Juan. I couldn't exactly confide in her. She worked for him before he brought me home with him, so who's to say she's really not just as bad as he is?"

"Or maybe, like you, she didn't have a choice. If she was kind to you, she probably has a good heart underneath, but she knows the type of man Juan is and is afraid of him. What if, like you, she came to be employed by your husband for a similar reason you were traded to him? Maybe he threatened her family if she didn't toe the line?"

"Yeah, you're probably right. At least I hope you are. She spends as much time with Mateo as I do. I'd like to think Juan wouldn't have someone evil teaching my son."

"Sadie, does Juan love Mateo?"

"Yes. If I know nothing else about Juan, I do know that. And the sad thing is Mateo loves him back. He has no idea what type of man his father is. Nora, do you think Hayden will be able to find Mateo?"

"If anyone can, it's Hayden and the family. Lucy has a friend who's even better with computers than she is, and the two of them are working hard to help Hayden."

"But why? I was supposed to be someone Hayden killed. Why didn't he do that when he found me instead of bringing me here?"

"Because you're innocent." Nora's voice was filled with conviction.

"But how does he know that? How does he know I'm not lying to save my own ass?"

Nora tilted her head to the side, her gaze boring into Sadie's. "Let's just say he and the other Hounds are skilled in interrogation."

"Hounds?"

"The Hounds of Zeus. It's the name of their motorcycle club. All the Hounds are in the family business. They're the good guys. The ones who will do anything they can to save whoever needs saving. Think of them as biker superheroes. Only instead of capes, they wear kuttes."

"What's a cut?"

"That's the black vest with all the patches on it."

"Oh, yeah. My brother had one." Sadie was young the last time she'd seen Dom, but she always thought his biker vest – his kutte – was cool as hell. She didn't remember him being a Hound. Something about gods instead. Sadie wondered if he was one of the good guys, or if he'd turned

126

out to be a loser like their father. She prayed he was still the sweet guy who took her for rides on his bike. The brother who taught her about good rock 'n' roll music. The one who threatened to beat every boy's ass if they mistreated her. She didn't let herself think about Dominic often, but when she did, it made her miss home as much as thinking about their mother.

"Your brother's a biker?"

"Yes. At least he was before I was taken."

"He still is." Hayden entered the room, his hands deep in his front pockets. "And he's never forgotten about you."

Hayden

LUCY HAD BEEN able to locate Juan Carlos in California. Only his meeting wasn't *with* Benning – he *was* Benning. He was using the alias to move about. And so far, the male hadn't left California to return to Texas. That was the good news. The bad news was neither Lucy nor Henry had been able to find the vehicles of the men who attacked the estate. They weren't giving up. Lucy had put her research with Jonas Montague on hold so she could work with Henry to try and locate Mateo. Henry had his own set of problems with a hacker who was targeting the Stone Society.

Hayden passed the information over to Spyder and Devon before returning to the living room to check on Sadie. When she mentioned Dominic, Hayden decided to give the female some good news to hopefully take her mind off Mateo, if for a little bit.

Sadie's amber eyes widened at his admission. "You

know Dominic?" She sat up, pushing the blanket off her legs.

"I do. Here, I want to show you something." Hayden thumbed through the photos on his phone. When he stepped closer to the sofa, Nora stood, and Hayden sat down beside Sadie and showed her the tribute bike.

"Is that...?" Sadie ghosted her finger over the screen. "That's me."

"It is. When I'm not out catching bad guys, I build custom bikes. I was commissioned by Dominic to paint your picture on the tank. The request came in a couple months ago, so he hasn't forgotten you. When this mess with Juan is over and we get Mateo back, Dom's going to be thrilled to see you."

"But why can't we tell him now? I mean, he's a biker, so that means he's tough, right? Maybe he could help you." Sadie was so hopeful, and Hayden didn't want to squash her dream of finally seeing her family again, but he had to.

"It's not that simple, Sweetheart. The more people who know where you are, the better chance Juan has of getting his hands on you. I can't risk that."

Sadie tossed the phone in Hayden's lap and surged to her feet. "This is my life, not yours. I'm the one who's been held captive for eight years. The one who was tossed away over a business deal. The one who had to marry a monster against my wishes!"

When Sadie grabbed her head, Hayden got up and gently urged her to sit back down. "I'm sorry. I don't mean to upset you. And you're right – it is your life. But you need to trust me in doing the right thing for you."

"Why should I trust you? I don't know you. Yeah, you and your family have been nice to me, but you kill people for a living. How does that make you any better than Juan?"

Hayden sucked in a breath. Her words were like a punch to the solar plexus. "I am better than him because I don't kill just anyone. I only take out those who keep skirting the law. Those who are killers, pedophiles, human traffickers. People who have no problem with harming innocent victims. People who take in young girls as payment, then force them to marry them. You said yourself you didn't care if I took Juan out. I'm not going to apologize for what I do. I'm not ashamed that I get rid of the trash of the world. But hey, if you want Juan to find you, to take you back to your prison, then you should walk out the door right now. Go back to him and back to the way you've been living." Hayden fisted his hands, his chest heaving. Instead of arguing more, he stormed out of the room.

CHAPTER TWELVE

Hayden

"EVERYTHING OKAY IN here?" Spyder stood in the doorway between the living room and kitchen.

"I'm going for a walk." Hayden had to leave before he said something he'd regret. He strode through the house and out the back door, ignoring the glances from Devon and his mate. Zeus, he wished he had his bike. Hayden wanted nothing more than to get on one of his Harleys and take off. Since he didn't, he opted for the next best thing. Striding into the woods, Hayden looked around to make sure he was alone, stripped down to his bare skin, then shifted into his Eagle. His Gryphon was itching to be turned loose, but that was too risky. Rarely did Hayden get to let the beast loose, especially when there were humans in the area. Seeing a large bird was one thing, but to see a half eagle-half lion? That was the stuff fantasy movies were made of, and Hayden couldn't risk it.

Leaving without taking his clothes with him was stupid, but Hayden needed to get away from Sadie. Her words stung, but the longer he soared above the trees, the more he calmed down. He reminded himself what she was going through. What she had gone through over the last eight years. On top of that, her child was missing. Thinking of the boy, Hayden turned toward the estate where he'd found Sadie.

When he landed on a branch of the tallest tree, Hayden searched the area. The house was cordoned off with yellow crime scene tape. Hayden wanted to shift and search the house for his own clues, but he couldn't risk being found, especially wandering around naked. While he was staring at the lounge chair where he'd found Sadie, his Eagle prodded him.

There's someone here.

Hayden focused in on the where the Eagle had spotted a human. A man dressed in camouflage was hidden on the other side of the property. He was peering through a pair of binoculars, his focus on the house. Without knowing where the security cameras were, Hayden couldn't shift and voice the male. Instead, he sat quietly, watching. Since he'd left his clothes and phone back at Devon's, he had no way of communicating with Spyder, so all he could do was wait.

The sun's shadows shifted over the trees, finally changing place with moonlight. Hayden figured he sat there for over seven hours before the man moved from his post. When he did, he passed off the binoculars to another man dressed in the same dark camouflage. Hayden didn't see rifles, but that didn't mean the men weren't armed. Still, he wanted to get closer, so he flew away from the house, taking a long loop around and coming up behind them. Instead of overhearing their conversation, he found the first man walking through the back of the property while the other one took up the post to watch the house. Hayden kept his eyes on the man walking, and when he was far enough away, Hayden launched from the branch he'd perched on and followed at a distance. Luck was on his side when the man got into an SUV Hayden hadn't seen during his flyover. He figured instead of leaving a vehicle parked, they were coming and going in shifts. Hayden memorized the tag number before flying directly overhead.

Hayden estimated the man drove approximately forty or fifty miles before coming to a stop at an old house which, from the air, appeared to be abandoned. Hayden circled high above as the man got out of the vehicle and strode toward the back of the house. Instead of going inside, he sat down in one of several chairs surrounding what appeared to be a fire pit. Hayden settled on a nearby tree branch and watched. The sun was just rising when movement from the house snagged Hayden's attention. His grip faltered when a little boy, followed by an older woman, came out of the house. The boy had to be Mateo. He walked right up to the man and climbed on his lap while the older woman took a seat next to them.

What the ever-loving hell?

At least we know he's safe.

If that's even Mateo.

Get closer.

Hayden flew lower and dropped down to perch atop the house. The boy was speaking rapid Spanish with the woman. Hayden's understanding of the language was lacking, so he couldn't follow the conversation. But the child was smiling, so if this was Mateo, he seemed happy and comfortable with both adults. After a few minutes, the woman stood and held out her hand for the boy.

"Ven conmigo, Mateo. Vamos a prepararle el desayuno a Tomás."

Hayden didn't know what the woman said, but he did recognize the two names – Mateo and Tomás. Yes! He had found Sadie's son. If only he had his phone. Hayden flew over to a tree at the side of the house so he could take a peek inside. As far as he could tell, the woman and Mateo were the only ones there. He continued around the house to make sure. When he didn't see anyone else, he took flight and headed for Devon's.

Sadie

SADIE STOOD AND headed to the kitchen, ignoring Spyder. Nora and Devon were whispering but stopped as soon as Sadie entered the room.

"Sadie, do you need something?"

"I'd like to go lie down in the bedroom."

"Of course, Honey. Do you want something to eat or drink? I have juice and tea."

"Just water would be nice, please." Sadie was hungry, but she didn't think she could keep anything down. She leaned against the doorframe while Nora got a glass out of the cabinet and placed it in the door of the fridge.

"Do you remember where the bedroom is? You were kind of out of it when we left earlier."

"I remember." Sadie took the glass and thanked the woman. Before she could turn away, Nora pressed her hand to Sadie's cheek.

"I know things seem bleak right now, but please remember Hayden's on your side, and regardless of what you think of his occupation, he's a good guy. All the Hounds are."

"Does your husband kill people for a living?" Sadie was tired, and her words came out harsher than intended.

Nora glanced at Devon's retreating back. "No. He isn't a mercenary, but if he were, I wouldn't have a problem with it. I've seen the evil in this world, and I appreciate those who put their lives on the line for those who are too weak to protect themselves. Like the military. They do the same thing as Hayden, only they're sanctioned by the government to go after bad men. Men like your husband who buy and sell humans so someone else can use them as slaves or for sex. Humans as young as your Mateo. Think about that before you judge Hayden too harshly." Nora squeezed Sadie's shoulder before turning away and walking out the back door where her husband had gone.

Sadie didn't want to think about it, but Nora had planted the seed, and now Sadie wanted Hayden there so she could apologize. She didn't want to go back to Juan. Didn't want to become a prisoner again. She should have asked Nora for more pain meds to have for later, but since she hadn't, Sadie took the water to the spare bedroom and closed the door. After taking a few sips of the cool liquid, she placed the glass on the nightstand, then curled up on the bed. When she closed her eyes, her precious Mateo's smiling face filled her thoughts. Wherever he was, she doubted he was smiling, and that hurt her heart. Tears ran down her cheeks, wetting the pillow. She was so sick of crying, but she couldn't help it.

Nora was right; Hayden's job, just because it was less than ethical, was important. If Juan was buying and selling people, he needed to be stopped. Before living with Juan, Sadie had never been around anyone who used anything harsher than marijuana. Some of her friends smoked pot, but they never abused it. Never got so strung out on something harsher where they would steal money just to have it. Yes, she had turned a blind eye to the fact that her husband sold drugs over the years, but she hadn't really had a choice. Now she did. Now there was someone who could stop him from ruining people's lives the way he ruined hers and her family's.

Hayden knew Dominic. Had met him. Had painted the most beautiful portrait of a younger Sadie. The gorgeous blond was freaking talented. Hayden hadn't mentioned her mother, and Sadie had to wonder if losing a child and husband had taken a toll. Sadie knew in her heart the man she'd called father was dead. Killed because of drugs. Because of Juan Carlos Alvarez. So yeah, she agreed her husband being taken out wouldn't be a big loss to the world.

Then she'd be free. She'd no longer be married to the man. She and Mateo would be able to have a new life wherever she chose. Except... How would she live? If Juan were killed, would all his money go to her and Mateo? Did the man have a will? Or would Antonia fight her for everything? Her sister-in-law could have the houses and cars. All Sadie wanted was her and Mateo's clothes and enough money to start over somewhere that wasn't Mexico.

If Dominic had a bike customized in her honor, he would want her around. Dominic would help her start over whether she had money or not. And if her mom was still around? Sadie could spend time getting to know her again, and Mateo would have a grandmother. He'd have a family who loved him. Dom and their mom would help them both in moving on.

A knock on the door roused Sadie. She had fallen asleep amid questions and tears. "Sadie?" Hayden stuck his head in the room. She'd expected the angry man who stormed out of the house to be the same one to return. It wasn't. Hayden was smiling. "I found him. I found Mateo."

"What?" Sadie jumped from the bed and grabbed Hayden's arms. "Where? Is he okay? Is he here?"

"Hold up." Hayden placed his hands on her shoulders, urging her to sit on the bed. "He's at a house about an hour from here. I couldn't bring him back, but we are going to go get him. He's with an older woman and a man named Tomás."

"Tomás? But he's one of Juan's guards. Why would he have Mateo? And what woman?"

"I didn't get her name. She's older with gray hair. But Mateo seemed like he knew her."

135

"It could be Ana Marie or Elena. Why would they have my son?" Sadie shook her head, bringing the pain back with a vengeance, but she ignored it. "Come on, let's go." She stood again, but Hayden stopped her. Again. "What are you waiting for?"

"We can't go in guns blazing. We have to make sure we have a solid plan so Mateo doesn't get hurt. The man – Tomás – he was watching your house. When a different man swapped off with him, I followed Tomás when he left. I have no idea if it's just the three of them. And you aren't going with us."

"Tell me. Tell me where my son is!" Sadie slapped Hayden's chest several times before he grabbed her wrists.

"Sadie, calm down."

"Don't tell me to calm down!" Her voice cracked as the tears fell. She broke free from Hayden's hold and took a step back.

"I'm going to get him. I promise, I'm going to bring him back to you. I had to come get Spyder and Devon to go with me. If I went in alone, I could have been shot or worse, and then no one would know where Mateo is." Hayden reached out like he was going to touch her but dropped his hand at the last second. "Your son is going to need things like clothes, so I want you to tell Nora his sizes so she can go shopping. You need clothes too."

"But I don't have any money."

Hayden did touch her then. He used his thumbs to wipe away her tears, and Sadie leaned into his touch before remembering she was pissed at the man.

"You don't need to worry about that. I'll take care of it. I'll take care of—"

"Havyk? You ready?" Spyder asked from the doorway.

Hayden closed his eyes and sighed, removing his hands from her face. Turning toward the other man, he said, "Give me a minute." Spyder inclined his head before backing out of the room, leaving them alone again. Sadie wanted to know what Hayden had been about to say before they were interrupted. She knew it was stupid to think this man could be interested in her, and Sadie wasn't sure she wanted that anyway. Yes, she'd dreamed of someone saving her, but this was reality. Not some schoolgirl fantasy. Hayden could have his own wife for all she knew.

"I need to make plans with the others so we can go get Mateo. Talk to Nora and tell her what you want her to get for you and Mateo. And not just clothes. Let her get him some toys or whatever will help keep him occupied while you're here. Okay?"

Sadie nodded. "I'm sorry."

"I'm sorry too. This is a stressful situation, but hopefully sooner rather than later, you'll be able to move on with your life with your son." Hayden stepped forward, cupped her face, and pressed his lips to her forehead. "I'll send Nora in." And with that, the man walked away, leaving Sadie wondering what his lips would have felt like against hers.

A few minutes later, Nora entered the room carrying a tray. "Hey, Honey. I brought you something to eat." Nora sat the tray on the dresser and handed Sadie a glass of juice. "Here's some pain medicine. You haven't taken anything since last night, and I just bet your head feels like it's about to burst open."

Sadie took the pills, washing them down with the sweet juice. "Oh, that's delicious."

"It's *agua de papaya*. I wasn't sure what you liked, so I made one of my favorites."

"That's very thoughtful. Do I taste lime juice?" Sadie took another sip.

"You do. As much as I love my tea full of sugar, I like my juices a bit less sweet. I hope it's okay. Plus, I made you a couple different sandwiches. It's technically time for

137

breakfast, but I wasn't sure what your stomach could keep down, so I fixed one with ham and cheese, and the other is a lighter one with cucumber and dill."

Sadie wanted to cry at the woman's thoughtfulness, but she was tired of the tears. "I can't tell you the last time I had a sandwich. Well, yes I can. I was fifteen. Is it crazy to miss something like that? I mean, who complains about having to eat something cooked for you at every meal?" Sadie picked up the triangle with cucumber and took a bite. She grinned at Nora who was watching her. "So good," Sadie muttered before taking another bite.

"What else do you miss? I was planning on cooking later, but if you want something simple, I'll get it for you. And what about breakfast? Did you have a favorite cereal? Do you like Pop Tarts? Toaster waffles?" Nora tapped her finger against her lips.

"Nora, it's fine. I'm not going to put you out any more than I already have. And I won't turn down a home-cooked meal. I'm sure whatever you fix will be different from what I'm used to. Everything I've eaten over the past eight years has been one Mexican dish after another. Don't get me wrong; Elena's a wonderful cook, but sometimes a girl just needs a cheeseburger or pizza. Mateo has never had pizza. Can you believe that?"

"I'm so sorry." Nora's eyes filled with tears.

Sadie sat down the sandwich and wiped her fingers on the cloth napkin. "I didn't say all that to make you feel sorry for me. I was just letting you know you don't have to go out of your way to fix something special. I'm going to enjoy whatever you cook."

Nora wiped her face and smiled. "Good to know. Now, Hayden wants me to go get you and Mateo some clothes. I can't wait to meet your little boy. It's been so long since Jericho and his sisters were small, it'll be good to have a young'un in the house again."

138

"And I still can't believe you and Devon are his parents. Devon and Jericho look more like brothers."

Nora smiled, but she changed the subject. "I need yours and Mateo's sizes. I figure shorts and T-shirts for him plus sneakers. Is that okay? And what about you? What do you like to wear?"

Sadie hated to tell Nora the way she'd had to dress, so instead of making the woman sad again, Sadie pointed at Nora's clothes. "What you're wearing is fine for me, but please, don't go spend a lot of money on us."

"Hayden's footing the bill, and he told me to spare no expense. He makes good money with those bikes he builds. He's even won awards, so he can afford to splurge on you and Mateo."

"But why would he? I'm just some woman he rescued. Heck, he was supposed to ki—"

"No." Nora shook her head. "Let's not think about that. As for why, Hayden sees how special you are, and as for Mateo? We're all suckers for kids in this family."

Sadie picked up the rest of the cucumber sandwich and took a bite. Now that she'd started eating, her stomach was letting her know how long it had been since the soup. The pills were already working, and Sadie wanted to regain the strength she'd lost since being hit over the head. God, had it only been yesterday when Hayden had brought her to Nora's house?

"Now, about those sizes."

CHAPTER THIRTEEN

Hayden

HAYDEN LEFT JERICHO at the house to watch over Sadie, while he, Spyder, and Devon went back to the house where Mateo was being held. Not that he thought anyone knew where the female was, but he didn't trust her not to try and reach out to her family. Not that she knew how after this long. Sadie didn't know if her mother was still in the area, or even alive, for that matter. But she knew Dominic was, and she was distraught.

As Hayden drove to the run-down house, his phone rang. He hit the button on the steering wheel to answer. "Hey, Lucy. You're on speaker. I've got Spyder and Devon in the car with me."

"Hey, guys. I ran the tag number you texted me, and it belongs to Alvarez."

"That kind of makes sense considering Sadie said Tomás is one of his guards. What doesn't make sense is why he has Mateo." Hayden called Lucy as soon as he returned to Devon's and gave her the license plate number of the SUV he'd followed.

"What if Alvarez is feeling heat from either the cops or some of his enemies? Maybe he had his guard take the boy to keep him safe."

"But why kill a handful of his own men?" Spyder

asked.

"To make it look like someone else did it?" Lucy huffed. "Who knows why these monsters do the things they do? I mean, look at what Rhiannon went through." Ryker's mate had lived in her own version of Hell after her mother died.

"Truth. What better way to make himself look like a victim?" Hayden drummed his fingers against the steering wheel. "Either way, I'm getting the boy back to his mother."

"Alvarez is still in California. He got a call from inside New Laredo General. Henry is tracking him, and so far, he isn't on the move. He's holed up in the hotel at the Bonaventure Casino in New Chula Vista."

"Is the sister still at the hospital? If so, she could have been the one to call him," Devon asked.

"Unless she checked herself out, she's still there. Last I checked, Antonia Dominguez had been admitted."

"Dominguez?" Spyder asked before Hayden could. "I thought she was Alvarez's sister."

"I knew that would be your next question, so I already did a little digging. It's harder to find out about Alvarez and his family since they're from Mexico. What I was able to find out is Antonia was the daughter of Jorge Dominguez, a man who was arrested twenty years ago."

"Let me guess? He was a drug lord."

"Yes, and guess who his protégé was? Juan Carlos Alvarez. Here's where it gets interesting. Jorge wasn't arrested for drugs but for vehicular manslaughter. From what I can tell, his assets weren't seized."

"So, Alvarez took over when his boss went to prison, and Antonia has been living with the man ever since?" Hayden flipped on the blinker to take the exit off the freeway.

"It would appear so. Oh, and Jorge was killed in a prison fight, so he won't be getting out and trying to take the business back from Juan Carlos. That's all I have so far.

141

I'm keeping tabs on Alvarez, and I'll let you know if he moves."

"Thank you for all you're doing. Oh, Lucy? Will you please get a copy of Sadie's birth certificate and Social Security card and send them to Devon's?" Hayden wanted to give Sadie every advantage once this mess was over.

"I'm on it. I'll text you when it's done."

"Thanks, Luce." Hayden disconnected the call. "No wonder Antonia hates Sadie."

"Do you think Antonia has a thing for her so-called brother?" Devon asked.

Hayden looked around, checking for the landmarks he'd seen from the sky. "Either that, or she's pissed she didn't get her daddy's business and all the money that went with it. When we were at the club, the guard arguing with her mentioned her doing her job, which I took to mean she too was a guard. Plus, the video from the attack on the house showed her with a gun. So instead of being partners with Juan Carlos, she's nothing more than the hired help. Fast forward twelve years from the time Dominguez went to prison. Alvarez takes Sadie into his home. When she's old enough, he forces Sadie to marry him and give him an heir. Alvarez now has a son to take over the family business when he's older, leaving Antonia in the shadows."

"Then why didn't Antonia take the kid instead of Tomás and the older woman?" Spyder asked.

"Who says she didn't? It's possible they're all in on it together." Devon caught Hayden's eye in the rearview mirror. "*Or* Antonia could be the one who ordered the hit. There's no one more dangerous than a woman scorned."

"Truth. Just ask Ryker." Spyder turned in his seat. "How are we going to play this? Are we going to question Tomás and the woman? Are we taking them out afterward?"

"They definitely need to be questioned. We need as

many answers as we can get. Not only are we up against Alvarez, but now we have to worry about Antonia as well. If she didn't have the kid taken, we need to find out who did. I say we determine their fate after we question them." Hayden pointed at a gravel driveway. "That leads to the house. It sits back a ways off the road. I'm going to find somewhere to park where we can hide the car." Hayden found another abandoned house a couple miles past the one where Mateo was being held. He parked behind the house so the SUV wouldn't be seen from the road should someone happen to drive by.

Instead of shifting and flying in, the three males jogged through the woods. The area they were in was heavily wooded, giving them the cover they needed. Daylight was fading, but their Gryphon vision allowed them to move through the dense trees. When they reached the edge of the property, Hayden held up a fist. He had already told Devon and Spyder the layout, and they had decided to split up with Hayden going in the front and the other two going in the back if Tomás wasn't sitting outside. As luck would have it, the man was sitting where Hayden had last seen him, only he wasn't alone. The woman and Tomás were watching as Mateo played with a dog.

"You didn't mention a dog," Spyder whispered.

"It must have been in the house." Before they could discuss next steps, the dog turned their way and started barking. "Fuck, that's not good." Hayden loved all animals, and he didn't want to hurt this one, but he wouldn't let it give away their presence.

"No! Come back," Mateo shouted and took off after the dog. That caused a chain reaction of Tomás following Mateo and the woman following Tomás, both calling after the boy to stop.

"Up!" Hayden said, releasing his Lion's claws to help climb the nearest tree. Devon and Spyder followed suit, and the three of them clung to branches while the dog barked and ran between the trees. It stopped at each one, putting its paws on the trunk, growling into the night. Tomás managed to grab Mateo before he reached the dense brush and handed him off to the woman.

"Mateo, no. It is too dangerous." The older woman was stronger than she looked. She turned back toward the house, holding onto the child, who was squirming to be let down.

"You were trained better than this. It's probably a squirrel," Tomás scolded in a clearly American voice. "*Platz.*" The dog, now focused on the man, sat down. "*So ist brav.* You're a good girl. You did your job and treed whatever it was. Let's get back to the boy." The man bent and gave her a couple ear scritches. "Go, Lina. *Geh raus.*" At the last command, the dog took off toward the house.

When Tomás turned to follow, Hayden jumped, landing on the man's back. The thirty-foot drop would have hurt had he not called forth his Gryphon wings to slow him. His T-shirt was shredded, but that was better than his body taking the brunt of the landing. Hayden figured he'd knocked the man out, but he still told him, "Don't move." When Tomás remained still, Hayden rolled off. Spyder held out a fist, and Hayden bumped the other male's knuckles.

"I've got him if you two want to go after the boy." Spyder placed his leather boot on the man's back.

Hayden looked toward the house. "What about the dog? From that command, I'd say it's highly trained."

Devon grinned. "I'll voice it, and if that doesn't work, I'll shift and show it who's boss. Come on."

Hayden followed his nephew out of the trees. When the dog became aware of them, it started barking.

"*Sitz,*" Devon commanded in both his Gryphon voice as well as what Hayden thought sounded German. The dog, Lina, sat, to Hayden's amazement. While they were watching the dog, they should have been paying attention to the older woman, because when they finally noticed her, she was holding a gun and pointing it their direction.

"Put the gun down," Devon said, still using his shifter voice.

The woman lowered the gun, and Hayden crossed the few feet to take it from her. When Hayden noticed Mateo was crying, he turned on his Gryphon's voice. "Mateo, my name is Hayden, and your mama sent me. She's worried about you, and I'm going to take you to her." Mateo nodded, and his sniffling turned silent.

The older woman frowned, and Hayden returned his attention to her. "Who are you?"

"Elena." So the cook.

Hayden didn't want to have this discussion in front of the child, but he would wipe his mind later.

"Why did you take Mateo?"

"Porque su padre es el diablo."

Little Mateo sucked in a breath, but Hayden had no idea what the woman said. "In English," he commanded.

"Because his father is evil."

"But his mother isn't. Why leave her the way you did? Why not take her too?"

"She's done nothing to protect Mateo for five years. If she were innocent, she would have taken Mateo and run."

"Do you honestly think she had the means to do that? She might be his wife, but she didn't have access to his money. She has no friends. No way of getting her son away from the house." Elena just stared at him. "If you believe Alvarez is a monster, why work for him?"

"I didn't have a choice. I worked for *Señor* Dominguez before he went to prison. When Juan Carlos took over, I remained so I could watch over Antonia, but it didn't matter. Juan Carlos's influence was greater than mine. He turned her into something just as bad as he was."

"So you and a couple guards decided to kill the others

145

and take the boy?"

"Havyk," Spyder interrupted. "We have a problem. Well, a couple actually." Spyder turned to Elena. "Sit down, don't move, and don't speak." Elena did as commanded. Mateo was still staring with wide eyes and shivering.

Hayden knelt in front of the boy. He hated using his voice on a child, but it was necessary. "You are safe, and you will forget this conversation." When Mateo nodded, Hayden stood and turned to Spyder. "What is it?"

"Tomás was supposed to check in with the other guard, and when he didn't, the other guard would have left his post to head here. Oh, and Tomás is undercover. The other man is not, nor does he know who Tomás really is."

"What did you tell Tomás?"

"I told him that five armed men came in and overpowered him and the woman, then took off with the boy. That will keep them looking for a while. It will also help Tomás keep his cover from being blown."

"How did he convince the other two to take the child?" Hayden picked Mateo up, ready to get the hell out of there.

"He didn't. The other guard and the woman are brother and sister. It seems they've been devising a plan for a while. They needed help, and Tomás had proven to be protective of the boy, so they took a chance and included him in their scheme."

"And a cop agreed to killing the other guards?"

"He states he knew nothing about the attack, so unless he's lying, the timing was coincidental. What do you want to do with her?"

"The way I see it, they were trying to do something good by getting Mateo away from his father. I say let Tomás and her brother deal with her. The siblings will probably go on the run, and Tomás will go back to being undercover. Not our problem right now." Hayden turned to Elena. "You will only remember that you were caught from behind then tied up, but you don't have to worry about Mateo. He'll be safe."

"You sure you want to tell her that? Five bad men were supposed to have taken him."

"Yes. She took the boy at risk to herself. She deserves to feel he isn't in danger."

Spyder inclined his head. "Yeah, okay."

Devon took Elena by the arm. "Come with me." He came back a few minutes later. "I used a phone charger to tie her hands behind a chair. I also gagged her."

"Good job." Spyder clapped him on the shoulder, then took off toward the woods.

The dog started whining, and Devon commanded, "*Bleib.*" Lina remained where she was.

"I didn't know you spoke German. That was German, right?" Hayden asked as he and Devon followed Spyder.

"Yes. I'm not fluent, but I know enough to get by. I am fluent in Spanish and French. I know a little Italian as well. Nora has cooking to keep her busy, so I took up learning languages as a hobby."

When they reached Tomás, he was lying on the ground unmoving. Spyder toed him with his boot. "I had to hit him to make it look realistic. He'll come around by the time the other guard gets here. Probably. Maybe."

They left him lying there as they made their way back to the SUV. Hayden placed Mateo in the back seat and secured the seatbelt around his small frame before sliding in next to him. The boy should've been in a booster seat, but there had been no time to grab one. Hayden wrapped his arm around Sadie's son, and the boy snuggled into his side. Hayden's heart did a little skip at how right that felt. Maybe not because of who Mateo was, but because Hayden wanted a child of his own. Sadie and Mateo couldn't be his, though. Once they took out Alvarez, Sadie would be reunited with her own family and Hay would go back to New York.

"Don't worry, Havyk. I'll make sure we aren't pulled over," Devon said from the driver's seat. Hayden gave him a small smile in the rearview mirror. Hayden was happy they had rescued Mateo, but they still had bigger hurdles with Alvarez being in California and Tomás being undercover.

"Did Tomás say how long he'd been on the case?"

Spyder turned sideways in his seat. "I didn't ask. Once I found out Jose, the other guard, was on his way, I knew our time was running out. If Alvarez trusted Tomás to stay at the house with Sadie and Mateo, I'd say he's been with him a while. Once Alvarez figures out which guards are dead and which ones are missing, Tomás will probably have to leave the area, but that's his problem."

"What does that do to our contract? If the cops have someone undercover, they've been watching Alvarez closely, and that won't change just because Tomás is no longer on the case." Hayden's previous contracts had been quick in-and-outs. He had no idea how to proceed, or even if they should.

Spyder glanced at Mateo. "Let's wait and discuss this once we have Mateo back with Sadie. We can call Ryker and get his opinion."

Mateo fell asleep against Hayden's chest a few minutes later, and the rest of the ride back to Devon's was made in silence other than Devon calling Nora to tell her they had Mateo. As Devon parked, Mateo woke when Hayden unbuckled him. The boy was confused, and when he looked up at Hayden, he blinked quickly. "Mateo, you're safe, and your mama is waiting for you." When Hayden pointed, Mateo turned and looked out the front window where Sadie was standing on the porch with her arms wrapped around her waist. As soon as Hayden opened the back door and helped Mateo to the ground, Sadie ran down the steps and didn't stop until she had her son in her arms.

The reunion brought a knot to Hayden's throat and a smile to his face. Sadie picked her son up and hugged him tightly, murmuring against his hair. When she got herself under control, she leaned the boy back so she could look at him. Devon had already told Nora Mateo was safe and unharmed, but Sadie had to see for herself.

Hayden took the T-shirt Devon held out for him and slipped it on. Once covered, he approached Sadie, and she smiled at him through teary eyes. "Thank you. I owe you everything."

"You owe me nothing. Let's get Mateo inside." Hayden placed his hand on Sadie's back and urged her toward the house.

Once they were in the living room, Sadie put Mateo on his feet and tugged him toward the sofa. She sat down, and Mateo climbed onto the seat beside her.

"*Donde estamos, Mamá?*"

Sadie pushed Mateo's dark hair off his forehead over and over. "We're at Miss Nora and Mister Devon's home." Sadie pointed to the couple standing at the doorway to the kitchen.

Mateo gave a small wave to the couple, then looked around. "Where's *Papá*?"

Sadie looked at Hayden, so he sat down on the coffee table. "Your *papá's* away on business. This is my family, and you and your mama are going to stay with us for a while. Are you hungry?"

Mateo frowned and asked Sadie, "Is it time for supper?"

"You can eat whenever you want to. Miss Nora will make you something if you're hungry."

"Is she the cook?"

Nora laughed. "I sure am. I can make whatever you like, whenever you like. We don't have strict rules about when we eat."

149

"Really?" Mateo's eyes were wide as he looked back and forth between Sadie and Nora. Hayden realized the child had a lot to learn about being in what Hay considered a normal household.

"Yes, really. Plus, I make a mean pizza. Your mama told me you've never had pizza."

Mateo scrunched up his face. "Why is the pizza mean?"

The adults laughed, and Sadie pulled Mateo into her arms. "That means the pizza is really good. Would you like to try it or maybe a hamburger? The food Miss Nora makes is like what I ate when I was your age. You get to try all these amazing new foods while we're here."

"What if I don't like it?"

"Then I'll find something you do like," Nora told him. "But I've never met a little boy who didn't like pizza."

"Can I, *Mamá*?"

"Yes, *Mijo*. I could go for some pizza too. I haven't had any in a long time."

Hayden stood and held out his hand. Sadie smiled at him and let him help her to her feet. She then took Mateo's hand and led him to the kitchen.

"Let's go to the office," Hayden told the males. Once they were behind closed doors, he walked over to where Devon had a line of liquor bottles and poured four glasses of whiskey. After passing them out, he took a sip and relished the burn down his throat. "We need to call Ryker and fill him in on what's happening. He'll know how to proceed, and if he doesn't, he can call Quinn and talk to her about it." His oldest brother was in charge of dealing with the handler. All their mercenary contracts came through to him, and he passed them out to the Hounds.

"I agree." Spyder sat in one of the armchairs, dangling his tumbler over the side. "I've taken a lot of contracts over the years, but I've never come up against anything like what we're facing." Spyder filled Jericho in on what they found

150

out while they'd rescued Mateo.

Jericho leaned against his father's desk. "You not only have Alvarez hiding out in Cali, but you have his sister who is a wild card. Then you also have the Feds involved. What a huckabuck."

Hayden thought the situation was far more fucked up than that, but he sighed and agreed, "A huckabuck, indeed."

CHAPTER FOURTEEN

Sadie

WHEN NORA TOLD Sadie the men had found Mateo and he was unharmed, she had been beyond relieved. Now that he was safely at her side, Sadie couldn't stop touching him. She wanted to ask her son about being taken, but she also didn't want him to have to relive the experience. Sadie watched Mateo as he watched Nora. The woman was patient as she explained what she was doing. She even let him help sprinkle the cheese over the sauce. Nora happened to have a couple pizza doughs in the fridge, and she admitted that it was one of Devon's favorite meals, so she made sure to keep dough ready for whenever he asked for pizza.

"*Mamá*, do you think *Papá* will let me have a dog? One like Lina?" Mateo was on his knees, staring through the window of the oven door as the pizzas baked.

"Who's Lina, *Mijo*?"

"Tomás's dog. She likes to play fetch." Mateo looked up at her with his big, brown eyes. "Can we get one?"

Sadie was torn. She wanted to tell her son yes, he could have anything he wanted. What she couldn't tell him was he would probably never see his father again. That their lives had been irrevocably changed the day before. On one hand, Sadie was grateful to be away from Juan. It was something she'd dreamed of since the day she went to live with him.

On the other, she was fearful. Scared Hayden would never catch Juan. Scared her husband would find her and Mateo should Hayden fail. Scared Antonia would exact revenge if she found out Sadie was with the man responsible for Juan's death if Hayden succeeded.

"We'll have to wait and see. While the pizza bakes, let's go look at the new clothes Miss Nora got you." Sadie held out her hand, and Mateo scrambled to his feet.

"Why did I get new clothes?"

"Because your old ones are at home, and we can't go back to get them for a little while." *If ever*, but she wasn't going to tell him that.

"Why can't we go home? Is it because of the bad men?"

"You remember what happened?"

"Uh huh. There were lots of loud noises, and Elena took me to the kitchen. Tomás told me to hide my face when he picked me up, but I peeked."

"Where was Ana Marie?" Sadie led Mateo into the room they were sharing. Once they were inside, she released his hand and picked up one of the shirts Nora had purchased.

"Hiding in the… the little room in the kitchen."

"The pantry?" Sadie helped unbutton Mateo's shirt, then pushed it down his little arms before replacing it with the new T-shirt.

"Yeah, that." Mateo looked down, pointing at the superhero print. "This shirt's silly."

"It is. Do you like it?"

Mateo nodded, but he looked up at Sadie with wide eyes. "*Papá* won't like it," he whispered. No, Juan wouldn't like it. He insisted Mateo dress like a mini adult. The only time he was allowed to wear something casual was when he was swimming or asleep.

"*Papá's* not here, *Mijo*. You and I are on vacation. That means we don't have to dress the way we do at home. See?"

Sadie pointed to her own clothes. "I'm not wearing one of my dresses." She understood her son's reticence at wearing something different. Sadie had changed from the sweatpants and too large T-shirt into shorts and a matching tee Nora picked out for her. Sadie never wanted to put on a dress again.

"Here. Let's try these shorts on." Sadie waited for Mateo to remove his shoes and pants, and when she handed him the shorts, he held them out.

"Are these to sleep in?"

"No, *Mijo*. They're to wear around the house. Go ahead."

"But where's the button?" Mateo's little face scrunched up as he inspected the elastic waist. They did look a bit like his pajamas.

"No button. They're what boys wear when they want to play ball or just lounge around the house."

Mateo pulled them on and wiggled his butt, fluttering the wide legs around his knobby knees, making Sadie laugh. Mateo glanced up at her, cocking his head to the side.

"What's wrong?"

"You laughed," he stated as though it was something that never happened. When Sadie tried to remember the last time she *had* laughed, she came up short. Surely, she had been amused by her son at some other point in time. Then again, Mateo was the perfect child according to how Juan expected him to behave.

"Well of course I did. You're a funny boy. Now, I bet the pizza's just about ready. Let's go check."

"Okay. I need my shoes." When he started to slip his feet into his loafers, Sadie tugged him by the arm.

"Why don't you go barefoot like me?" Sadie wiggled her foot. Mateo reached down and removed his dark socks. Sadie took them from him and placed them atop his old clothes that needed washing. "Ready?"

"Yes. Do you think I'll like pizza?"

"I do. I used to eat pizza all the time when I was younger. I can't wait to have it again."

"Do you think *Papá* likes pizza?" Mateo stopped at the end of the hallway. Hayden and the other men were standing around the living room.

Hayden squatted so he was on Mateo's eye level. "Hey, Buddy. Wow, I like your shirt. The Avengers are so cool."

"Who's Buddy?" Mateo asked, looking up at Sadie. "And what's Avengers?"

"Buddy means friend. It's a nickname, kind of the way I call you *Mijo,* so Hayden's calling you his friend. The Avengers are a group of superheroes in movies. That's who is on your shirt."

"Oh. *Hola,* Buddy."

Hayden laughed and ruffled Mateo's hair. "I hear you helped Miss Nora make pizza. Are you ready to try it out?"

"*Si.tengo hambre.*" When Hayden looked up at Sadie for translation, she smiled down at him.

"He said he's hungry."

Hayden stood and patted his flat stomach. "That makes two of us. After you." Hayden gestured for her and Mateo to go ahead of him. Sadie placed her hand on Mateo's neck and rubbed her thumb under his hair as they walked to the kitchen. She knew she couldn't touch him constantly, but the need was there. She didn't know what she would do if she ever lost him the way she'd been lost to her mother. Sadie wanted to call her mom, but she wouldn't until she knew the threat from Juan and Antonia was gone.

Nora had already removed the pies from the oven. One was cheese only, and the other had several types of meat but no veggies. Sadie had loved pepperoni as a teen, so she placed one of each on her plate and cheese on a plate for Mateo. Several drinks were lined up on the counter including soda, tea, and what looked like another juice.

155

Sadie opted for soda and poured juice for her son. Nora, Devon, and Hayden sat with them at the table. She was glad Spyder didn't join them. He had tried to talk to Sadie when Hayden left the day before, but she got the feeling he didn't like her much.

Mateo stared as everyone picked up their slices. Sadie wanted to cry over the fact that her son didn't know how to eat pizza. "Just pick it up and take a bite. It's a little messy, but that's what napkins are for." Sadie made a show of taking a bite, and when the flavorful sauce hit her tastebuds, she couldn't hold back a moan. "Oh, God, this is so good." She took another bite before she'd finished chewing the first. It was then she noticed Hayden staring at her. She swallowed and wiped her mouth. "Sorry."

His eyes were heated, but she didn't understand... Oh. Now she got what an article she'd read referred to as food porn. Sadie felt her face heat up, and she looked away from Hayden. Mateo had taken his first bite, and he was nodding as he chewed. He didn't slow down until his first slice was devoured.

"I like pizza. Can I try yours? It's chunky."

Sadie grinned and held out her piece with meat on it. Mateo chewed the bite, and after he swallowed, he said, "I like mine better. Is that okay?"

"That's perfectly fine. Here, try this." Sadie held her glass filled with Coke up to his lips. He took a sip, and his eyes widened.

"What is that? It's yummy."

"That is called soda. It comes in all sorts of flavors, but this one is Coke. It has caffeine in it, so you can't have too much, or you'll be buzzing around like a little bee."

"I like Coke. And I like pizza. Why don't we eat pizza at home?" Mateo picked his second slice up and took a bite.

Sadie realized everyone was watching them. Nora's eyes were wet. Devon looked sad, and Hayden... He looked angry. She didn't understand why, though. It wasn't like Mateo had been starved. They ate well, they just didn't eat anything other than the Mexican dishes Elena cooked every meal.

"Maybe Elena didn't know how to make pizza. There are all kinds of food you'll get to try now that we're staying with Miss Nora. I'm going to introduce you to all the things I liked when I was your age. Spaghetti. Hamburgers. Hot dogs. French fries." Sadie hadn't thought about all the foods she'd missed over the years, and now she couldn't wait to eat them all.

Mateo dropped his pizza onto the plate. "*Mamá*! I don't want to eat a dog. That's mean."

Everyone laughed, and Sadie brushed her son's hair off his forehead. "It's not a real dog, *Mijo*. It's like a sausage served in a long bun. I'm not sure why it's called a hot dog, but they're really good."

The rest of the meal was done with Mateo asking questions about the foods Sadie had mentioned. Nora promised to make whatever Sadie desired and even offered to let her help in the kitchen when Sadie mentioned cooking with her mother. That brought another round of questions from Mateo.

"You have a *Mamá* too?"

"I do. Her name is Gloria. I haven't seen her in a long time, but I'm hoping you and I will be able to visit with her soon." Sadie looked at Hayden when she made the comment to gauge his reaction. He had told her she needed to wait, and when he shook his head, she knew he hadn't changed his mind. Sadie sighed, but if he thought it was too dangerous to contact her mom, it probably was. She hadn't seen her in eight years, so what was a few more days or weeks?

"Come on, *Mijo*. Let's wash your hands, then there's something I want to show you." Nora had already insisted

Sadie make herself at home while they were waiting on Mateo's return, and she couldn't wait to show him all the cartoons and animated shows available.

Hayden

THE PHONE CALL with Ryker went as Hayden expected. He was ready to get on a plane and fly down to Texas to help out. Hayden convinced his older brother to stay home with Rhiannon, but he didn't argue when Ryker said he was sending Judge down to help. With all the moving pieces, Hayden was glad to have the backup. Before stating he would send Judge, Ryker called Quinn to update her on the situation. Being a handler, she wasn't at liberty to tell who took out the contract if she knew who it was. As far as Hayden knew, most were taken out anonymously. Quinn then did initial research on the mark before offering the job to the Hounds. The Lazlos weren't the only mercenaries in the world. Nexus, the group they had worked with before, had several handlers and even more assassins on call. When one of their operatives turned out to be a psycho bitch who used Ryker, the Hounds had severed ties with the group. Quinn's father, Trenton Shepherd, was a friend of Sutton's. They went way back, having served in the Army together. Shepherd also knew the truth of what the Hounds were. Sutton trusted the father-daughter team, therefore Ryker did as well.

Considering Sadie was an innocent party, Quinn promised to do some digging into the identity of the person who contracted the hit. She admitted to Ryker this wasn't the first time someone was targeted who shouldn't be. But, like the Hounds, she would rather be out the fee than to take an innocent life.

Another issue they discussed while in Devon's office was whether or not to move Sadie and Mateo to a different city. They weren't far enough away from Alvarez's house for Hayden's comfort. They didn't have safehouses in Texas. What they did have was a boatload of family willing to take in the mother and son, but Hayden wasn't sure about risking his family, Gryphons or not.

Devon finally convinced him to let them stay where they were. He and Nora didn't have small kids at home, and they were willing to watch over the pair while Hayden and the others did their job. Their home was situated on five acres, so it was fairly secluded. As long as Sadie and Mateo didn't leave, nobody should be able to find them there. With that decided, Hayden and Spyder made their plan to meet Judge in Cali.

They left Devon's office and were in the living room when Sadie and Mateo returned from their bedroom. Mateo looked cute in his Avenger's T-shirt. He looked more like a five-year-old should now he wasn't wearing a button-up and khakis. Hayden wanted to know all about the boy. He was so different than Major and Marshall. Mateo had none of the devil-may-care personality of Major. He was quiet like Marshall, but there was something missing behind those big, brown eyes. Something Hayden couldn't quite put his finger on.

While they were sitting around the large pine table eating pizza, Hayden figured out a small part of what was missing. Mateo and Sadie had strict rules at home. They ate at certain times and only what was laid out before them. Not only had Mateo missed out on things like pizza and burgers, Sadie had as well. She explained to Nora how she hadn't had what she deemed American food for the last eight years. Sadie's moan around her first taste of pizza was sinful. She chugged her soda like a man in the desert dying of thirst. Sadie had been denied all the things she'd enjoyed in her earlier years. The way she and Mateo kept tugging at their clothes indicated they weren't used to wearing shorts and T-shirts.

Hayden's first glimpse at Sadie had been of a woman who looked like a million dollars in her fitted black dress, high-heel shoes, smoky makeup, and diamond jewelry that Hayden doubted came from a department store. Sitting in Devon and Nora's kitchen, the woman was just as stunning with no makeup, her hair pulled back in a loose ponytail, and her feet bare except for the bright red polish on her toes. Hayden did his best to focus on the pizza, but his Gryphon was sure Sadie was their mate, and it wouldn't let him take his eyes off her for too long.

The one thing that bothered Hayden about Mateo more than anything was the way he mentioned his father constantly. Even though Alvarez wasn't there, his presence was. Mateo worried about what he wore. What he ate. More than once, the child looked over his shoulder as though his father would appear out of nowhere and chastise him for the things he was doing. Had Mateo been allowed to be a kid at all? He got the answer to that question when Sadie took Mateo into the living room to watch TV.

"This television is magic, *Mamá.*"

"It sure is, *Mijo.* There are so many shows I think you'll like." Sadie had to get Hayden to help her with the remote, but once he explained how to scroll through the channels, she lit up as much as her son did. After Mateo was situated on the floor in front of a show featuring a talking dog, Sadie took a seat on the sofa next to Hayden and explained how they weren't allowed to watch television. They were only allowed certain movies, and then only on special occasions.

"I'm interested in learning more about your life. But if

you don't want to talk about it, I'll understand." Hayden thought she was going to refuse, but Sadie turned and bent her leg so she was facing Hayden.

"When I first got to Juan's house, I was schooled in etiquette. I was taught how to dress. How to apply my makeup. The only outside source I was allowed were fashion magazines so I could emulate the looks of the models. The jeans and T-shirt I had on when I was taken were tossed, and the next day, dresses filled the closet along with heels to match. I went from a teenage girl who spent time in the kitchen with her mother learning to bake to a teenage girl who was groomed to be a trophy wife. Juan didn't touch me until I turned eighteen, but the day of my birthday, everything changed." Sadie glanced down at Mateo when the boy laughed, and her eyes filled with tears. Roughly brushing them away, she turned back to Hayden.

"Juan came to my room that morning saying he had a surprise for me. I stupidly thought it would be cake and presents. Instead, he laid out a long, white dress and announced we were getting married. I grabbed the dress and threw it at him, saying I would never marry him. I got in his face, shouting how I hated him for taking me. For keeping me prisoner and ruining my life. Up until that point, I had kept my head down and did what was expected. I always thought Dominic would come for me. Every day for almost three years, I waited for my big brother. For *someone* to come rescue me. But that day... I lost every bit of hope I'd clung to. Juan picked up the dress and laid it out on the bed. When he turned toward me, I saw something in his eyes I'd never been subjected to, at least not from him – cold eyes and a colder voice. He told me if I didn't marry him, he would kill my family.

"I had no choice. He'd already had my father killed. At least I'm pretty sure he did. When we were driving away after my father gave me over to Juan, I heard a gunshot. In

161

that moment, I prayed it was my dad being killed. If that makes me a bad person, so be it. He was never a good dad. Sure, we had a decent house, and I never had to worry about going hungry. I had a normal life up until that point. When he was home, he wasn't kind to me, but he never beat me. Never laid a hand on me in an inappropriate way. He wasn't kind to my mother, but he didn't hit her either. He was gone a lot, and those times were the best. My mom would teach me to cook. We would watch TV together at night. Before Dominic moved out and joined the motorcycle club, he was the best big brother. He would take me out to the movies or for ice cream." Sadie stopped talking and began rubbing her temples.

Hayden reached out and touched her arm. "Do you need something for your head?"

"Yes, please." She smiled, but it didn't reach her eyes.

Hayden stood and went into the kitchen where Nora and Devon were drinking coffee at the table. "Just getting Sadie something for her head." He opened the cap and tapped out two pills before filling a glass with water. He returned to the living room where she was scrolling through the channels again.

"I changed my mind. I want a dog like that instead of Lina." Mateo was on his knees with his hands resting on Sadie's thigh. "I'll be good; I promise."

Hayden held the pills out, and Sadie took them, popping them in her mouth. She took a few sips of water, then placed the glass on the coffee table. Hayden sat down, leaving plenty of room between them.

"I know you'll be good, but I'm not sure how long it will be before we can go home. Let's wait and talk about getting a dog then. Now, do you want to watch another episode of 'Sprocket,' or do you want to see what else is on?"

"Something else. Are there talking cats too?"

"I'm not sure. Let's look." Hayden pulled out his phone and searched the internet for talking cat shows. He didn't find one, but he did find an animated show with a porcupine. "No cats, but there's one called 'Mr. Prickles.' It's about a porcupine and his friends."

"What's a porcupine?" Mateo asked Hayden.

"It's like a big ol' rat with spiky hair."

Sadie handed over the remote. Hayden reached out to take it, and their fingers brushed. Sadie looked away quickly, but Hayden didn't miss the way her cheeks blushed. Nor did he miss the way his Gryphon preened inside when his dick jumped at the barest of skin touching.

Get it together. It was just a touch.

And it was electric. Can you imagine—

No. I can't.

Hayden searched for the show, and when he found it, he handed the remote back to Sadie. "Here you go. In case he doesn't like it, you can switch over to something else. I need to go make a call." Hayden lunged off the sofa and didn't look back.

CHAPTER FIFTEEN

Hayden

"HEY, LUCY. HOW'S it going?" Hayden hated bothering his niece. She always called immediately if she found anything useful, but he told Sadie he had to make a call, and he didn't want to look like a liar if she saw him wandering around outside without his phone to his ear.

"There's been no movement from Alvarez, but I just received an alert. Antonia has checked herself out of the hospital. I'm going to do my best to keep track of where she's going, but if I had to guess, I'd say she will return to Nuevo Laredo. With the house in Texas being watched, I don't see her going back there."

"Who's watching the one here?"

"The same guard who was helping Tomás and Elena. He and Tomás are still rotating shifts, even without having Mateo."

"That's Jose, Elena's brother. I don't get why they would continue watching the house now."

"Maybe they're waiting on Alvarez to return."

"Zeus, this is a clusterfuck." Hayden ran his free hand through his hair.

"And you still don't think they're the ones who took out the contract?"

"At this point, anything is possible. Ryker called Quinn.

She said the contract was done anonymously, and she feels really bad that Sadie was listed as a target. Luce, are you certain Alvarez is still in California?"

"Yes. Henry has a facial recognition program running. Unless he somehow changes his appearance, we'll get a notification if he leaves."

"Fuck. Okay. I think our best bet is to go after the man there. Once we take him out, we'll move on to the next part of our problem."

"And that is?"

"Keeping Sadie and her son safe. Someone wants her out of the picture." Hayden had a feeling that person was Antonia, but if Alvarez was no longer alive, would she back off? Or would she come after Sadie?

"Whatever you decide, stay safe."

Hayden's phone vibrated, indicating another call. He ignored it for the moment. "I will. How are you and Jonas coming along with the journals?" Lucy had traveled to New Atlanta when she found some of Lucius's journals with notes about prolonging life. Lucy, being Gryphon, didn't have to worry about longevity, but the Gryphons who had human mates would benefit from such a discovery.

"It's slow going. Even once we get the formula perfected, we can't just test it on a human. We'll have to try it on a lower lifeform. If that works, then we'll have to find someone willing to be a guinea pig. Pardon the pun."

"Okay. I'll let you get back to it. I'll text you when we leave for California. Talk to you soon." Hayden disconnected and checked to see who had called. When he saw Jericho's name, Hayden bristled. His nephew had gone to Sadie's mother's house to keep an eye on the woman. Before he could call Jericho back, a noise behind him caught Hayden's attention. When he turned around, Spyder was standing on the top step, leaning against the post.

The male pushed off and walked down the steps to join

165

Hayden in the yard. "Since we have time before we leave for Cali, I thought I'd take a look around Alvarez's place."

"Tomás and the other guard are still taking turns watching the house."

"That doesn't make sense. I..." Spyder ran a hand through his beard as he looked over Hayden's shoulder. "I voiced the Fed. Why wouldn't he have left the area?"

"What exactly did you say to him?"

"I told him five armed guards took off with Mateo, but they vowed they wouldn't hurt the child." Spyder pulled the band out of his long hair, then retied it, grabbing the loose tendrils that had fallen out.

"Maybe that makes his job easier. If he's undercover to get Alvarez, having Mateo out of the picture is one less thing for him to worry about. It's Elena and her brother who wanted to get Mateo away from Juan Carlos."

"Yes, because they don't want the boy to turn into his father. Tomás could be waiting on Alvarez to return, and Jose could be looking for some sign of Mateo. What aren't we seeing?"

"Did you tell Tomás specifically his cover was blown? That he admitted to being undercover?"

"No, I didn't." Spyder blew out a breath. "Elena and her brother wanted to get Mateo away from Alvarez. If they had put out the hit, they would have made sure Sadie was dead and not merely injured during the attack on the house. The attack wasn't a last-minute hit, which means either Elena and Jose are responsible and had already been in contact with the attackers, or they got really lucky with their timing. A plan was already in place, so whoever was responsible had access to Alvarez's schedule. Elena worked for Dominguez before Juan took over. It's possible he shared his trip with her thinking she was a trusted employee. And what if Jose was Dominguez's second-in-command and is pissed Juan took over the family business?"

166

"But why wait all this time? That happened almost two decades ago."

Spyder threw his hands up. "Fuck! I don't know. There are too many moving parts with no diagram. I say we take out Alvarez and let the rest of them deal with the fallout. That seems to be the common thread here – getting Juan out of the picture."

"And the contract on Sadie? That's not going to go away."

Spyder grinned. "Then you'll just have to protect her, won't you?"

Hayden groaned aloud, while his Gryphon murmured in agreement inside his head.

"Hayden!" Devon ran out the door. "I just got a call from Jericho. He tried to call you, but you didn't answer." Devon looked back toward the house. When he turned back around, he lowered his voice. "When he got to Gloria Rodriguez's home, it had been ransacked, and the woman's nowhere to be found."

"Shit. Shit! I need to call Dominic."

"And tell him what?" Spyder asked.

"The fucking truth. If Alvarez somehow got hold of Sadie's mother, it makes sense he'll go after Dominic too."

"The male's going to be pissed you didn't immediately tell him you found his sister."

"That's the least of our worries. I'll take a pissed male as long as he's a breathing one." Hayden tugged his phone out of his pocket and pulled up Dominic's contact information. The call went straight to voicemail, so he told the guy to call him as soon as he got the message. Hayden wished he'd put Kodiak's number in his phone. "I need to go back to Jericho's. I left Kodiak's card on the dresser."

"Here." Devon handed Hayden his keys. "Take my car. That way you'll have two vehicles."

"Thanks, Dev. Spyder, once I get hold of Kodiak, I'll call

you."

Spyder inclined his head and jogged to their SUV. Hayden returned to the house to talk to Sadie. When she saw his face, her smile faltered.

"Is everything okay?"

"I need to leave for a little while. You'll be safe here with Nora and Devon."

"What about you? Will you be safe?" Sadie bit her bottom lip, and it was all Hayden could do not to reach out and touch her.

"Always. I'll be back as soon as possible." Hayden backed away, keeping his eyes on the female until he had no choice but to turn around before he hit the wall. If he didn't know better, he would think Sadie was interested. Knowing she was married should have been a deterrent. It wasn't. Not when Hayden knew what she'd been through at the hands of her husband. That was the deterrent. Sadie deserved a better life than the one she'd been given. As he strode to the garage where Devon's sleek sports car was housed, he allowed himself a brief moment to think he could be the one to give her a better life. Her and Mateo. He knew she would be glad to be free from Juan Carlos, but Mateo was another story. The boy clearly loved his father.

Hayden was used to the rumble from his bikes. He relished the feel of power as he rode whichever Harley he chose for the day. But the purr Devon's car elicited had its own brand of enticement. The low chassis hugged the road, taking curves with an ease Hayden had never experienced. He flexed his hands around the leather steering wheel, the suppleness a stark difference from the nubbed grips of his bikes. Yes, the sports car was a dream machine, but Hayden couldn't see himself owning one. He preferred two wheels unless it was storming. He didn't mind riding in a little rain. It could be refreshing. Cleansing. He wondered if Sadie had ever ridden with her brother, or if she would turn her nose up at riding the wind. He could just imagine her snugged up against him as they rode together.

The ride to Jericho's was short, and Hayden rushed into the house to find the card Kodiak had given him. He punched in the number, and after ringing several times, he was ready to leave a message. The phone was answered with a brusque, "What?"

"Kodiak, this is Hayden Lazlo. I was actually looking to talk to Dominic, but if I caught you at a bad time, I can call back."

"That's going to be a problem. Dominic's gone missing."

"Fuck. This is bad." Hayden paced the living room of his nephew's house. He didn't know Kodiak. Didn't know if he was honorable, but Dominic probably wouldn't ride with the club if the male wasn't aboveboard. He had to make a judgment call, and he hoped it wouldn't come back to bite him in the ass. "His mother's missing too."

"What the fuck did you say?"

Hayden cringed. "Not over the phone. Are you at the clubhouse?"

"Yes. I've got my crew out looking for Dominic, but I'm waiting here in case he shows up or calls."

"I'm on my way." Hayden disconnected, then called Spyder. When the male answered, Hayden didn't waste time with pleasantries. "Dominic's missing too."

"How much you want to bet Alvarez sent someone after them?"

Hayden locked the door on his way out to the car. "But why now? With the hit on the house, it appeared Sadie and Mateo were taken." Hayden set the Bluetooth on his phone to pair with the car, then navigated to the clubhouse from memory.

"I doubt he's thinking rationally right now. But if he is responsible, it's possible he sent a couple guards from Cali to take Dominic and Gloria."

"Or he has more men on his payroll than we're aware of. If we take him out before they're found, what happens to them then? Will whoever has them kill Sadie's family or turn them loose?"

"Fuck, Brother. This keeps getting more convoluted."

"Truth. I'm headed to the Norse Gods' clubhouse to talk to Kodiak. And before you ask, yes, I'm going to tell him what's going on, but not until I ask him a few questions about his integrity. My gut's telling me he's one of the good ones, but I have to know for sure. I won't put our family in danger by talking without knowing first."

"I trust you, Havyk. I may have been a dick to you regarding Sadie, but I was out of line."

"Already forgiven. If you see anything at the house, give me a call. If I don't hear from you, I'll call you once I've spoken to Kodiak."

"Ten-four."

Hayden turned the AC on high and the radio up. He would have preferred to roll down the windows. Being an air Gryphon, Hayden loved the wind. The feel of it on his face. The way it howled through the trees during a storm. The way it pushed his Eagle when he was flying. But this far south was like a sauna, even in November. He was used to the weather in Upstate New York where they had already had snow flurries. Hayden wondered if Sadie had ever seen snow. Texas wasn't immune to the white stuff, but it rarely snowed in the southern part of the state.

He would love to take her and Mateo home with him. Show her how a female should be treated. Introduce her to the other mates so she could have friends close to her own age. He wanted Mateo to meet the twins and have a chance to act like a little kid. Hayden chuckled thinking of the buttoned-up little boy getting a dose of Hayden's nephews. Talk about culture shock. Major and Marshall had play dates with some of the Hounds' kids, but Mateo had no one other than Sadie and the nanny, and that broke Hayden's heart. Even if Sadie weren't interested in a relationship once this was all over, he would still offer to be her friend. He'd just have to do it from a distance, because being around her without touching would be difficult. It already was.

Gryphons didn't have fated mates the way the Gargoyles did. There wasn't one being the fates or gods decided was the perfect partner. Hayden was glad because if that were the case, two of his older brothers would be alone now, having lost their wives early on. Both Ryker and Warryck had again found someone to spend their lives with. Maveryck hadn't lost his partner; she'd walked away from Mav, taking his two unborn sons with her. Hayden couldn't imagine life without Major and Marshall. The two little dudes had already burrowed their way into the hearts of each family member. Hayden wanted that. He wanted the love of a child, or children, and the companionship of a good woman. Someone who loved him the way he was.

Hayden knew he could be good for Sadie. Good to her. Both her and Mateo. He couldn't give her the same lifestyle she was accustomed to, but he had quite a bit of money saved. Being one of the best bike builders in the country meant he could ask top dollar for his work. His house was paid for. If by chance Sadie did want to be with Hayden, he would sell that house and buy her one of her choosing. And if she wanted to stay in Texas with her family? Would Hayden be willing to move away from New York? He had his sisters and all their kids and grandkids, so he wouldn't be without family. He could still take on mercenary jobs. Could still customize bikes. He could be a Hound in the MC with Devon and Jericho.

Holy shit. He absolutely would. But he was getting way the fuck ahead of himself. Was it Sadie herself making him ready to take that leap? Or the fact that he wanted love and

171

a mate so desperately? Yeah, he needed to do a little soul searching. And get rid of her fucking husband.

When Hayden arrived at the Norse Gods' clubhouse, he could feel the tension as soon as he got out of the car. Several males stared him down until they realized who had driven up in a fancy sports car.

"Havyk, come inside." Kodiak stood in the doorway, taking up the whole of it with his massive size. If Hayden weren't a Gryphon, he might have been intimidated.

"Can we talk privately?" Hayden knew that was asking a lot of the MC President, but he didn't want to have to voice a bunch of males at the same time.

Kodiak frowned at the request, but he didn't object. Instead, he led Hayden to a conference room with a large table much like the one at the Hounds' clubhouse. Kodiak shut the door, but he didn't take a seat.

Hayden didn't give the male a chance to start questioning him. Instead, he asked him several of his own questions to determine whether or not Kodiak was honorable. The one question he wanted to ask but didn't was whether or not Kodiak was a shifter. That was none of Hayden's business. Once he knew he could trust the male, Hayden wiped the last few minutes from Kodiak's memory. "Thank you for allowing us some privacy. What I'm going to tell you needs to stay in this room."

"I'm listening." Kodiak crossed the room to where a bar was set up, pouring them both a couple fingers of whiskey.

"I'm not only in Texas to deliver Dominic's bike. I was also sent here to go after a Mexican drug lord by the name of Juan Carlos Alvarez."

"I've heard of him. He's recently moved to New Laredo."

"He has, and with him he brought his wife and son. His wife was traded to him in exchange for money owed by a man named Ricardo Rodriguez. Dominic's father traded

Sadie when she was fifteen for nearly half a million dollars when he couldn't come up with the money. Alvarez forced Sadie to marry him and give him an heir. He told her if she didn't marry him, he'd kill her family. For the last eight years, Dominic's sister has been forced to live in seclusion."

"How do you know all this?" Kodiak swirled the liquid in his glass before downing it in one swallow.

"Because I have her and the boy somewhere safe." Hayden recounted how he and the others went to the Alvarez home and what they found when they arrived. "As far as we know, Alvarez is still in California. I have someone watching him, but since he is no doubt aware his wife and son are both missing, I have a feeling he's behind Dominic and his mother going missing."

"Why didn't you call Dom as soon as you knew who Sadie was?"

"To keep him safe. The same reason I didn't let Sadie call her mother."

"Well, that didn't work too well, now did it?" Kodiak stood to his full height. Hayden's Gryphon was ready to come out, but Hayden pushed it down.

"No, it didn't, but I'm not going to apologize. We had no reason to believe Alvarez would go after Sadie's family. He doesn't know who has her and the boy. The hit on his house was done by someone who wants him out of the game as much as we do."

"How do you know that? You don't know who those men were."

"Yes, we do. Juan Carlos worked for Jorge Dominguez, and twenty years ago, Dominguez went to prison. Alvarez took over the business. A brother and sister team worked for Dominguez, and Alvarez kept them along with everyone else who worked for his former boss. Dominguez's daughter, Antonia, was one of those people, only when her father went to jail, she was young. Instead of allowing her to be a normal teenager, Alvarez turned her into one of his guards. Elena couldn't protect Antonia from Juan's influence, but she and her brother agreed they would protect Mateo from turning into his father. So, they devised a plan to get the boy out of the house."

"So that's who put out the contract on Alvarez?"

"No. At least we don't think so. The hit was on both Juan and Sadie, only when the house was hit, they didn't kill Sadie. They only wounded her. We believe the contract was taken out by either Antonia or someone else who wants Juan out of the way."

"Antonia would make sense. Or maybe one of the other men on Dominguez's crew who felt they should've been in control once the man went to prison."

"Exactly."

"What's your play?"

"We're still going after Alvarez. I have another Hound coming in, and as soon as he gets here, we're headed to California. Once Juan's out of the picture, whoever wanted him dead will more than likely move into the lead role and get what they wanted."

"Yes, everything except Sadie." Kodiak grabbed the bottle and poured another glass, this one full. He downed it as well before leaning back against the table. Even though he appeared to be calmer, Hayden could feel the anger rolling off the male.

"We'll keep Sadie safe. Her and the boy. My family is large enough we can hide her until we figure out who took the contract out on her and eliminate them."

"And how are you going to get Dominic and Gloria back? Or are you even worried about them?" Kodiak's voice was eerily low.

"Of course I'm worried about them. It's why I was calling Dominic in the first place."

"If you had called them both when you found Sadie,

174

they wouldn't be missing now!" Kodiak pushed off the table and threw the empty glass against the wall. Shards of glass sprayed the air. Muscles rippled, and Hayden's Lion rumbled in his chest. Kodiak snapped his head around at the sound. "What the fuck was that?"

Hayden opened his mouth to voice the male, but Kodiak held up his hand. "No. Do not try and pull that bullshit you used when we first came in here. I don't know what the fuck you are, but it's not human." Hayden had never met anyone who was both aware of and unaffected by Gryphon voice. Kodiak now knew things he shouldn't.

Before he could figure a way out of the situation, the door flew open, and one of the Norse Gods stormed into the room and rounded on Hayden. "Koda? You okay?"

"Stand down, Saber."

Saber frowned at his Pres, and Kodiak ran a hand through his thick hair. "Gloria's missing too."

"Oh, fuck. Do you think Dom grabbed her and took off?"

"No. Shut the door." Saber did as told, and Kodiak turned to Hayden. "Gloria's my mate."

"Koda, no. He's not—"

"He is. Well, he's something, I just haven't figured out what exactly."

"What the fuck?" Hayden muttered. "Is your whole MC... different?"

"No. Just a handful of us. We've stayed off the radar this long, and we'd like to keep it that way."

"Same. But if Gloria's your mate, why are you standing here talking to me? If that was—" Hayden closed his mouth before he let it slip he felt Sadie was his.

"If it was your mate who was missing, you'd be tearing the world apart to find her? I'm old, Son. I've got enough years in me to keep my anger under control." Hayden glanced down to where the glass sprinkled the floor. Kodiak tracked his eyes and waved a hand. "That's me in control."

"Does Gloria know what you are?"

"No. Neither does Dominic or anyone else in the Club who isn't like us. Now, enough about that. Considering we both have a stake in this, how about you go do your job, and me and the Club will worry about finding Gloria and Dominic?"

"As soon as I have Alvarez, I'll ask him if he had a hand in their disappearance. If he did, I'll call you."

"And if he didn't?"

"We'll work together until we find them and bring them back home." Hayden prayed the two were still alive. If they weren't? He had a feeling he would see Kodiak's inner beast let loose, and Hayden doubted that was a good thing.

"Once this shitstorm is over, Sadie needs to be with her family. Dominic gave up hope she was alive, but Gloria never did. Seeing her daughter will go a long way in helping her heal."

"Sadie's alive? What the fuck?" Saber took a step toward Hayden, but Kodiak moved between the two of them.

"Stand the fuck down. I'll explain later, but yes, she's alive." Kodiak gripped Saber on the shoulder. "Our Sadie's alive."

Saber's eyes shined, but he quickly blinked the wetness away. Hayden was missing something, but he didn't get the chance to ask what. Kodiak ushered him to the door. "Go take care of Alvarez and keep me posted. If I hear from Dom or Gloria, I'll call you."

Hayden inclined his head and left without saying anything else. He didn't know what *to* say. His head was spinning. He knew other shifters existed because of the Gargoyles. Kodiak didn't give off that vibe, though. And his comment about "our Sadie" left Hayden more perplexed than before. Sadie had mentioned her brother being in an

MC, but she never said anything about the rest of the Club. There was something off about the whole scenario, but Hayden didn't have time to figure out what. He had to get back to Devon's, check on Sadie and Mateo, then he and Spyder would fly to California and meet with Judge.

The one thing that stood out the most was the fact that Kodiak hadn't completely flipped his shit when he found out his mate was missing. As he drove back to Devon's, Hayden tried to imagine any of his family being so calm in the same situation, and he couldn't. Like Kodiak said, they would tear the world apart looking. Sadie wasn't his, but Hayden knew already if it were her and he couldn't find her? Not even Zeus himself would get in Hayden's way.

CHAPTER SIXTEEN

Sadie

HAYDEN WAS ACTING weird when he returned from wherever he went earlier. Sadie didn't know the man well enough to pry. She had learned early on when Juan was in a mood to leave him alone or else she would feel the brunt of his ire. She didn't think Hayden was the same way, but she couldn't be sure. When he walked in the door, his eyes searched the room until they landed on her. He relaxed briefly, then he excused himself, and he and the other men had locked themselves away in Devon's office. Nora didn't seem to mind or be worried. Instead, she sat with Sadie and Mateo in the living room watching movies Mateo hadn't seen. Sadie felt a little rebellious in letting her son stay up late, watching one show after the other. When Nora offered to make popcorn, Sadie readily agreed. Hell, she had missed the salty snack, and it was another thing from her past she could share with Mateo.

Sadie had just gotten Mateo settled in bed and was singing to him when she realized they weren't alone. She looked over to find Hayden peeking around the door. If Sadie didn't know she had a decent voice, she would have been embarrassed.

"Sorry to interrupt. I just wanted to make sure everything was okay. Do you need anything?"

"No, we're good. Nora's been the perfect hostess."

"How's your...?" Hayden pointed at the back of his own head. Sadie had shown Mateo her staples when he almost hit them on accident.

"It's better. The medicine is doing its job."

"*Mamá* got an owie," Mateo said, already snuggled underneath the covers. The heat outside was still sweltering, but inside the house was nice and cool from the air conditioner.

"She did." Hayden's eyes softened while he was talking to Mateo. "How about you, Buddy? Did you have a good night watching cartoons?"

"*Si.*" Mateo yawned, rubbing his eyes.

Hayden hesitated, but he didn't say anything else. He stared at Sadie a moment, then left the two of them alone. Once she got Mateo to sleep, Sadie padded out of the room and went in search of the man. When she walked into the living room, Nora looked over the back of the sofa and pointed toward the kitchen. Sadie frowned, and Nora cocked an eyebrow, grinning, before snuggling back against Devon. Sadie wondered if Nora could read her mind. Probably. The woman had been amazing in giving Sadie and Mateo everything they needed, most of the time without asking. When Sadie didn't find Hayden in the kitchen, she glanced out the back door. He was leaning against the railing of the deck, looking up at the stars. He turned her way when she opened the door.

"Everything okay?"

Sadie nodded and walked over to stand close to him, turning her gaze upward, feeling it was safer to stare at the inky sky instead of the man beside her. "I had forgotten how amazing the stars can be."

"Is where you lived not secluded?"

"Oh, it is, but I wasn't allowed outside at night unless we were going to a club. When I left the house, I was always ushered straight to the car." Hayden angled his body towards hers, giving her his full attention. "Other than that, the only time I got to go outside was when Mateo wanted to swim, and that was only a few hours during the day. Juan tried to teach me to play tennis early on, but I sucked at it. When Mateo was with the others, I had to stay in my suite. I had my music, but that was it. I only ate in the dining room when Juan was home and in a good mood." Sadie turned her head from the stars to find Hayden staring. "Do you live close by?"

"No. I live in Upstate New York. I have a house in a neighborhood, so unless I get on my bike and take a ride, I don't get to see the stars like this either." Hayden took a step closer and brushed a knuckle down her cheek. She leaned into his touch, but he shook his head. "Sorry. I shouldn't have done that."

"Do you have a girlfriend? A wife?"

"No. I—"

Sadie pressed her fingers to his lips. "Then don't apologize." She ran her thumb across his bottom lip, wondering how it would feel pressed against hers. She'd never had a real kiss from someone other than Juan. Sadie didn't consider the few pecks from her one boyfriend in high school to be real kisses. The rare times Juan kissed her was usually a hard crush of mouths during sex.

"Sadie, we can't." Hayden's voice was strained.

"Sorry. I thought…" She thought he was interested, but what the hell did she know about men? With Juan her only source of comparison, Sadie knew nothing.

Hayden sighed deeply. "Sadie, look at me." He tipped her chin up using the side of his finger. "You are an exquisite creature. I'm deeply drawn to you, but I won't take advantage."

"Advantage? Because I'm married? Damaged? Used goods?"

180

"What? You're not damaged nor used goods. I just said you're exquisite, and I meant it. Normally, I wouldn't ever consider looking at a married woman, but knowing who your husband is and what he's put you through, I can overlook that. But you've been hurt, and your son was kidnapped." Hayden pressed his palm to her cheek, his eyes searching hers. Sadie leaned into his palm and closed her eyes. For just one moment, she wanted to feel his touch. Wanted to know what it was like to be with someone who wasn't Juan. When his other hand cupped her neck, Sadie opened her eyes.

"Please," she begged on a whisper.

Hayden hesitated, and just when she thought he was going to step away, he leaned down and pressed their lips together. It was a ghost of a touch, and she wanted more. Sadie wrapped her arms around his waist, bunching his T-shirt in her fists. Hayden kissed her again, and Sadie opened for him. He angled her head and pressed in, his tongue seeking hers. It was the softest kiss she'd ever had, while at the same time, the most electric. Juan's kisses were bruising. Demanding. Hayden's was searching. Learning. Tentative yet thrilling. This man was a biker. A mercenary. The hands cradling her gently had killed. That should be alarming, but it wasn't. It was exhilarating. That should have been a big red flag. It wasn't. Sadie stepped closer, pressing her soft chest to his hard one. His chest wasn't the only thing hard. His erection was evident against her hip. If they had been anywhere else, somewhere alone, she might have found the courage to touch him.

"Havyk, are you ready? Oh, shit. Sorry." Spyder had snuck up on them from the darkness.

Hayden released her mouth and pressed his forehead to hers, sighing.

"I'll just... Yeah. Let me know when you're ready to ride," Spyder said as he turned and walked away.

"You're leaving?" Sadie ran her hand through Hayden's hair, scratching his scalp with her nails.

"Not if you keep that up. Damn, that feels nice." Hayden practically purred as Sadie continued gently clawing his head. He grabbed hold of her wrist and brought her knuckles to his lips. "Yes, I'm leaving. We're going after Juan. It shouldn't take more than a couple days, and then I'll be back. You and Mateo will be safe here with Devon and Nora."

"I'm not worried about us. Promise you'll be safe."

"I will. I have both Spyder and Judge with me." Hayden pressed another quick kiss to her lips, then pulled away. "I'll be back before you know it." He bopped her on the nose, then took off down the steps, following Spyder into the darkness. Sadie leaned against the railing, looking up at the stars once again.

"Please bring him back to me," she whispered, sending her prayer to the heavens. Sadie stayed outside a little while longer, enjoying the peacefulness. She was used to being alone for long stretches, but being outside alone was freeing. At least she didn't think anyone else was outside, but one of Hayden's family members could be strolling around in the dark without her knowing. If they were, it was to keep her and Mateo safe, not confined. Rescuing people was what his family did, along with killing others. That was hard for her to wrap her brain around.

Hayden had been the white knight she had always dreamed of. Well, after her brother. Sadie had thought it would be Dominic who came for her and saved her from her life of imprisonment. She couldn't wait to see her big brother again. And her mother. She often wondered if they'd moved on with their lives, thinking Sadie was dead. Once this was all over, Sadie could get her life back. She wanted to introduce Mateo to her family. Figure out who she was as a person and not Juan's prisoner.

Hayden lived in New York, so he would go back to his life, leaving her in Texas. But he had family here, so maybe he would come visit her. Sadie shouldn't let herself become attached to the mercenary. He had rescued her and Mateo, but that didn't mean he was interested. And she really shouldn't be thinking about him romantically. He had been torn over kissing her. And what a kiss it had been. Sadie wanted more of his lips on hers. His hands on her face. His hands everywhere. Would he be a gentle lover? Or would he be rough and demanding like Juan? Hayden was a dangerous man, but he was kind to her. Gentle with her.

She realized she was probably reading too much into her feelings toward Hayden since he'd rescued her, but she felt something for him. He wasn't the only one in on the rescue. Spyder and Jericho had been there. Devon too, but Sadie didn't feel drawn to the shorter biker with his long hair. Yes, he was hot. As were Devon and Jericho, and yes, that was a little weird considering they were father and son. Sadie hadn't seen Judge, but she had a feeling he'd be just as stunning as everyone else in Hayden's orbit.

Laughter from the kitchen brought Sadie out of her musings. She turned to find Nora and Devon standing at the island. Nora had her chin propped on her fist, smiling at her husband while he said something to her. Sadie watched the couple, an ache forming in her chest. She wasn't used to seeing that type of connection. Her parents had never laughed with one another. She had certainly never laughed with Juan. Yes, she had smiled whenever he joked with Mateo, but it was always because of her son's happiness, not from being charmed by Juan. Sadie wanted that. Wanted to have a man who made her smile. Looked at her like she hung the moon. The way Hayden had looked at her briefly. Maybe that had been wishful thinking on her part, but his kiss said otherwise.

"Sadie, you okay?" Nora asked from the open door. She

183

had been so caught up in thoughts of Hayden she hadn't seen the woman move from the island.

"Yes. Just enjoying the stars." Sadie entered the kitchen, and Nora closed the door behind her.

"Nothing like a big Texas sky." Devon leaned against the counter and held out his arm. Nora didn't hesitate to stand next to her husband, leaning into his embrace.

"It's one of the things I've missed most about home. That and my mom."

"And I'm sure she's missed you as much," Nora said.

"I can't wait to see her. I wish Hayden would let me at least call her, but I get why he wants me to wait."

Nora's smile faltered. "What else have you missed?" Devon pressed a kiss to his wife's temple. Something was off about the gesture.

"Freedom to walk outside whenever I want. To stand around the kitchen like this, talking. To be able to choose my own clothes. To wear shorts and T-shirts and not dresses all the time. To roll out of bed and not worry about my hair sticking up." Sadie laughed at the thought. "All the little things. Watching TV. Having popcorn and chocolate or soda at all or whenever I feel like it. Going to school. Not that I like sitting in class all that much, but the routine of getting out of the house every day and seeing my friends. I missed out on so much. Dances. Prom. Football games. I used to love going to the games every Friday night. Dominic would drive me to school when he lived at home, then after he moved out, my mom would take me. I miss my big brother. He's several years older, but he never made me feel like I was in the way."

Sadie wiped at the tears she hadn't realized were falling until her vision blurred. "Dominic was the best. Once he joined the MC, he would come by the house on Sundays if our dad wasn't home and take me for a ride on his bike. I miss riding with him. That freedom of being on two wheels with the wind whipping my face. There's nothing like it."

Nora beamed at her. "I know exactly what you mean. Riding with Devon is one of my favorite things in the world. You know, Hayden has several bikes. When this is all over, I'm sure he'd love to take you out on his bike."

"But he lives in New York. I don't see him hanging around after this job is over just to take me riding."

"He might surprise you. Our family is extensive, so he'd have plenty of reason to hang around a while."

"*Mamá?*" Mateo was standing in the doorway, twisting a knuckle over one of his eyes.

"I'm here, *Mijo.*" Sadie crossed the room and knelt before her son, rubbing his arms. "Can't sleep?"

"I had a bad dream." He leaned into her, and Sadie wrapped her arms around him.

"I'm sorry, Baby. Do you want some milk or juice? That always helped me when I had a nightmare." Sadie didn't ask him what the dream was about. She wanted to get his little mind off whatever it was.

"How about I make some cocoa with marshmallows? Would that be okay?" Nora offered.

"What's cocoa?" Mateo asked.

"It's a warm chocolate drink, and the marshmallows melt, making it gooey."

Mateo's eyes widened. "Can I, *Mamá?*"

Sadie stood and took his small hand, leading him over to the island. "You sure can. As a matter of fact, I think I'd like some too."

Nora winked at Sadie before turning to grab the ingredients she needed. Sadie helped Mateo onto one of the tall stools, pulling it closer to hers so she could rub his back. Nora explained everything she was doing, and Sadie appreciated it. The other woman's chatter helped keep Mateo's mind off the dream and Sadie's off Hayden.

185

Hayden

THE LATE FLIGHT into New San Diego was quiet but anything other than boring. The flight attendant in first class spent more time flirting with Spyder than doing her job. Hayden was sitting by the window, and when she first set her sights on him, he politely took his drink, then turned his attention to the window. Of course, Jude soaked up the attention, shamelessly flirting back. By the time the plane landed, he had the woman's number and promised he'd try to get together with her during her three-day layover. Hayden knew it wouldn't happen. Not with them on a job.

Judge met them on the lower level, and they rented two cars as soon as they made their way through the airport. Hayden and Spyder checked into The Rialto, a nice hotel down the strip from where Juan was supposedly holed up. Since Alvarez had seen Hayden and Spyder at the club, Judge checked into the Bonaventure Hotel where he would do the recon. Instead of dressing like the bikers they were, all three wore shorts and T-shirts. They needed to blend in, and wearing their MC gear or mercenary clothes would bring too much attention. The suite Hayden booked had two bedrooms, a common living room, and kitchen/dining combo. At least they'd be comfortable during their stay should it take more than one night. Hayden walked over to the sliding glass door looking out over a large balcony. The room was situated so they had a good view of the casino. With their Eagle vision, they didn't need binoculars to see the few blocks.

Henry was on standby back in New Atlanta,

monitoring the hotel and waiting for their call. Judge had managed to get a room on the same floor as Alvarez. He checked in with them less than twenty minutes later, stating he'd already found the man's suite. He had heard two voices coming from the room, one of which belonged to a woman. Judge settled in by his own door, waiting to see if Alvarez or the woman left the room. If there was no movement, Judge was going in. Hayden and Spyder were going to be waiting in the stairwell until he got into Alvarez's room. Doing the job in the middle of the night was preferable when most guests would be asleep and housekeeping wouldn't be wandering the hallways.

Hayden wanted this part over with. He wanted the cheating bastard out of Sadie's life. Then he would concentrate on finding who had taken the contract out on her life and put an end to them as well. During the flight, he'd had time to think about that. Whoever contacted Quinn either didn't know Sadie well or didn't care that she had nothing to do with her husband's dealings. If it was the former, they needed to be put down because they hadn't done their own due diligence when it came to ordering a hit on an innocent woman. At least, that was Hayden's thoughts on the matter. He wasn't going to allow someone to remain in Sadie's life who had no regard for her well-being. Someone who was willing to make Mateo an orphan.

While they waited, both males changed out of their shorts into jeans and button-ups. The hotel where Juan was staying was attached to a casino, so they could dress casually and still fit in. They stuffed a change of clothes into a messenger bag in case they got blood on what they were wearing. If it were up to Hayden, there would be a lot of blood. He wanted to make Alvarez pay for what he'd put Sadie through these last eight years.

Hayden and Spyder left their hotel and walked across the street to a bar. It was almost closing time, but they needed an excuse to be on the street so late. Hayden texted Henry when they left, giving the Gargoyle time to put the hotel security footage on a loop so they wouldn't be caught on camera. He texted back and let them know everything was good on his end. He had it set for an hour, but he was monitoring the feed just in case someone in the hotel noticed the glitch.

Hayden and Spyder each downed a couple beers before making their way toward The Bonaventure. They strolled through the opulent lobby as though they belonged at the hotel and hit the stairs. When they reached the fifth floor, Hayden sent Judge a text letting him know they were in place. Spyder propped the door open just enough they could see through the crack. Judge came out of his room and walked the few feet to Juan's suite. He cocked his head to the side, listening for movement within the room. Judge nodded, and Hayden leaned against the wall of the stairwell, fisting his hands.

CHAPTER SEVENTEEN

Hayden

JUDGE JIGGLED THE door handle, mumbling to himself. He knocked softly, then jiggled some more.

"Who is it?" Alvarez demanded.

"Is me, *Papi*. Open up," Judge slurred in a crazy falsetto, knocking again. "Can't find my key." A room down the hallway opened up. An older woman stuck her head out, shook it, then retreated back inside.

"You've got the wrong room."

"Come on, *Papi*. Don't do me dis way. I's sorry. Please, Baby..." Judge thunked his head against the door. Hayden was both horrified at the thought of Judge standing where Juan could shoot him and amused at the male's acting job. The door was flung open, and Judge stumbled forward, effectively knocking Alvarez backwards. "*Papi*! Who's in your bed?" Judge asked loudly, letting Hayden and Spyder know the woman was still in the room. Sadie had assumed her husband had other lovers, and she'd been right.

Hayden and Spyder ran to the room before the door could close. Judge hadn't mentioned a gun, so Hayden knew the man wasn't armed.

"What the fuck?" Alvarez, clad in a pair of black boxer briefs, rushed to the bed where a woman was gaping at the three of them, her naked body on display. Before Juan could

189

reach for a weapon, Hayden was on him. Tackling him to the bed, they landed in a heap on top of the woman who was now screaming.

"Shut up," Spyder demanded in his Gryphon voice. The woman immediately clamped her lips shut. Spyder dragged her out from under Hayden and Alvarez. Hayden had one of Alvarez's arms trapped behind his back, while Hayden snaked his other arm around Juan's neck. The man was a fighter, Hayden gave him that, but he was no match for a Gryphon.

"Go in the bathroom and don't make a sound," Spyder commanded the woman. Hayden didn't know if she was a prostitute or someone Juan had met possibly in the hotel bar. He didn't care. They would make sure she didn't come to any harm. They wouldn't kill her for being stupid enough to get caught up with a drug lord. Once the female was safely enclosed in the spacious bathroom, Hayden had to keep his Gryphon from slaying the man. They needed to question him first. Hayden kept his arm around Juan's neck but relieved the pressure so he wouldn't pass out. Judge, wearing gloves, searched the room for any weapons. He found a loaded Glock 9mm under the pillow, and another in the bedside table drawer atop the ever-present Bible hotels deemed necessary reading material.

"Stop fighting me," Hayden commanded. Alvarez stopped struggling, and Hayden released him.

When Juan turned around, Hayden pointed. "Sit there and don't move." Juan sat on the side of the bed, resting his fisted hands on his bare thighs. Hayden took in the bite marks on Juan's neck and chest. "You have a beautiful wife at home, so why would you cheat on her?"

"*Mercedes es una niña.*"

"In English."

"Mercedes is a child. She knows nothing about pleasing a man."

"Yet you married that child," Hayden seethed. "Had a child with her."

"She was pretty enough, and I only needed her to produce an heir. Who the fuck are you?"

"I'm the male sent to kill you and Mercedes."

"Mercedes? She is dead? Where is my son? If you hurt Mateo, I will—"

"I don't kill innocent people. Mercedes was attacked by someone else."

"Is she dead? Where's my son?" Juan's body was fighting against the command to remain still. The rage in his eyes would have shaken a lesser male, but Hayden wasn't worried. Even if his Gryphon voice didn't work on the drug lord, Spyder and Judge had his back.

"I'm surprised your sister didn't tell you."

"Antonia? She told me the police raided my home, and I should stay out of town for a few more days."

"She lied. Armed men attacked your guards, attacked your wife, and took off with your son."

"If that is true, why isn't Antonia dead also? She's a guard."

"You'd need to ask her that. Maybe she was behind the attack. I mean, she isn't really your sister, is she? She's the daughter of your mentor. Maybe she felt she should be the one at your side instead of Mercedes. The one to give you an heir. Or maybe she wanted you out of the way so she could take over."

"No. Antonia is loyal to me. I took her in when her father went to jail. Gave her a job."

"Maybe it wasn't a job she wanted."

"She loves me. Antonia would do anything to be by my side."

Hayden rolled his eyes. The man was delusional. "What about Mercedes's family? Where are they?"

"How would I know?"

"You honestly want me to believe you don't keep tabs on them?" Hayden knew Juan was under the influence of his Gryphon voice, but he doubted the man was telling the truth.

"It's been eight years. After Mercedes became my wife, they no longer were a threat."

Hayden looked at Spyder who shrugged.

"Someone is a threat. Someone offered a lot of money for us to kill you and Mercedes. I still think it's Antonia. If she loved you like you say, she wanted you all to herself. When that didn't happen, she did her best to make Mercedes's life hell. She hates your wife as well as your son."

"How do you know this?"

"I spoke to Mercedes before getting her out of the way. She told me all about what it was like being your wife. Told me about Antonia and how she treated Mateo. Did you know your son is scared of your sister? Trembles whenever she's near?"

"If what you say is true, I will kill her. Nobody touches my son or threatens him."

"Sorry, but you won't get that opportunity. Like I said, I came here to do a job." Hayden released his claws, and Juan gasped.

"What the hell are you?"

"Nothing you'll remember." Before he could take a swipe at the male's neck, Judge grabbed his arm.

"No." Judge held up Juan's gun, which was fitted with a suppressor. "He's a known drug lord and aspiring human trafficker. This will be easier to explain." Hayden nodded and stepped back.

"I shouldn't, but I will give you one thing before you die... Mateo is safe. So is Sadie. And I'm going to make sure your influence over both of them dies along with you."

Judge didn't hesitate to pull the trigger. The impact of

192

the bullet into Juan's brain knocked him backwards onto the bed. Blood escaped the exit point, coloring the pristine white pillowcase scarlet. The copper scent reached Hayden's beast, and it roared in his head. It, too, was glad Sadie's husband was dead.

"Let's get out of here." Judge tossed the gun onto the floor where the police would find it.

While Judge wiped his prints off the door handle, Spyder opened the bathroom door with his shirttail and voiced the woman with a story to tell the police. In twenty minutes, she was to call 911 and tell them her lover had been shot by one of his own guards.

Hayden picked up the messenger bag they hadn't needed and followed Judge back to his room to grab his things. He hadn't unpacked, so within minutes, the three of them were headed down the stairs and out the door. They walked behind the hotel and down the block where they crossed over to The Rialto. Using his keycard, Spyder let them in a side door. They didn't speak until they were securely in their suite. Hayden sent a text to Henry telling him their job was done and thanking him for the assist.

"You didn't give the woman much of a story for the cops," Judge said while pouring them all a drink from the minibar.

Spyder leaned against the back of the sofa, his legs crossed at the ankle. He paused tapping on his phone. "Didn't want to make it easy on her. She was in bed with a criminal. Literally. She was wearing three-carat diamond earrings. Unless prostitutes make better money in California than they do elsewhere, I figure she was someone Juan knew or picked up. She should've been more careful in choosing a sex partner." Spyder put his phone in the back right pocket of his jeans. "There. I changed our flight back. We leave later today instead of Monday."

"Thank you. We need to get back and find Antonia. I

193

bet if we find her, we find Dominic and Gloria." Hayden unbuttoned the dress shirt and slid it down his arms, leaving him in a T-shirt.

Judge poured himself another drink. "You said the Norse Gods' Pres was looking for them."

"Yes, but I haven't heard from him. I'm going to ask Lucy to help out."

"Well, it is four in the morning. I doubt he'd text you this late." Spyder stood and stretched. "I'm going to grab some shut-eye. Our flight back is now at ten fifteen."

Since Judge had returned to their hotel, that meant either bunking together or one of them sleeping on the sofa. Hayden had slept in worse places. "You can take the other bed. I'll sleep out here."

"Or we could share the bed. I think I can keep my hands off you for one night." Judge winked. He was as straight as Hayden, even if he was as big a flirt as Spyder.

Spyder turned when he got to the door of his bedroom. "Just come sleep with me, Judge. I'm the smaller out of all of us, so there'll be more room in my bed. If you think you can keep your hands off all this." He waved a hand down his tight body.

"Yeah, I think I can manage." Judge clapped Hayden on the shoulder. "See you in a few hours." The male followed Spyder into the room, leaving the door open. Hayden wouldn't have been bothered sharing. He'd slept in the same bed as his brothers, and Judge was like another sibling. All the Hounds were.

"Goodnight," Hayden called after them before retreating to his own room. Stripping down to his briefs, he climbed under the covers, tucking one arm behind his head as he stared at the ceiling. Amber eyes, plush lips, and a nice, round ass called to him. Sadie was soft in all the right places, and her mouth... Closing his eyes, he thought back to the way she kissed him. He wanted more of that. More of

194

everything. Now that Juan was dead, Sadie was free to be with whomever she wanted. But things weren't that simple. Unless he had a will, Juan's death was going to bring a whole new set of problems to her life. All the male's assets would go to her. She had at least one house, possibly two. Juan Carlos hadn't been the biggest drug lord around, but he'd made a name for himself, and with it, a shit-ton of money.

But with Juan's death came an opening for someone else to step in and take over his business. Was that Antonia? Was the woman ruthless enough, savvy enough, to continue where the man left off? Or was there someone else who had their sights set on what Juan had? When Juan had taken out Ramirez, he had seized the other man's home and possessions. That kind of thing didn't happen through legal channels. Sadie was going to need legal counsel, and Hayden knew just the person to help. With their family being so extensive, there was someone in just about every profession. One of Dahlia's sons, Nolan, was an attorney up in Dallas. Hayden would call him in the morning. Well, later in the morning since it was already after four. Hayden fell asleep feeling a little better about Sadie's predicament.

Antonia

"MALDITOS CABRONES!" ANTONIA tossed the papers onto the desk in Juan's office. The fucking asshole thought he was better than his rivals. Thought if he didn't put anything onto a computer, no one would be able to find where he had his money. She'd learned from the best – her father. From a young age, Antonia had observed Jorge Dominguez as he built his empire, thinking she would one day follow in his

footsteps. But when he brought in Juan Carlos Alvarez to be his second, his protégé, Antonia got pushed to the side. She still watched and listened. Learned everything she could, so one day, *she* would be in charge.

Now, not only had Juan left a sizeable amount of money in an account for his kid, he'd also set aside a large sum for Mercedes. Oh, he had his own bank account. One that was small enough it didn't raise any red flags. That would *not* be enough money for Antonia to disappear on.

"*Señorita*, we have company." One of the new men Antonia had hired stood in the doorway to the office.

"I'll be right there." She shoved the papers back into the drawer in the hidden compartment and replaced the books Juan thought would conceal the false bottom. She grabbed the handgun from the desk and slid it into the holster on her hip. When she reached the front room, a couple of large bikers were waiting.

"Can I help you?" Antonia might be dressed as a guard, but she used her sultry voice. The one that brought many a man to his knees.

"I think we can help each other." The man was over six-and-a-half feet tall. His biceps were larger than most men's thighs, and if this were any other circumstance, she'd want to find out if the rest of him was in proportion. She'd long ago given up on her and Juan being together. The two of them had burned the sheets many a night, but that was before he married Mercedes. Once he put a ring on it, Antonia was pushed to the side. Again.

"Would you gentlemen care for a drink?" Antonia walked over to the sideboard, giving them her back. If there weren't six armed guards in the room, she'd never have made such a daring move, especially since she had no idea who the bikers were or what they were going to propose. She looked over her shoulder and raised her eyebrows.

"Sure. Why not?" the man answered, his posture

relaxed like he hadn't walked into a lion's den.

Antonia poured hefty amounts of top-shelf bourbon, carefully picking up all three glasses and passing them out. She should be intimidated by the man's size, but she wasn't.

"Now, gentlemen. May I ask why you've come into my home without an appointment?"

The smaller man smirked, and Antonia almost reached for the weapon on her hip. Who the fuck did he think he was besides some low-life biker?

"How is it you're walking around a crime scene?" the larger man asked.

Antonia shrugged. "Money talks. And now so should you. What do you want?"

"I believe you have something of ours. Or should I say someone."

"Who is it you think I have?" Antonia sipped the alcohol, keeping her eyes on the shorter man. He was the one with the attitude.

"Dominic and Gloria Rodriguez. Tell me where they are, and I'll give you something you want."

"What could you possibly have that I want? Look around you." Antonia waved her hand toward the rest of the house.

"If this was yours, maybe. But it belongs to Juan Carlos who took it from Hector Ramirez. I happen to know you lost something valuable of Juan's, and when he finds out, will you still be welcome here?"

Antonia's insides chilled. These men knew where Mateo was. If she could get the boy back, she could continue with her plan instead of running.

"What makes you think I know where your friends are?"

"Leverage. Bargaining chips. Call it whatever you want. You needed some, and now you have it. You tell me where they are, and I'll tell you where to find Mateo."

197

Antonia strolled over to the sideboard and refilled her glass. She took a sip, then turned. "Let's talk."

Hayden

BY THE TIME the plane landed in New Laredo, Hayden was ready to crawl out of his skin. He knew Sadie was fine, but he wanted to see her for himself. He'd called Devon before their flight took off and told him everything. Nolan was meeting Sadie at Devon's, and he was bringing Grayson to play with Mateo at Hayden's request. The boy needed to be around other kids. He couldn't wait to introduce him to the twins. Yes, he was getting ahead of himself thinking of taking Sadie and Mateo home to New Troy, but damnit, he wanted that. Wanted her to meet the other mates. His brothers and his parents. He wanted Rory to wrap Sadie in her arms and give her all the love his mother possessed. There was just something about Aurora Rose Lazlo, and Hayden was blessed to have her and Sutton as parents.

Hayden was already designing a sidecar in his mind for when Sadie and Mateo rode with him. Already thinking about getting a puppy for Mateo. Animals were skittish around shifters, but Hayden could ask Tamian to work his magic. Lucy's Gargoyle had a special gift of talking with animals.

"Earth to Havyk." Spyder nudged him on the shoulder. "You gonna sit on the plane all day or get back to your female?"

Hayden unbuckled and stood, taking the bag Spyder was holding. He didn't bother correcting the male about

Sadie being his, because if he had his way, she would be. Sooner rather than later. Hayden knew in his heart she was meant to be his. Now he had to figure out how to keep her safe.

On the drive from the airport, Lucy called to check in. "I have movement on Antonia. She's back at the house in New Laredo, and she isn't alone. She has six men with her. Tomás and Jose haven't been seen since last night. The nanny, Ana Marie, showed up, and after what appeared to be a heated discussion with Antonia, Ana Marie packed a couple bags and left. Since there's no audio, I have no idea what was said. And that's not all. A group of bikers showed up this morning. Two of them were escorted into the house, and after about an hour of civil discussion, they rolled back out. Since there's no audio feed, I have no idea if they're working together or not."

Hayden and Spyder looked at one another. "What did these bikers look like?" Spyder asked through the Bluetooth.

"Mostly Hispanic, but there was one really big male. Towered over everyone."

"Could you see the name of the MC on their kuttes?" Hayden asked.

"I never saw their backs. I'm sorry I can't give you more."

"No, Lucy. You're doing all you can. I appreciate it." Hayden leaned harder against the passenger door. Her description sounded like Kodiak, but Hay was assuming when he didn't know for sure. If it was Kodiak and the Norse Gods, what was the male playing at? He knew Hayden had Sadie and Mateo, but he wouldn't offer that information up to Antonia, would he? If it meant he could find his mate, then maybe. "I have to make a call, Luce. Keep us posted if you see anything else."

"Will do."

The line disconnected, and Hayden punched in Devon's

number. As soon as his nephew answered, Hayden asked, "Have you seen any bikers in your area?"

"No. Things have been quiet. Why do you ask?"

Hayden recounted the call with Lucy. He had a bad feeling in his gut, and his Gryphon was rattling around his head, shouting to hurry up and get to Devon's house. "Call the Hounds. Get them to your house now."

"I have Jericho, Oscar, and Reid here with me. I think we can handle some humans."

"Dev... Fuck. They aren't all human."

"What?" Spyder and Judge shouted at the same time Devon said, "Come again? If they were Gryphons, they'd be riding with the Hounds."

Hayden scrubbed a hand down his face. "They aren't Gryphons. I have no idea what they are, but I do know they aren't human."

Spyder slapped the steering wheel. "And you didn't think we needed to know that?"

"At the moment, no. When I met with them yesterday, I voiced Kodiak, but it didn't work. One of the others, Saber, burst into the room when Kodiak threw a glass against the wall. After a heated discussion where it was hinted none of us were human, they admitted some of their club were like them, but not all. Kodiak also admitted Sadie's mother is his mate."

"Fuck, man. He was probably telling Antonia you have Sadie." Spyder growled low in his throat, but Hayden ignored it.

"I don't think so. Kodiak called her 'our Sadie.' You saw how emotional all the Gods were when they saw the tribute bike. She means something to them. There's no way he'd sell her out."

"Even to get his mate back if Antonia has her? You know mate trumps everyone else."

"Fuck! Devon, get on the horn and call in the Hounds. I

want as many as you can get guarding the house. We'll be there in twenty."

"I'm on it. We won't let anyone near your female."

CHAPTER EIGHTEEN

Sadie

"GOOD MORNING." SADIE padded into the kitchen. The aroma of coffee tempted her senses, and Nora looked up from the island, where she was working a crossword puzzle.

"Good morning. Have a seat." Nora poured a mug and handed it over, pushing the sugar bowl and creamer toward Sadie. "I have some news."

Sadie spooned some sugar into her cup, giving Nora her attention as she stirred. "Hayden's on his way home?" When Nora grinned, Sadie blushed. As a married woman, she shouldn't be worried about someone who wasn't her husband, but damnit, she hadn't asked to be married to Juan.

"Yes. Their mission was successful."

"You mean Juan's dead?" Sadie whispered. She looked behind her toward the hallway. As glad as she was to be out of the man's clutches, her son would be devastated.

Nora nodded. "Hay's on his way back, but now's when things are going to get complicated for you. Someone else is going to be ready to step into your husband's shoes once they find out he's dead. As things stand, what he owned technically belongs to you. But we both know that's not how things work in that world."

"I don't want any of it. The house, the cars, the money… Okay, maybe a little money for Mateo's future, but the rest of it? Whoever takes over can keep it. There is nothing in either house that was truly mine. All the clothes are dresses, and I'd rather burn them than wear them again. Although I will miss the nice skincare products, but I'll be fine shopping at the local pharmacy for those things."

Nora tilted her head. "You're really not going to miss the fancy house? The expensive jewelry?"

"Not at all." Sadie sat her mug down harder than she should have, but she needed the woman to know she was serious. "I didn't ask for any of those things. I lost eight years of my life, and all the flashy shit is a reminder of what I lost. I was happy wearing jeans and cowboy boots. T-shirts and shorts with flip-flops. Going the weekend with no makeup and my hair in a messy bun. I had friends. I got to leave the house and go to school. To the movies. To watch whatever I wanted on TV. To spend time in the kitchen with my mom learning to cook. All that was taken from me, and those are the things I want back."

"I'm sorry, Sweetheart. I didn't mean any offense." Nora's eyes were shiny, and that made Sadie feel like crap.

"No, I'm sorry I snapped at you. You've been nothing but kind to Mateo and me. I do worry about what this is going to do to him though. He's so young."

"Yes, he is, but kids are resilient. He'll miss his papa, but he'll have you full time now to make sure he's okay. You're a wonderful mother, and you've got a lot of people in your corner to help make his new life better."

"I really don't. I mean, yeah, I'll have my mom and Dominic, but everyone Mateo was used to is gone. I don't even know where Ana Marie got off to after the attack on the house. She could be back in Mexico, or she could be waiting for Juan to come back from his trip, expecting everything to go back to normal. She's worked for him a long time. The woman doesn't realize she's out of a job. That her employer is dead. Ana was just as big a part of Mateo's life as I was. Heck, she spent more time with my son than I did." Sadie pressed her palms to her eyes. Nora was right. Things were more complicated than before. Not only did she have to worry about someone taking Juan's place, but there was still the matter of who wanted her dead.

"Sadie, look at me." When Sadie raised her head, Nora leaned across the counter and took one of her hands. "Yes, you'll have your mom and brother, but you also have our family. And let me tell you, it's a big one. Hayden has ten siblings. Most of those siblings have mates and kids and even grandkids. I can't tell you how many Lazlos there are because honestly? I've lost count. You and your son have the extended group who will welcome you both with open arms. Some of us already have."

"But why? I mean, yes, you and Devon opened your home to us, and I'll be forever grateful to you. But the others? They don't know us."

"Because you mean something to Hayden, and he means the world to the rest of us."

Sadie's heart beat a little faster. She meant something to Hayden? No, she was a job. He had a life in New York.

"I can hear you thinking from over here." Nora laughed and turned loose of the grip she had on Sadie's hand. Nora picked up her coffee and took a sip. "I'm a firm believer in everything happening for a reason. And I think Hayden was meant to be the one to take this particular job. He was meant to find you and Mateo."

"But my life's a mess. Why would he or anyone else want to get mixed up in all the craziness? Like you said, my life is just now getting complicated. Who would want to take that on? What man wants a woman with a past like mine? A woman with someone else's child? A woman who for all intents and purposes has nothing to offer? I have a ninth-grade education. I have no job. No marketable skills. For all I know, my mother could have had me declared dead, and then what?"

"You are an amazing person. You're strong. Brave. You're kind. Let's not talk about how stunning you are, even with your crazy bed hair." Nora winked again. "You have lived through your own hell and came through the other side. It doesn't matter about your education. That can be fixed. From the way you speak, you're intelligent. You don't need money or a job. The right man will take care of you and Mateo. If you want to stay home and take care of a household, there's nothing wrong with that. If you want to find a job that makes you happy, you can do that too. You're young, Sweetheart, and you really do have your whole life ahead of you. Now, how about you and I get breakfast started?"

"You want me to help you?" Sadie's throat was tight from Nora's kind words, and now she was willing to let her help cook.

"Only if you want to."

"I'd like that." Sadie was truly gratefully for this woman. *She* was the kind one, and Sadie was glad Hayden had been the one to get the contract too. Anyone else could have not worried whether she deserved to be taken out. Mateo could be an orphan, not just a fatherless child. But she wasn't going to let herself think that just maybe Hayden was interested in her other than she had been a job. She couldn't get her hopes up.

Nora showed Sadie how to make homemade biscuits and gravy. As good a cook as her mom had been, even Gloria couldn't get the hang of biscuits. She'd more often than not bought the frozen kind. They had been good, but the ones Sadie took out of the oven looked and smelled like heaven. Sadie loved carbs of all kinds, but bread was her weakness. Always had been. Living with Juan, she hadn't exercised much other than swimming and dancing when she was alone in her suite. A few of the videos Juan had allowed Sadie to have were how-tos on Salsa dancing. She had watched them over and over until she was able to do the moves flawlessly. Sadie had always loved to dance, so it wasn't a hardship to learn.

Mateo walked slowly into the kitchen, his hair as askew as hers had been before she excused herself earlier. While the biscuits had been in the oven, Sadie had gone to check on Mateo. While she was in their room, she took the opportunity to brush out her hair, taking care not to bump the staples. Her scalp was tender, but the pain had lessened. She dreaded having the staples removed, but she looked forward to it as well because that meant she would be healed up.

"Good morning, Mateo. Would you like some juice or milk? Breakfast is almost ready." Nora had already pulled a small plastic cup down from the cabinet. It had cartoon characters on it. When Sadie asked about it, Nora explained that there were a lot of small kids in the family who came to visit.

One thing Sadie couldn't wrap her head around was how Nora was old enough to have grandkids. Jericho wasn't married, but Nora had mentioned she had daughters. She said they had good genes, but Sadie felt there was more to it than that. She had seen family photos scattered around the house, and all the adults appeared young. Sadie couldn't tell the parents from the kids unless they were younger like Mateo or teens. And there wasn't an ugly one in the bunch. That wasn't Sadie being cruel. She knew not everyone could look like a model. Her best friend growing up had been about as plain as a girl could be, but Sierra was a beautiful soul on the inside, and to Sadie, that counted more than what a person looked like on the outside.

"Milk, please." Mateo climbed up on the same stool

he'd used the night before, his eyes following Nora's every move. When she set the cup down, he smiled. "Thank you."

"You're welcome."

The back door opened, and Devon, Jericho, and a couple other men walked in. Devon went straight to Nora and kissed her on the cheek before snagging a biscuit. Nora didn't chastise her husband; she just grinned and shook her head. Now Sadie understood why they had cooked such a large breakfast. The two newcomers glanced at Sadie, but neither man's eyes lingered too long.

"Sadie, this is Oscar and Reid, two of Devon's cousins," Nora said, introducing the men. "This is Sadie and her son, Mateo. You boys wash up, then grab a plate. Breakfast is ready."

All four men took turns at the kitchen sink washing their hands. They each grabbed a plate, but none of them made a move for the stove. Nora explained she didn't usually set the food on the table to be passed around. Said it was easier to eat buffet-style.

"Sadie, come fix your plates. If we don't get ours first, there won't be any food left once these Lions get through with theirs."

"Lions? Where?" Mateo asked, looking around.

Nora and Devon shared a look, but it was Jericho who answered. "All us men have the appetite of a big cat. It takes a lot of food to fuel these muscles." He flexed his bicep, and Mateo giggled.

"*Mamá*, I want to be a lion," the boy said as he climbed down from the stool.

"Then you need to eat a good breakfast."

Mateo held up his hands like claws and roared. All the adults laughed at his antics, but Sadie's heart swelled. Her son never felt at ease enough to play around. Always afraid he'd be chastised for not acting proper. Being around Hayden's family was good for him. She wished some of the grandchildren could come over and show him how to play like a regular boy.

They all filled their plates, then moved to the dining room. Nora made sure everyone had something to drink, then sat down next to Devon.

"These are yummy," Mateo said around a mouthful of biscuit.

"Your mama made them." Nora gestured at the bread clutched in the boy's hand.

"Really?" Mateo scrunched his little nose, and Sadie couldn't help but laugh.

"I did. Miss Nora showed me how."

"Do you think you can teach *Señora* Elena how to make them when we go home?" Mateo's question was innocent, but it caused the food to sit like a rock in Sadie's stomach. How could she tell her sweet boy they didn't have a home to go back to?

"We'll see," was all Sadie could manage. She would have to figure out a way to tell her son his papa was gone.

"Mateo, how would you like to play with someone your age today?" Nora smiled softly at Sadie as though she knew where her mind had gone.

"A boy?"

"Yes. Devon's cousin, Nolan, is driving down from Dallas to talk to your mama, and he's bringing his grandson with him. Grayson is five, just like you."

"Can I, *Mamá*? Can I play?"

"You sure can. But first, you have to finish your breakfast."

Mateo shoved a big bite of biscuit in his mouth. Sadie had tried to get him to cover it with gravy, but he insisted on eating it plain. When he finished that one, he eyed the stack of them in the middle of the table. He had never before asked for seconds, having been told he had to clean his plate first, so she reached out and grabbed another for him.

The men at the table were watching them closely, but there were smiles on their faces as they did so. Sadie didn't know if Devon had told them about Sadie and Mateo, but she figured he had since they weren't asking questions. She was pleased they weren't looking at her with disdain considering who her husband was. *Had been.* That was going to take some getting used to.

When Mateo went back to focusing on his food, Nora reached out and touched Sadie's arm. "Nolan is an attorney. Hayden called him this morning and asked him to meet with you."

Sadie set her fork on her plate and laced her fingers together in her lap. "Do you think he can help us?"

"Yes. There's still the small situation of why Hayden was here in the first place, but while he and the others are working on that, Nolan will start working on getting what you want out of the... deal."

"I really appreciate that." Sadie had been thinking that maybe she and Mateo might need new names. She didn't know if that were possible, but if someone was still after her, she thought maybe it best if she and Mateo left Texas. She considered asking Hayden to take them to New York. Surely that was far enough away that whoever was after her couldn't find them at the other end of the country, but she couldn't do that. His family was already going out of their way to be kind.

After they finished eating, Sadie insisted on helping with the dishes. Devon and the two newcomers took their coffee out onto the deck, and Jericho offered to get Mateo settled in the living room. Her son went with the man without question. He was such a trusting boy, and that worried her. He was only five, but he had no real life skills. He had been just as sheltered as Sadie, but she knew how ugly the world could be. Sadie watched the door as much as she did the dishes she was washing, knowing Hayden was on his way back.

"His flight lands at 1:30," Nora said without looking at Sadie.

"I wasn't... I just..." Sadie sighed and stopped lying. She absolutely was watching for the blond.

"It's okay, Sweetheart. If you're worried about me or anyone else judging you, don't. You didn't ask to be married to Juan."

"No, I didn't, but I should be focused on what happens next. Do you think...?"

"Do I think what? You can ask me anything." Nora took the platter Sadie was rinsing and began drying it.

"Do you think I should change my name? Maybe disappear? I mean, what if Hayden can't figure out who's after me? I don't want to be out somewhere with Mateo and always looking over my shoulder, wondering if the people I'm passing on the street are out to get me."

"That's certainly a possibility. Another is you could take Mateo away from here and hide out somewhere safe until the person after you is caught. Then you could come back as Sadie Alvarez, not someone different."

"I don't want to be Mercedes Alvarez. I never did. Maybe Nolan can help me at least get back my last name. For eight years, I have wished I could go back to being Sadie Rodriguez. As for getting away, I have nowhere to go or the means to get there."

"Oh, but you do. When I said our family had your back, I meant it. You don't have money now, but you will. And even if you never had another penny to your name, you don't have to worry about that. I know Hay makes good money between his bike business and the jobs he takes on the side. He's not going to let you and Mateo want for anything. And I don't mean the way Juan did. You'll have choices, Sadie."

"But he doesn't know me. I'm just a job to him." Sadie

knew she sounded like a broken record, but she was trying to be realistic.

"You really aren't. This may sound odd, but sometimes you meet the right person at the right time. Take me and Dev, for instance. I was engaged to my high school sweetheart. We dated for years off and on. Just like any other teenagers, we'd have a fight, break up, then get back together. My dad and I were like oil and water because we had the same temperament. Both stubborn. I thought by marrying Donnie it'd get me out of the house, away from my father. It wasn't like I was madly in love with the boy, but he was nice enough. Handsome. Set to graduate college with a good job. Then one day, I was headed to the florist to talk about flowers for the wedding. I tripped on the sidewalk, and the most stunning male I'd ever seen caught me before I could hit the pavement. One look in his dark eyes and I knew. *He* was the one I was meant to be with."

Sadie handed over the last dish and unplugged the sink, rinsing the suds until the basin was clean. She glanced over at Nora. "Then what happened?"

Nora got a dreamy look in her eye as she dried the dish. "He asked me out for coffee. I explained that I had been on my way to the florist to pick out flowers for my wedding. You know what he said?" Sadie shook her head. "He said, 'No,' then he grabbed my face and kissed me right there in front of Zeus and everyone. And it wasn't a chaste kiss either. Devon Ellis kissed me like a male possessed, and I guess he was. Or maybe obsessed is a better word. Then he dragged me into the florist and proceeded to tell them I wouldn't be needing their services."

"And? Don't keep me hanging here," Sadie complained, but she did so grinning.

"Let's just say we didn't make it to the coffee shop." Nora wiggled her eyebrows.

"No!"

211

"Oh, yes. If I thought his kiss was possessive, the way he—"

"Nora!" Devon yelled through the back door. Sadie jerked around to look at him, fully expecting him to be pissed, but he was wiggling his finger back and forth at his wife.

Nora threw her head back, laughing. She then blew her husband a kiss before leaning against the counter, her smile beaming. "Several hours later, I called Donnie and told him the wedding was off. Devon took me home to pack my things, and I moved in with him that night."

"What did your parents do?"

"There wasn't anything they could do. I was twenty-two. My father was pissed, but that was nothing new. My mother was smitten by Devon's charm. That might have been part of why my dad was so bent out of shape. I think if Devon had crooked his finger at her, she'd have left my dad. I think even if I'd met Devon after I married Donnie, things would have turned out the same."

"You'd have left your husband?"

"Without a doubt. Devon and I were meant to be. We aren't the only ones in our family with similar stories. When you meet that one perfect being, things just kind of fall into place. Maybe it's the same for you and Hayden, maybe not. What I'm trying to say is don't worry about what anyone else thinks. If you have feelings for him, don't hold back."

"But what if he doesn't feel the same way?"

Nora reached out and brushed a tendril of hair behind Sadie's ear. "I don't think that's something you have to worry about. Now, why don't you go sit with Mateo? Unless you'd like to help me bake a cake? I happen to know Hayden loves red velvet."

Sadie peeked into the living room where Mateo was sitting in Jericho's lap. "I think Mateo is fine where he is."

CHAPTER NINETEEN

Hayden

THE NEXT SEVENTEEN minutes were the longest of Hayden's life. Spyder pulled down the long driveway, and Hayden was out of the SUV before the male had it in park. Several Hounds were stationed around the house, but Hayden only acknowledged them with a chin lift before striding inside. Something sweet filled the air, taking his feet straight to the kitchen when he didn't find Sadie in the living room, where Mateo was playing with Grayson. Hayden had only met his little cousin once, but the boy looked exactly like Nolan's son, Jonah.

Sadie was sitting at the island with Nolan while Nora stood leaning against the counter. Hayden nodded at Devon's mate as he crossed the room. With no hesitation, he strode up to Sadie and pulled her to her feet, wrapping her up tight. He buried his face in her hair, inhaling deeply.

"Hayden?" Sadie hugged him back, running her hands up and down his back. "You okay?"

"I am now." Hayden released her and pressed his lips to her forehead. "Sorry." He took a long look at her amber eyes before stepping back. Nora was smirking.

Nolan, however, was frowning. "Everything okay?"

"Yeah. How are things going here? Do you think you can help Sadie?" Hayden couldn't tell them what was going

213

on. Not yet.

"I'm not going to lie; it won't be easy. If Juan set up any accounts in Sadie's or Mateo's names, that money is theirs. I've put a call in to a friend who lives across the border. He is going to do some digging for me. Looking at previous similar incidents, the government will likely seize his assets. At least those in his name. If he didn't go through the proper channels after taking over Ramirez's house here, then it and everything in it will be up for grabs. His men and sister could step in and claim it, setting themselves up against rival cartels. Since we don't know who his second-in-command is or was..." Nolan held his hands up.

Hayden pulled out his phone and sent a text to Lucy, asking if she or Henry could do some checking into the bank account situation. "What else?" he asked, once that was done.

"I asked Nolan to help get my name changed. I never wanted to be an Alvarez, and now that he's *dead*," Sadie whispered, "I don't want to be associated with him in any way."

Hayden could understand that. He knew it was too soon to be thinking about her last name becoming Lazlo, so he kept that to himself.

"I need to let Lucy know about the name change. She's looking into getting your birth certificate. Right now, we need to discuss something else." Hayden rubbed the back of his neck. He hated to tell her about her family, but she needed to know the truth. He stepped closer and took her hands. Her eyes widened, and he gripped her hands tighter. "Your mom and brother... they're missing."

"What? How...? When...? What?" Sadie's knees buckled, and Hayden grabbed her before she could fall. He banded an arm around her waist, and she grabbed a fistful of his T-shirt.

"With both you and Mateo missing from the attack on

214

the house, we sent someone to watch over Gloria, but when Jericho got there, she was gone. The house had been ransacked. I called Dominic to tell him about you, but Kodiak informed me Dominic was also missing."

"Y-you talked to Koda?" Sadie's voice was barely a whisper.

"You know him?" Hayden shouldn't be surprised. Not with the way the large male had spoken about Sadie.

"Yes. He came to the house a lot with Dom when my dad was out of town. He was like a father to me, and I think he was secretly in love with my mom. They never did anything like touch or kiss, but I often caught looks they shared when they thought I wasn't watching."

"I think you're probably right. And I'm pretty sure they got together after your father was killed. He mentioned she was important to him. But here's the thing. Lucy said some bikers went to the house here in New Laredo and met with Antonia and the guards she has with her. I told Kodiak I have you and Mateo. Sadie, I can't be sure he didn't give your location up."

"No!" Sadie pushed away from Hayden. "He wouldn't do that."

"You don't understand. Your mom is..." How could he explain about mates without telling her the truth of himself and his family?

"Hayden, I think it's time," Nora said.

"Time for what?" Sadie asked.

"Do you want me to leave?" Nolan lowered himself to his feet. "I can go sit with the boys."

"Please. We don't need Mateo walking in during show and tell."

Nolan inclined his head and left the room. Hayden looked at Nora, and she assured him with her eyes this was the right thing to do. Hayden took a deep breath and released it.

215

"There's something you have to know about me. About my family. It's going to be hard to believe, but after I've told you, I'll show you proof."

"Show me what?" Sadie took a step back, her pulse quickening and her eyes dilating.

Nora moved over to the island, resting her forearms on it. "Remember when I mentioned Lions and Jericho made a joke about it? He wasn't kidding. My family, we're shifters. We are Gryphons – half Lion, half Eagle. We can change into either animal or both at the same time. We were put on Earth by Zeus to watch over humans."

Laughter bubbled from Sadie's throat as she shook her head. She looked from Nora to Hayden. "Do you believe this?" she asked him. In response, his Lion rumbled. Sadie gasped and took another step back. "Oh, my God. How did you do that?"

"Because he's Gryphon too, Sweetheart. Most of our family are shifters. I know it sounds impossible, but it's the truth. We can show you if you like."

"By turning into a-a-an animal?"

"Well, we can't shift into our Gryphon inside the house without wrecking it. They're pretty big, but we can show you our Lion or our Eagle." Nora let her Lion's fangs elongate, and when she held her hands out, they were no longer human but her Lion's paws. Claws and fur were on display.

"Holy shit! Is this some sort of trick?"

"No. Hayden, why don't you show her your Lion?"

"Sadie, do you want to see me? The real me?"

"I-I-I don't know. This is all too much." Sadie looked around the room, and Hayden followed her eyes as they locked on the block of knives on the counter.

"Would it make you feel better to be armed? Nora, hand Sadie the butcher knife."

Nora didn't hesitate. They both knew they could defend

216

themselves were Sadie to try and swipe at one of them. Sadie took the knife and held it in front of her. Her hand was shaking so hard Hayden was afraid she was going to hurt herself instead of one of them.

"Do you want just a partial glimpse or the whole shebang?"

"Partial. No, the whole thing. Holy crap on a cracker, I can't believe I just asked you to turn into a jungle cat."

"Technically, lions don't live in jungles, but then neither do I. Except when all my brothers are around. Then it can get a little crazy." Hayden tried using humor to lighten the mood, but Sadie was still shaking. He prayed the female didn't have a heart attack when he shifted.

"Okay, I'm going to shift. I want you to know I would never hurt you. Not in my human form and not as a cat. I'll sit really still, and if you want, you can pet me. I vow on all that's holy, I will not hurt you."

Sadie's head bobbed up and down, but her grip tightened on the knife. Instead of stripping, Hayden toed off his boots, then he let the beast loose, shredding his clothes. Once his Lion was free, Hayden sat back on his haunches and waited. Sadie gasped, her free hand covering her mouth. She looked from him to Nora and back.

Nora walked around the island and set her hand on Hayden's back. "He's still Hayden. He can hear you and understand you in this form." Hayden swished his tail back and forth across the kitchen floor and waited. Sadie lowered her hand and reached toward his massive head. He kept his eyes on the knife because it was still pointed his direction. "It's okay, Sweetheart. He won't hurt you." Nora leaned against his back, wrapping her arm around his neck. It was odd to be hugged in this form, but he knew what Devon's mate was trying to do.

"Havyk! We've got... Oh, hell." Spyder stopped just inside the back door. "Sorry to interrupt, but we've got incoming. Four SUVs. Guess that answers our question as to whether or not Kodiak would give up Sadie for his mate."

Hayden's Lion roared, and Sadie screamed right before she fainted. Hayden shifted back, and Nora waved him off. "Go. I've got her. Nolan! Bring the kids. Hayden, go grab some of Devon's clothes. You can't go outside like that."

Hayden rushed down the hallway to his nephew's room and threw open drawers until he found a shirt and pants. The sweats were a little tight, and he didn't bother grabbing underwear, but modesty was the least of his worries at the moment. When he left the bedroom, Nora was ushering the boys to the back of the house, while Nolan carried an unconscious Sadie. Hayden bristled at the sight of his female in another male's arms, but he pushed back against wanting to rip her away from his nephew's hold.

"I've already called the police. Stall as long as you can," Nolan said.

When Hayden got to the front door, it was like a scene from a movie. Gryphons were mighty creatures, but they were no match for the weapons aimed at them. Four black SUVs were parked haphazardly. Hayden counted seven males holding rifles, and leading the group was Antonia.

"Give me my nephew," Antonia commanded. She was standing beside the open door of one of the vehicles, a handgun pointed at Hayden's chest. The Hounds Devon had called were scattered around the property, some standing and some among the trees in their Eagles. Hayden had to hope the cops weren't on Alvarez's payroll.

Stalling, he crossed his arms over his chest. "Your nephew? Who the fuck are you?"

Antonia snarled. "You know who I am, and I know you have Mateo in that house. Juan Carlos doesn't take lightly to his son being kidnapped. Either you send him out now, or we start shooting."

"Juan is dead, so his thoughts on the matter don't count

218

now, do they?" Hayden wasn't sure whether or not Antonia had received word of Juan's demise, but he needed her focus on something other than Mateo.

"You're lying. My brother is safely tucked away."

"Are you sure about that?" Hayden wanted to tell her the truth, but he couldn't without incriminating himself, Spyder, and Judge. "When's the last time you heard from him? And he's not really your brother, is he? He's the man who took over when your father went to prison. The man who turned you into a guard instead of taking you into his bed where you really wanted to be."

"Shut up! You don't know anything."

"I know what I saw. What I heard. That night in the club, you stood closer to Juan than his wife did. You wanted to be the one on his arm, being admired. I saw the way you glared at Mercedes. The way you couldn't take your eyes off them while they commanded the dance floor. But you were there to do a job, weren't you? You were there to make sure Juan's wife was safe."

"Shut up! If you don't shut the fuck up, I'll kill you all and that bitch too." Antonia pulled the trigger, the bullet hitting the house less than a foot from where Hayden stood. He dove onto the porch, and the other Hounds scattered.

"FBI, drop your weapons!" a voice shouted from the cover of the trees. Antonia and her men turned toward the voice and fired. They had remained beside their vehicles, but their focus had been on Hayden and the house. Hayden remained on his stomach as several agents returned fire from various locations around the property. He was torn between going in the house to check on Sadie and remaining where he was so he didn't become a target. When Antonia's pistol was out of ammo, she reached into the vehicle and pulled out an assault rifle. Before she could pull the trigger, a bullet slammed into her shoulder from behind. The female stumbled, but it didn't stop her. Antonia turned the rifle in

Hayden's direction, and he knew then he would never have the chance to be with Sadie. He didn't close his eyes, though. If death was coming, he wanted to see it.

Antonia's eyes widened when a bullet hit her in the chest. She dropped to her knees, then her body slumped to the ground. Hayden released a shaky breath, but he still didn't move. Even when the air around him went silent, he lay frozen against the porch. Only the rumble of several motorcycles broke him from the stupor he was in. Hayden rose to his knees when Kodiak parked his bike. The large male stood and walked over to where the FBI agents were looking down at the dead bodies of Antonia and every male but one she'd brought with her. Hayden remained where he was as Kodiak shook hands with one of the agents. When Kodiak turned toward Hayden, his face was lined with worry. That was what brought Hayden to his feet. What sent him rushing the larger male, claws out.

"Havyk, no!" Spyder yelled, but Hayden's Lion was on a mission to take down the bigger male who'd put Sadie in Antonia's sights. Hayden shifted midair, oblivious to the FBI agent pointing a gun at him. Kodiak lunged. Not at Hayden, but at the human. Hayden landed, sliding to a stop a foot from where Kodiak had shielded Hayden from the gun shot. Kodiak grunted, holding onto the agent's hand. Now that Hayden wasn't trying to kill Kodiak, he got a good look at the other man. Tomás. Hayden shifted back, and stepped around Kodiak. Tomás's eyes were wide, and he was struggling with the large biker.

"Th-that was a l-lion!"

Hayden called on his Gryphon. "There was no lion."

"Uncle Hayden?" Jericho stepped up beside Hayden and held out a pair of sweatpants. Hayden grabbed them and slipped them on.

"Kodiak? You mind telling me what the fuck is going on here?"

Instead of answering Hayden, Kodiak turned to Tomás and began barking instructions. "Tommy, you and the men get this cleaned up. Take that one" — Kodiak pointed to a still-breathing guard — "to the hospital. I'll handle the rest."

"Yes, Sir." Tomás turned and corralled the rest of the agents into doing what he was ordered to.

"*Sir*? Who the fuck are you?" Hayden demanded.

"Let's go in the house. I'll explain everything."

"No. You're not getting anywhere near—"

"Koda!" Sadie yelled from behind Hayden. He turned to find his female running toward them. Only she bypassed Hayden and launched herself at the larger male.

"Hey, Baby Girl." Koda wrapped his arms around Sadie and buried his head in her hair. "God, I thought I'd never see you again." He set her on her feet and held onto her arms. "Look at you. All grown up. Just as beautiful as your mama." Koda kissed Sadie's forehead, and Hayden's Lion growled. Koda looked over at Hayden, smirking. "It's like that, is it?"

"Yeah, it's like that, so I'd appreciate you taking your hands off my mate."

Koda rolled his eyes. "Sadie, girl, your mama is going to be so happy to see you. Dom, too."

"Where are they? Are they here?" Sadie looked around.

"No, but they're waiting on you. I just have to talk to Hayden for a few, then I'll take you to them."

"Now wait just a minute. She's not going anywhere with you. You were the one who told Antonia where Sadie and Mateo were. You put them both in danger."

Sadie's eyes widened, and she moved away from Koda. Hayden held out his hand, holding his breath. When Sadie laced their fingers, he exhaled as softly as possible, not wanting Koda to know how new or unsure this thing with Sadie was. Sadie had fainted because of Hayden's Lion, but she seemed to trust him.

"I did. It was all planned out. As you can see" — Koda swept his arm around — "everything turned out fine. Tommy and I were already in place when Antonia arrived. There was never any threat to Sadie."

Hayden took a step, putting himself between Koda and Sadie. "No? What if she'd been on the porch with me instead of hiding at the back of the house? What if one of those numerous bullets being sprayed at me hit her? And what the hell was that with Tomás calling you Sir?"

"I'll tell you everything if you calm the fuck down." Koda's own shifter rumbled in his chest, but Hayden didn't back down.

"Uncle Hayden, why don't you take this discussion inside?" Devon suggested.

Sadie tugged at Hayden's hand. When he glanced back at her, she placed her palm on his cheek. "I have so many questions, and I'd really like to see my family. Please?"

Hayden couldn't deny her anything when she looked at him with those big, amber eyes. Plus, her touch calmed his inner beast like nothing else could.

Hayden nodded, then gestured to Koda. "After you."

Koda strode toward the house, not looking back. Once inside, he stood off to the side, allowing Hayden and Sadie to pass by him. Sadie sat on the sofa, but Hayden remained standing.

"Start talking."

"I've been working with the FBI to bring down Hector Ramirez. When Alvarez took him out, we turned our focus on Juan Carlos. Tommy, or Tomás as you know him, has been undercover. He's a federal agent who went on hiatus so he could cross over into Mexico and go after Alvarez. When he got word that Elena and Jose were plotting to take Mateo while Juan was out of town, he went along with their plan to keep an eye on the boy. Their plan was almost fucked up during the attack on the house. That was

222

Antonia's doing, by the way. She had her own vision of getting rid of Juan and taking over his business. The hit on Juan and Sadie? That was her doing as well."

"She just volunteered all this information to you?"

"You aren't the only one with the power of persuasion."

"So, you what? Told her you'd trade Sadie and Mateo for Gloria and Dominic?"

"I did, but I already knew where Gloria and Dom were. They are both safe at my home. After you told me who Mercedes really was, I hid them away just in case Juan made a play for them. With Sadie missing, the first place Alvarez would look for his wife was with her family. It was better to make him think someone had taken them."

"Why did you lie to me then? Why not tell me the truth?"

"Plans were already in motion, on both sides. When you told me the real reason you were in Texas, I thought it best to let you follow through. We already knew from Tomás that Antonia was unhappy. She's been going behind Juan's back for a while now gathering her own little army. Promising certain guards they'd be King to her Queen, one of them being Jose. It was how he knew when the attack would happen. He and his sister, along with Tomás, already had an exit strategy for Mateo, but the attack happened sooner than it was supposed to." Koda ran a beefy hand through his thick hair. "Antonia was a snake. She wanted to run the empire. She wanted all the money, but it wouldn't be hers with Sadie still in the picture. I'm sorry if this upsets you, Sadie."

"You aren't telling me anything surprising. She's never liked me or Mateo."

Hayden's heart was thumping wildly. If Koda betrayed him, he would be going to prison. Him, Spyder, and Judge. "Did you share with your FBI friends what I did?"

"No. Maybe we talk about this somewhere more

223

private?" Koda glanced at Sadie.

"She knows the truth."

Koda's eyebrows shot up. "All of it?"

"Yes. Once I rescued her from the house and brought her back here, I told her about the hit."

Koda once again turned to Sadie. "And you were okay with that?"

Sadie stood, placing her fists on her hips. "More than okay. That man took me across the border when I was fifteen. Made me a prisoner. He forced me into marrying him and giving him an heir. I don't regret Mateo for a second, but the life he and I have lived? I wouldn't wish that on anyone. He took everything from me, and if it weren't for Hayden being a decent human... uh..." Sadie cut her eyes to Hayden.

"It's okay, Gorgeous. He knows."

Sadie's eyes widened. Her anger dissipated a fraction, but she jutted her chin at Koda. "If it weren't for Hayden being a decent being, I wouldn't be standing here. He didn't just take the contract and do the job without all the facts. If it had been anyone else who got that particular job, they might have pulled the trigger without asking questions first. But yes, I'm quite okay with being a widow." She walked over and stood next to Hayden. "I'm more than okay with it."

"If you didn't tell the FBI about the hit, what did you tell them?" Hayden asked.

"Nothing. As far as anyone knows, Alvarez was killed by one of his guards. That was the story the woman in his room told the cops who showed up. Sorry, Sadie."

"Don't apologize. I knew in my heart he wasn't faithful. Men like him only care about themselves. He never loved me. If he did, it wasn't the kind of love I want. Now, I'm going to check on my son. You two please finish hashing out whatever it is you need to, then I'd really like to go see my family." Sadie gripped Hayden's hand, squeezing it before turning and walking out of the room.

CHAPTER TWENTY

Sadie

SADIE WAS HAPPY to see Koda. He had been part of her life for a couple years before she was taken. He visited with Dominic whenever he came to supper, but only when her father wasn't home. It didn't take a rocket scientist to see Koda was in love with Gloria. The way he smiled softly. The gentle touches when he thought no one was watching. Her mother's smile was just as loving, but with her Catholic upbringing, Gloria would never divorce her husband. Sadie's romantic heart hoped the two of them had gotten together after her father was killed.

When Hayden accused Koda of selling out Sadie for his mate, she knew what he meant by mate. While they were hiding out, Nora had explained a bit about shifters and their significant others. Sadie had heard the term mate over the last couple days and thought it odd. Now it made sense. But if Hayden mentioned Koda having a mate, that meant he was also a shifter. Did Gloria know? Was she aware the man she let into her home was other than human?

Sadie now also understood the immediate connection she felt with Hayden. Nora said Sadie was Hayden's mate, or she could be, if that's what she wanted. The conversation was quick, and Sadie had so many questions. Like how the Gryphon voice worked. Nora used it on Mateo so the boy wouldn't be scared when he was ushered to the back of the house to hide. Had they used it on her? Was she doing things against her will because she'd been commanded? Was her affection for Hayden something conjured, or did she truly want the male? Male, not man. That was another term she now understood.

No, Sadie had been drawn to Hayden from the first moment she laid eyes on him in the club. No one had spoken to her in Gryphon voice or human. Her attraction was genuine. Maybe it was because she was his mate. At least she hoped so. She knew going from a marriage right into another relationship was probably foolish, but as Nora said, it was no one's business but hers if she did.

When gunfire sounded outside, Sadie had rushed to the front of the house against Nora's wishes, but she couldn't sit by while Hayden was out there defenseless. Yes, he was Gryphon, but his shifter was no match for guns. Nora had said as much. It was why she couldn't *not* go after him. Nora had held onto her arm until the gunshots stopped. It had been the hardest thing she'd ever done – waiting to see if Hayden was okay. Instead of going to him immediately, though, she'd rushed into Koda's arms. She needed to apologize to Hayden for that misstep. She never wanted him to feel as though he was second in her life. Well, after Mateo. Her son would always come first. If Hayden didn't understand that, he wasn't the male for her.

With both Juan and Antonia dead, the only business left for Sadie was finding out if any of the money was available or if some other drug lord would waltz in and take over the way Juan had when he set up residence in Hector Ramirez's home. Nolan promised to figure that out for her. Nora said money was no issue. Hayden would take care of both her and Mateo. But would he want to do that in Texas? Sadie was excited about seeing her mom and Dominic. They all had a lot of catching up to do. Mateo had a grandmother and uncle to meet. The child also had to deal with the loss of his father when Sadie found the courage to speak to him about it. Maybe Hayden could soften the blow with his Gryphon voice. Then again, maybe Mateo needed to deal with it the way all other humans did. Death was a part of life, and even though she never wanted her child to hurt, she couldn't - shouldn't - shelter him from certain things.

If Hayden didn't want to remain in Texas, Sadie would go with him to New York after she'd spent time with her mom. She already knew in her heart she and Hayden were meant to be together, and if Gloria was aware of what being a mate meant, she'd understand. If not? Sadie would promise to visit.

Mateo and Grayson were playing with toy cars while they watched a cartoon movie about talking vehicles. He didn't look up when she walked into the room. Her son had quickly latched onto the other little boy. Having never had a friend, it was a joy for Sadie to see Mateo having fun.

Nora rose from the chair where she was watching over the boys and met Sadie at the door. "Everything okay?"

Sadie tilted her head to the hallway, and Nora followed. She didn't want Mateo to overhear the conversation. "It is now. Antonia showed up with several guards. Koda, a friend of the family - mine, not Juan's - has been working with the FBI for years, and he led Antonia here. Hayden was pissed about that, but Koda swore they had everything under control. I guess since Antonia and all but one of her men are dead, that was the truth."

"I'm surprised Hayden let you out of his sight."

"I think it's only because he knows I'm in the house. When Koda said he'd take me to see my family, Hayden told him I wasn't going anywhere with him. It was kind of hot."

Nora grinned. "I bet. I love it when Devon's shifter gets riled up."

"What about yours? Does your Gryphon ever want to come out because it's jealous or upset?"

"Oh, yes. Not that I have anything to be jealous about because that male is mine. But when we're out and other women don't care he has his female on his arm, I'm tempted to let the Lion rumble. Or the Eagle loose with its talons." Nora held out her hand, and sharp talons took the place of her fingers. She retracted them just as quickly. "Talk about plucking some eyeballs out." Nora laughed maniacally, and Sadie couldn't help but grin. "That's one thing you'll have to get used to. Shifters are much more territorial than humans. Although, we do have some human mates in the family, and they can be just as fierce when it comes to their mates. The connection in shifters is stronger. Deeper. While Gryphons don't have fated mates, the bond isn't any less intense."

"I think I can get behind someone loving me that much. Having lived in a forced marriage for eight years has me yearning for the kind of bond you're talking about." Sadie turned to see Hayden standing at the end of the hallway, his eyes narrowed on her. He stalked toward her, and when he was close enough, Hayden tagged her wrist and yanked her against his hard body. Obviously not caring that Nora was standing right there, Hayden fisted Sadie's hair and tilted her head before crashing his lips to hers. The kiss the night before had been hot, but this was all-consuming. As if he could suck her soul out through her mouth, and in turn, offer his to her the same way.

Hayden backed her against the wall and continued the onslaught. If kissing were battle, he'd brought a mighty army to slay her. Warm tingles started in her chest, snaking down her stomach, and into her core. Never had she been turned on from kissing. Never had she burned from the inside with a need to lay herself bare. Sex with Juan had been a chore. He gave her orgasms, but that had been a biological response to stimuli. She hadn't wanted her husband. She didn't want Hayden – she needed him. Needed his hands on her. His skin rubbing against hers. His cock filling her.

"Havyk— Well, hell." Spyder groaned. "I swear my timing is better."

Hayden released Sadie's lips, but he didn't step back. Maybe he didn't want his friend to see the erection that was pressed against her hip. Sadie thunked her head against the wall, then sucked in a breath, having forgotten the staples. Hayden's eyes were heated, lids half-open. His hand was still in her hair, but his fingers were caressing her scalp, close to where the staples were.

"Give me a minute."

Spyder gave a two-fingered salute before he turned on his heel and strode off.

"Soon, Gorgeous. Very soon, it's going to be just you and me. Somewhere we won't be disturbed." Sadie shivered at Hayden's promise. Hayden's hand in Sadie's hair relaxed, and his exhale ghosted across her face. "I was coming to tell you Kodiak and I got things squared away and to see if you're ready to go see your family."

"But?" Sadie felt there was something more happening because that kiss was unlike anything she'd ever encountered.

"No buts. This right here..." Hayden brushed his thumb across her cheek. "This will still be here when you get back."

"You're not going with me?" Sadie trusted Koda. Well, she had before today, but she couldn't forget he'd brought the enemy to Hayden's family's doorstep.

"Do you want me to go with you? I figured you'd want some privacy."

"I want you." Sadie swallowed hard when Hayden's eyes narrowed. "I want you with me, unless you have something else you need to do?"

230

"Let's get something straight, Gorgeous. I want you too, for as long as you'll have me. Having said that, you need to know that *you* are my first priority. You and Mateo. If you want me with you, then there's nowhere else I'd rather be."

"But what about your job? Your home in New York?" Sadie asked before she could stop herself. She shouldn't come across as needy. That probably wasn't attractive, but she needed to know how things were going to be for them.

"You come first. Period." Hayden pressed a kiss to her forehead. God, he was going to kill her with kindness. Tears welled in her eyes, and she tried to blink them away. "Hey, what's this? Why are you crying?"

"You're too sweet."

Hayden took a step back. The gentleness in his eyes was gone in an instant, and Sadie had no idea why. Before he could walk away, Sadie grabbed his wrist. "Hayden, that's a good thing. I'm not used to tenderness or caring. I'm not used to being someone's priority. God, you have no idea how that makes me feel. You being too sweet? That's what I want more than anything."

Hayden sighed. "I'm sorry. It's a sore spot with me. Women I've gone out with have wanted anything but sweet. They expect me to live up to the reputation of being a badass biker."

Sadie didn't want to hear about other women he'd dated, but that would be a little hypocritical considering she'd been married for the last five years. "Then their loss is my gain. At least I hope it is. God, this is crazy. Isn't it?"

"What's crazy?" Hayden slid his hand down into hers and laced their fingers together.

"All this. We just met. Until last night, I was still married. And you..." A sharp laugh escaped, but Sadie couldn't help it. It had been a few days since she met Hayden, and here she was already planning their future together. Nora said it happened that way in Hayden's family, but still. "You and I don't know each other very well, but what I do know about you I like. A lot. Your job as a mercenary and you being a biker doesn't define who you are, Hayden." Sadie placed her free hand on his chest. "Your heart does."

Sadie thought Hayden was handsome before, but when he smiled at her words, his whole face lit up.

"*You* are my heart, Sadie Rodriguez," Hayden whispered before leaning down and pressing their lips together. If a kiss could talk, this one spoke volumes. It said she was his heart, his mate. Too fast or not, Sadie knew in that moment, she had found her forever.

Hayden

HAYDEN WAS NERVOUS. He didn't get nervous, but here he was. Sadie was in the passenger seat, and Mateo was buckled safely in a booster seat behind them. They were following Koda to his house where Sadie would be reunited with her family. He was worried how they would feel about Sadie going from one relationship to another with no time in between. He couldn't explain to them she was his mate. They didn't know about shifters. Hayden still had no idea what kind of shifter Kodiak was, but he guessed him to be a bear. Both his nickname and size would make sense if he were.

Sadie still hadn't told Mateo about his father's demise. Hay had no idea how she would handle it, but he would be right there with her, if she wanted him to be. He planned on being at Sadie's side every day going forward. If that's what she wanted. If not? He'd somehow deal with it. They needed time alone to discuss their future. Time to figure out if they were staying in Texas or if Sadie was interested in moving to New York. Hayden hoped it was the latter because he already had a house there. It's where his equipment was. Where his parents and brothers were. But he wasn't so selfish to demand it. She was the one who'd lived the past eight years of her life as a victim. She was on her way to be reunited with her own family, and if she needed time with them in Texas, that's where they would stay.

When they pulled down a long driveway, Hayden was surprised to see a large sprawling estate. Koda didn't come across as someone with a lot of money, but if he was a shifter, it was possible he'd already lived a long life and amassed a small fortune over the years. Maybe he was good at investing. Before Hayden could further contemplate how Koda made his money, the front door flew open, and Hayden was staring at Sadie thirty years into the future, if Lucy didn't come up with a way to slow that rate at which human mates aged.

Gloria Rodriguez flew down the front steps and didn't stop until she was at the passenger door. Sadie pushed it open and fell into her mother's outstretched arms. Giving the two women time to get reacquainted, Hayden unbuckled and exited the SUV, then went to the back door and unlatched a wide-eyed Mateo.

"That's your grandmother. Your mama's mama."

"She's pretty." Mateo allowed Hayden to lift him into his arms, and the two stood watching. Dominic exited the house a lot slower than his mother had. He turned to Hayden, his brown eyes glistening. When his steps brought him within arm's length, he halted, staring at the boy in Hayden's arms. "Hello, Mateo."

Mateo clung to Hayden, and even though the boy was

233

timid about the newcomer, it felt good to have his arms around Hayden's neck. His weight was perfect, and in that moment, Hayden knew he'd found a piece of his forever.

"Mateo, this is your Uncle Dominic. Your mama's brother."

Dominic reached out to touch Mateo, but the child shrank away. It was no surprise, considering how most of the men in Mateo's life had been hardened guards. "It's okay, Buddy. Dominic loves you, and he would never hurt you. I promise."

Mateo met Hayden's eyes, the doubt shining. Before Mateo could decide whether or not Hay was telling the truth, Sadie and her mom were there. Sadie held out her arms, and Mateo went to her. *"Mijo,* this is my *mamá.* Mom, this is my son."

Gloria swiped at the tears, but it did no good. They continued to fall as she took in her grandson. *"Hola, Mateo. Es un placer conocerte."*

"It is good to meet you too… *Mamá,* what do I call her?"

Sadie laughed and looked at Gloria. "What would you like to be called?"

"Oh, my. Well, I'm too young to be Nana, so how about GiGi?" Gloria asked Mateo.

The little boy giggled, and it was the best sound in the world. It reminded Hayden of the twins' laughter. He couldn't wait to introduce Mateo to the two little dudes.

Sadie turned to her brother. "Dom…" Her voice caught in her throat as she stepped into his open arms. Mateo clung tightly to Sadie's neck, but he seemed to accept his uncle more easily with his mom hugging her brother with her free arm.

Koda, who had been standing off to the side, eased his way closer until he was standing next to Gloria. She smiled up at the large male, and his eyes softened for his mate. "How about we head inside and get out of the heat?" Gloria put her small hand in his larger one, and the two of them led the way toward the house. With their arms wrapped around each other's waist, Sadie and Dominic followed. Hayden wasn't sure what to do. He wanted to go with them, but Sadie might want time alone to become reacquainted with her family. When they reached the steps, she turned loose of her brother and looked back at Hayden. She held out her hand to him, and the tightness in his chest eased. She wanted him with her, and there was no place he'd rather be.

It didn't take long for Dominic to single Hayden out. Sadie and Gloria sat on the sofa with Mateo between them. Although Koda was giving them space, his presence filled the room. He remained quiet when Dominic asked Hayden to go for a walk. The two of them headed through the house toward the back. When they reached the patio just off the kitchen, Dominic turned to Hayden.

"Kodiak told me why you were here. The real reason. I'm forever in your debt, Havyk. If it had been anyone else who took that contract, I might be burying my sister instead of getting her and my nephew back."

Hayden almost said that anyone else would have done the same thing, but he knew it would be a lie. Not all mercenaries had a conscience. Some would have taken out Sadie along with Juan and not blinked an eye. Hayden shrugged one shoulder. "I realized who she was at the club. Even if she hadn't been your long-lost sister, I would have done my homework. I don't take out innocents."

"Don't think I missed the way she reached out to you. Is there something going on between the two of you?"

Hayden couldn't tell Dominic the truth of mates, so he gave him another truth. "We've gotten close these last few days. Your sister is a magnificent woman, and I care for her deeply. I only want what's best for her and Mateo."

Dominic crossed his arms over his chest. "And you

think you're what's best? A mercenary?"

"Yes. I take out the trash. I rid the world of people like Juan Carlos Alvarez. People who have no remorse in taking a teenage girl in trade. Forcing them into marriage when they're barely legal. I may be a mercenary, but I'm a good male. I have a good heart. I know what Sadie's been through these last eight years, and I'm just the kind of male she needs. Someone who will put her wants and needs first. Hers and Mateo's. Someone who has a softer side when it comes to women. Is it too soon to move forward with a relationship? For some. I'm not rushing Sadie. I care about her enough that she can have all the time in the world to make her own decisions regarding what's best for her and Mateo."

"But how does she know what's best? She's been sheltered. Hidden from the world. Who knows what Juan Carlos put her through? Don't you think she's latching onto you because you rescued her? She's not had any outside contact for eight years. I don't think she's in the right mindset to make a responsible decision."

"And that's why I just said I would give her all the time she needs. I'm not going to force Sadie to do anything she doesn't want. I've waited my whole life for someone like her, so waiting a few weeks, months, or even years isn't going to do any harm." That was a lie. Hayden nor his beast would be able to stand being away from their mate, but if it's what she needed, he'd find a way.

"So, what's your plan? Are you headed back to New York?"

"Not right away. I have plenty of family here I can stay with. If Sadie decides she wants to remain in Texas, then I'll move my business here so I'm close to her and Mateo. There is nothing I wouldn't do for her, and that includes leaving my home so she can stay close to hers. I understand why you doubt what Sadie and I mean to each other. It's only

236

been a few days, but I know enough about your sister to know she's the one for me. If after a while of us seeing each other it turns out she doesn't feel the same, I'll do the right thing."

Yes, we'll kidnap her and tie her to the bed until she sees reason.

You're an idiot. We're not tying her to the bed.

But we will kidnap her?

Maybe take her on a long vacation where it's just the three of us.

I can handle that.

Hayden had to bite the inside of his jaw to keep from laughing aloud at his Gryphon. Sadie had been taken against her will once, so that was out of the question. Hayden didn't think it would come to that, though. He'd encountered her passion when they kissed. Her softness when they embraced. The surety in her eyes when she smiled at him. No, it wouldn't take months or years for Sadie to convince her family Hayden was the one she wanted, too soon or not.

Dominic ran a hand through his dark hair. "I believe you. But man, I just got her back. Mom's beside herself with worry about Sadie's state of mind. She's gonna need time to see for herself Sadie's okay."

"I think once you talk to your sister, you're both going to see she's a strong woman. She's had to be for Mateo. Yes, things will be different for her now that she'll be free to come and go. She's going to have some catching up of her own to do with regards to life outside her prison. But she's got a whole passel of Lazlos to help with that. My family is extensive, and those who have met Sadie have already seen to it she gets the best start on her new life. Sadie had to grow up fast. She's not the fifteen-year-old girl you remember. She's a remarkable woman considering what she's been through."

Dominic sighed. "Koda told me the same thing. He also said you would be good for Sadie."

That surprised Hayden. He and Koda had come to somewhat of a truce, but he never expected the other male to go to bat for him. It had to be because the male was a shifter and knew about mates. He knew no one else would ever be better for Sadie than Hayden.

"I will be. I vow to you on all that's holy Sadie will never want for anything. Not love, money, family, whatever her heart desires. If it's within my power to give it, I will. Freely."

"Then I'll do my best to see her as the woman she is."

Hayden felt the other male meant his words. Now, if Gloria would do the same, everything would be okay.

Hopefully.

Chapter Twenty-One

Sadie

As much as Sadie loved being back with her mother, she kept glancing toward the back of the house where Hayden and Dominic had gone. She figured her brother was giving Hayden the third degree, and it worried her. She didn't want Dom to get all protective where Hayden was concerned. There was no need for it. Then again, Dominic didn't know Hayden was a Gryphon. A shifter who thought of Sadie as his mate. If she could only explain that to her brother, it would make sense as to why the two of them were so close after only a few days.

"Mama, I'm hungry." Mateo had been speaking English more the longer he was away from Juan and their former home.

Gloria jumped from the sofa. "I'll make lunch. What would you like?"

"Pizza!" Mateo shouted, pumping his little fist in the air.

"Oh, Lord. Miss Nora has created a monster." Sadie tickled Mateo's sides, and the boy squirmed on her lap, laughing and begging her to stop.

When Sadie ceased tormenting him, Mateo sat up and looked at Gloria. "Gigi, can you make pizza?"

Gloria's lips turned down for a second, then she just as

quickly smiled, though it didn't meet her eyes. "I don't have the ingredients. If I had known you were coming, I'd have gone to the store. I could make you something else instead."

Koda stepped away from the wall he was leaning on, and put his hands on Gloria's shoulders. "Gloria, there's a frozen pizza in the freezer. I'm sure Mateo will be satisfied with that until you can go shopping." Gloria leaned her head back against his stomach and reached a hand out to rest atop one of his. Koda threaded their fingers and brushed Gloria's hair off her shoulder. The love between her mom and Koda was tangible, and Sadie wanted that for herself.

Sadie turned her head toward the back of the house just as Hayden and Dominic returned. Sadie smiled at Hayden, hoping to convey her support. No matter what he and Dominic spoke about, Hayden was her first priority. Yes, she loved her brother, but he wasn't her future. He wouldn't be the one who held Sadie at night. Made love to her. Kissed her awake. Besides, her brother had his own life. He would probably spend time with her in the beginning, becoming reacquainted, then Dom would go back to whatever life he had been living the last eight years. Gloria had her life with Koda, and in that moment, Sadie knew what decision she would make when it came to staying in Texas or going to New York.

OVER THE NEXT week, Sadie split her time between Koda's house, spending time with her mom, and Nora's. When she was with her mother, Hayden gave them space to bond. She and Gloria returned to the house where Sadie had grown up. Walking back into her childhood home had been harder than she expected. Her room was the same as it had been the day her father took her to Juan. Sadie spent hours looking at all the mementos of her former life. None of her clothes fit any longer, but her favorite pair of cowboy boots slid over her feet like old friends welcoming her home. Sadie gathered a few photos, but other than that, there was nothing she needed from the house to carry with her into her new life. She and her mom looked around the house one last time before Gloria shut the door and locked it, planning on putting it up for sale now that Sadie said she didn't want it.

Sadie finally explained to Mateo that his father wasn't coming home. She refused to tell him Juan was in heaven with the angels because Sadie knew if there was a Hell, that's where her husband was. Mateo didn't cry. He didn't ask questions. He seemed to take it in stride, but Sadie figured at some point, it would hit him his papa was really gone. Hayden and his family, along with Dominic and his MC, made sure to keep Mateo occupied so he rarely had time to think about his father.

Nolan and Grayson remained in New Laredo. Nolan worked on Sadie's legal situation while Grayson played with Mateo. Even when they went to Gloria's, Nolan allowed his grandson to accompany them. The male knew Mateo needed the distraction, and Grayson loved being around Mateo. Sadie kept an ear on the boys when they were off in another room, and she'd often hear them chatting in Spanish.

Also during that week, Hayden had located Ana Marie. The older woman had returned to the house only to find it empty. Instead of going back to the hotel, she had remained there alone. Waiting. Hayden explained what happened, and Ana had been distraught. Having worked for Juan over twenty years, she had no idea what to do with her life. Hayden, being the wonderful male he was, offered to either

241

send her back to Mexico or put her in touch with some of his family who would find her a place to live and retire, if that's what she wished. After speaking with Sadie, Hayden mentioned allowing Ana to remain with them and Mateo. The boy loved his nanny like another grandmother. Rory would take to Mateo like she did all the kids, but she wouldn't begrudge Ana stepping in and helping with Mateo. Ana sobbed when Hayden made the offer, begging him to let her remain in their employ.

Gloria was skeptical at first, asking how a woman could work for such a monster and be a good person at the same time. It was Ana herself who explained how she came to work for first Dominguez, then Juan when he took over the business. Like Sadie, Ana had been given to the drug lord. Like Sadie, Ana had been forced to produce Dominguez an heir when his wife failed. It was sitting in Gloria's kitchen that Ana Marie admitted to being Antonia's mother. When she learned of her daughter's demise, the woman wept silent tears, but when she composed herself, she explained that Antonia never knew Ana was her mother. Jorge's wife had claimed the title up until the day she disappeared. At that point, Ana was just the nanny in Antonia's eyes, and she didn't see what good it would do to tell the girl otherwise.

Mateo was visiting with Gloria, and Ana was there too, bonding with Gloria as Sadie's mom helped them learn about life in the States. Sadie was sitting at Nora's dining room table with Nolan seated across from her and Hayden at her side where he usually was. Not only had Sadie spent time with her mom, she'd also met a bunch of Hayden's family. When he said he had plenty of support in Texas, he wasn't kidding. His six older sisters, who didn't look much older than Hayden, had welcomed Sadie with open arms. As had their kids and the older grandkids. Mateo had yet to meet them because Sadie was giving Gloria time to bond

242

with her grandchild. Once Mateo got entrenched in all the other boys and girls his age, she was afraid she'd never get him to leave.

Over the last few days, Sadie and Hayden had grown closer. They shared stolen kisses whenever possible, but that was as far as Hayden had allowed things to go. Sadie was going crazy wanting more. She was appreciative to Hayden for taking things slow, but if the erection pressed against her whenever they were kissing was any indication, he was having a hard time not moving things to the next level. Sadie smirked inwardly. He was definitely hard. She often caught him staring at her ass or her chest, then rearranging his hard-on when he thought she wasn't looking. Being a little on the thick side, she was glad he found her enticing.

"I have good news," Nolan said, bring Sadie back to the present. "I filed the paperwork to have your last names changed to Rodriguez. Since Juan isn't alive to contest the change, it should go through rather quickly. Lucy was able to locate a couple bank accounts in yours and Mateo's names. She was also able to get into Juan's accounts and move the money into new accounts in a fake name. That way the government can't track it back to you. She doubts she found everything, but at least you will be set going forward. As far as the house here, it was never changed from Hector Ramirez's name, so we can't touch it. Now, we just need to decide what to do about the house in Nuevo Laredo. According to my friend down there, it looks like someone has already moved in, but it's technically yours."

"I don't want the house. All I wanted was a little cash for Mateo and me. We have that. Let the Mexican government deal with whoever moved in."

"Sadie, you don't have a little cash." Nolan grinned, and Sadie frowned.

"But I thought you said—"

"You have millions."

Sadie squeezed Hayden's hand tighter. "Say what?"

"Not counting the small accounts Juan set aside for you and Mateo, Lucy found four-point-seven million dollars. Drugs are a lucrative business."

"Four-point-seven... But that's drug money." Sadie turned to Hayden. "I don't want it."

"I understand, Gorgeous. But before you turn it down, think about all the good you could do with it. Whenever we complete a job, Lucy transfers the money from the mark into accounts that our family uses to help those people we rescue from the cults we take down. We have a few charities we donate to as well. Nolan, how much was in the smaller accounts?"

"Half a million."

"What?" Sadie shrieked.

"Each." Nolan laughed. "I told you the two of you were set for now. You can live on the money in your account and invest Mateo's. By the time he's ready for college, he'll have a nice little nest egg waiting on him."

Sadie figured that money had come from illegal gains as well, but damnit she was due *something* for what she'd been through the last eight years. If keeping it made her a bad person, then so be it. Maybe giving the millions to Hayden's family to use for their endeavors would make up for it, and Karma wouldn't come back and bite her in the ass.

Hayden brought their hands to his mouth and kissed Sadie's knuckles. "Don't forget, I make a really good living. Everything I own is paid for. Even if you turned down every penny of Juan's money, you and Mateo don't have anything to worry about."

That was one of the topics Sadie had discussed with her mom – Hayden and how he was ready to take care of Sadie and Mateo. Instead of the doubt Dominic held, Gloria understood. She had lived over twenty years in a loveless marriage with Ricardo. As soon as he'd been found dead – and Sadie had been right about hearing the gunshot that fateful day – Koda had stepped in, declaring his love, and the two of them had been together ever since. She had moved in two days after getting the call about her husband. During their talks, Gloria admitted to keeping the house Sadie had grown up in for no other reason than in case Sadie made her way home somehow. Sadie had already made up her mind to go to New York, but knowing her mother approved of Hayden made it that much easier. With Hayden having family so close to Gloria, they could visit both families often.

"You don't have to decide what to do with the money today. It's not going anywhere." Nolan stood and stretched his arms overhead. "Now, unless you have any questions, I'm going to stop by and pickup Grayson, then go see my mom."

"No questions. Thank you for everything, Nolan," Sadie said.

"No thanks needed. You're family." Nolan winked at her, then clapped Hayden on the shoulder.

Hayden turned to Sadie as soon as the door closed. "Do you hear that?"

"Hear what? Everything is quiet."

"Exactly. I happen to know we have the house to ourselves for the next few hours." Hayden pressed his palm to Sadie's cheek, rubbing her bottom lip with his thumb. "I've been trying to take things slow, but I need you."

"Yes." Sadie pushed her chair back and grabbed Hayden's hand, tugging him out of his seat. Hayden chuckled, but Sadie cut the sound off with her mouth. God, she wanted this male. Hayden wrapped his arms around her waist, sliding his hands down her ample butt until he grabbed her thighs and lifted. Sadie gasped. He picked her up as though she weighed no more than Mateo. Then again, he was a shifter. She had seen his Lion, but... "I want to see your Gryphon."

"Now?"

"No. Right now, I want to see the man. All of him. But later, as soon as we find a good time and place, I want to see the rest of you."

Hayden walked them down the hallway to the bedroom Sadie and Mateo had been sharing. She and Hayden had yet to spend the night together, and it was something she was looking forward to. Now that Lucy had everything squared away with regards to the money, there was no reason to wait on heading to New York.

Hayden closed the door behind them, then set her on her feet. He lifted Sadie's T-shirt and licked his lips when he got a look at the black lace bra she wore. Sadie returned the favor, removing the white tee over Hayden's head. He had to bend forward since he was quite a bit taller. She had been dying to get a good look at all the ink adorning his body, but she was too interested in getting him inside her. There would be plenty of time later for studying his tattoos.

By the time they were both naked, Sadie was shaking with need. She knew how to please a man, but this was Hayden. The male she planned to spend the rest of her days with. The male she wanted to make as happy as he did her. Sadie raked her nails down his bare chest, relishing the way his abs bunched under his skin at her touch. She wrapped her hand around his erection and stroked.

"Sadie." Hayden's voice was low, but she ignored the warning tone. Never had she wanted to give Juan a blowjob, but the need to taste Hayden was imperative. Sadie lowered herself to her knees and licked at the liquid on his tip. Hayden slid his hands into her hair and fisted the long strands. Her staples had been removed, but her scalp was still tender. Hayden always took great care not to hurt her, but in that moment, she welcomed the little bit of pain.

Sadie didn't want to think about all the times Juan demanded Sadie blow him, but she was thankful for the practice she'd received. She also didn't want to think of Hayden's many lovers who'd come before her. She would do what she'd learned and prayed it was enough to satisfy her male. Sadie knew Hayden was hers. He'd told her as much. He explained about the mate bond, and she was ready for his bite. Ready to seal their fates together. Hayden's dick was longer than Juan's, so she couldn't take him all the way into her mouth. She used her fist to help with the friction. Her saliva mixed with the fluid leaking from his slit, and her hand stroked easily over his hot skin. The hand not stroking his cock was braced against his muscular thigh, and it bunched beneath her palm. Hayden's breathing sped up, as did her bobbing up and down. She wanted him to come in her mouth. For the first time in her life, Sadie wanted her partner's release shooting down her throat.

"Sadie... Gorgeous... I can't... Fuck, you're good at that."

Hayden was holding back. She'd had her throat ravaged too many times to count, so she knew he was taking it easy on her. Sadie tightened her fist and sucked harder, paying special attention to the spot just under the head. She released his thigh and reached between his legs to cup his balls. Sadie gave them a tug, and Hayden's grip on her hair tightened.

"Shit, Sadie. You gotta... I'm going to..." Sadie tugged harder on his sac, and Hayden came with a roar. Salty cum coated her tongue, and she swallowed it all down. When she let his still half-hard dick fall from her mouth, she looked up to see the most wondrous sight in the world. Hayden's smile brightened his whole face. His blue eyes were full of heat and longing and what she hoped was love.

Hayden

FUCK, HIS FEMALE was good at giving head. Hayden didn't want to think why that was, because he already knew. He had much to thank Juan Carlos for, including teaching Sadie about blowjobs. Teaching her how a woman *shouldn't* be treated. Keeping her as a wife instead of handing her off to his men to pass around. So many things could have happened the day Sadie's father traded her for the money he owed. Yes, Sadie's life had been traumatic, but it could have been so much worse.

He was eager to get inside his mate, but Hayden was glad she'd gotten him off. Now he wouldn't be ready to come as soon as he buried his cock inside her. Hayden tossed the covers back before urging Sadie to lie down. She was the most exquisite creature he'd ever seen, and she was his. After today, she'd be his mate. He would ask permission again, but she'd already agreed to the bite when the time came.

Hayden never thought he had a type when it came to females, but seeing Sadie spread out against the bedding, her wide hips, her full breasts, her lush mouth... Yeah, he had a type. But more than her enticing body was her strength. Her perseverance. Her heart. Hayden had fallen quickly, as had most of those in his family when finding their mates. Wasn't that the tell, though? The immediate connection to another being letting them know they were the perfect choice as a life partner. Hay refused to believe it had been his recognition of her as Dominic's little sister. It was his own recognition of her soul calling out to him and his Gryphon. His beast had latched onto Sadie the moment their eyes met in the club.

Hayden started at her feet and kissed his way up Sadie's legs. He nibbled the inside of her knee before licking a stripe up her inner thigh. Her core was right there. Her essence calling to him to taste. To feast. And he would. Later. Right then, Hayden needed inside Sadie more than he needed to breathe. Climbing atop his female, Hayden's cock rested at the juncture between her spread thighs. He held himself aloft on his forearms, his eyes searching hers. He found what he was looking for in her amber depths. Acceptance. Acquiescence. Love. Yeah, she felt it too.

Sadie raised her knees toward her chest, urging Hayden silently to take her, so he did. His dick was so hard, it bordered on painful. Using his knees for leverage, he raised his hips, and without using his hands, he nudged at her entrance. The tip of his dick met slickness, and he pushed in slowly. Sadie's hands moved from his shoulders down his arms, gripping his biceps. Her head tipped back when he was fully seated in her heat. Moaning, Sadie placed her feet on the bed and pushed against him, trying to take him deeper. He got the message.

Hayden rolled his hips, filling her before retreating to do it all over again. And again. Sadie was an incredible dancer, and the way she moved beneath him was like a slow seduction. She kept her eyes glued to his as she moved in time with his gentle thrusts. Her fingertips skimmed his arms, the scratch of her nails sending shockwaves down his spine. Women had scratched him before, but it had never felt like this. Before, it had been nothing more than animalistic rutting. A means to an end. Before, they had expected him to be rough. Demanding. This was so much more. This lovemaking with Sadie was everything he'd been missing. Everything he needed.

The tingle in his spine hit quickly. He wanted to draw

this out, their first time, but he couldn't. Being wrapped up in his mate's slick heat was more than he ever dreamed possible. His Gryphon was pushing at him to take her hard. To bare his teeth and strike. He understood the possessiveness. He felt it too, but he was doing this his way, by Zeus. The way Sadie needed. Deserved.

"I want your bite," Sadie muttered between moans.

"Yes," Hayden hissed. He squeezed his eyes shut for a moment as he did his best to keep from coming before she did. Her pleasure was what mattered. But the harder he tried, the less he managed to keep the sensation from rolling down his spine to his balls. Hay opened his eyes and dropped his fangs. Sadie's eyes widened at the long canines, but there was no fear there. Excitement glittered her irises, and Sadie licked her lips.

"Do it, Hayden. Make me yours." Sadie's fingers tightened on his arms, most likely in anticipation of the pain she knew was coming. What she would quickly figure out was the pain would be overridden by pleasure when his Gryphon saliva entered her system. Sadie wrapped her legs around his hips, pressing closer. Hayden lowered his head, inhaling the scent of shampoo, body wash, and his mate. The mixture was intoxicating. Hayden nudged her head, and Sadie angled her neck giving him full access. As Hayden's orgasm barreled its way through his lower body, he sank his teeth into the tender flesh of her neck. Blood flooded his mouth, and Sadie's core tightened, and she yelled out as she came around his cock. Their mutual releases converged. They hadn't discussed having more kids, but Hayden wouldn't hate it if their lovemaking resulted in a baby. He wanted that with Sadie. Wanted to see her belly swell with their child. He wanted Mateo to grow up being surrounded by siblings he could love, mentor, and torment in equal measure, the way his brothers did him.

Hayden retracted his fangs and licked the spots on her shoulder. The wounds closed, leaving two pink proofs of the mate bite. It was done. Sadie was his. Now and forever. He took her mouth, and Sadie opened for him, her tongue finding his in a dance as sensual as her lovemaking. Hayden threaded his fingers in her dark hair, loving the way the silky strands felt in his grip.

When he broke the kiss, Sadie was smiling. "Is it always like that?" she asked.

Hayden almost said no, thinking about the other times he'd bedded women, but he didn't think that's what she was asking. "It will be different each time. The mate bite makes things more intense, so we won't have that. But I promise to make it just as good for you."

"It was beyond good. That was..." Sadie's smile enlarged, and her eyes shifted from sated to dreamy. "Magical," she whispered.

"I agree. You wove a spell on me the moment our eyes met in the club, and I knew I'd do anything to make you mine. My Gryphon fought with me right there to grab you and run."

"Why didn't you?" Sadie carded her fingers through his hair, her nails scraping his scalp in a soothing motion. His Lion rumbled in appreciation.

Sadie gasped, then she laughed. "Is your Lion purring?"

"Lion's don't purr. We're not house cats." Hayden's haughty tone made Sadie laugh harder. Hayden called forth his feline, and his head morphed into that of his Lion. He shook his long mane in her face, and Sadie shrieked. When the Lion retreated, Hayden was grinning at the awe on his mate's face.

"You are a treat, Hayden Lazlo. A surprising wonder."

"And you are an exquisite creature in your own right, Sadie Lazlo."

Sadie's eyes widened again. "Lazlo? Did I marry you and not know it?"

"For all intents and purposes? Yes, you did. Legally, you are still Sadie Rodriguez, but I wouldn't be opposed to wedding you. I would love for you and Mateo to have my last name."

Sadie sighed, cupping Hayden's cheek. "We would be honored."

The honor was Hayden's. He spent the next couple hours showing Sadie his appreciation.

CHAPTER TWENTY-TWO

Hayden

WATCHING SADIE SAY goodbye to her mother had been gut-wrenching. They had only been reunited a couple weeks, but Hayden promised Gloria he would bring her back soon. He reminded Gloria and Dominic it was Sadie's choice where to live. If she got to New Troy and hated it, he would pack them up and be back in Texas as soon as she said the word.

Hayden left the SUV with Spyder so he could drive back whenever the male wanted. Jude had decided to remain in Texas a while longer, stating he was rather enjoying the warmer weather. Since Sadie had never flown, Hayden chartered a private jet to get the three of them to New York. He wasn't surprised to see his parents waiting at the airport. He was surprised they were alone.

"Welcome home, Son." Sutton pulled Hayden in for a fierce hug, slapping his back a few times before turning him over to Rory.

Rory's embrace was just as welcoming if only a little less bruising. "Hey, Mom. There's someone I'd like you to meet." Hayden held out his hand to Sadie, and she laced her free hand with his. Her other was full of a wide-eyed Mateo. The boy had been thrilled at flying, and his excitement hadn't waned now that they were standing on the ground once more. "This magnificent creature is my mate, Sadie. And this handsome young man is Mateo. Sadie, please meet Sutton and Rory, my parents."

Rory's grin was wide until Sutton whistled low. "Damn, Son. How'd you manage such a beauty?" Sutton winked at Hayden, then Rory backhanded her own mate in the chest.

"Behave, you beast." Rory's smile returned when she approached Sadie. "Welcome to the family, Sadie. *Hola,* Mateo. I'm Rory, but you can call me Grammy. It's what the twins call me. Or you can find your own name for me if you'd like."

Mateo smiled at his mom. "I have a Gigi and a Grammy."

Sadie hugged her son tighter. "You sure do."

Hayden had talked about Major and Marshall on the plane ride home, so Mateo was looking forward to meeting them. "Speaking of, where are the two little dudes?"

"Everyone is waiting at our house. Let's grab your things," Sutton said, already headed toward the plane to retrieve Sadie and Mateo's luggage. The two of them didn't have much, only what Nora had purchased. Hayden planned to take them shopping in the next few days, after they got settled into his home. Whether or not they stayed in New Troy remained to be seen, and Hayden was okay with that. He loved his parents and brothers. He was fond of the mates and all the kids, but Sadie was his priority now, and living in Texas surrounded by his sisters and all their offspring wouldn't be a hardship.

Hayden wrapped his arm around his mate. "Let's go home."

Sadie

HAYDEN HAD WARNED Sadie about his family. On the plane, he had talked about his brothers, their mates, the few kids, and his parents. Sadie had been nervous about meeting the matriarch of the family, but being around Rory was like coming home. The female didn't look much older than her sons and daughters, but she had an air of strength about her. She commanded respect without saying a word. But it was evident from watching Hayden and his brothers they offered their respect willingly. Sutton might have been the army veteran. The former cop. The previous president of their MC, but it was Rory who had that silent influence born from years of her maternal love and acceptance of her children. Even the unruly Major and Marshall were different with the female.

As soon as they walked in the door, Major and Marshall had latched onto Mateo and taken him under their proverbial wings, and her son was enthralled. Sadie was as well, but it was the mates who held her interest. Kerrigan, Natalia, and Rhiannon couldn't have been more different from one another, but Sadie found herself admiring each woman. The three of them took Sadie aside while Hayden met with his brothers to recap what happened on his latest job. She had no doubt they would be discussing her, but she didn't mind because she was dishing on him to her new sisters. And that's what these three women were. There was an instant bond when they sat around telling how they each came to be part of the Lazlo brood. Each story was different. Each one rife with its own tragedy, but the one thing that rang true between the four of them was how they were saved by their Gryphon mate.

As much as Sadie appreciated Nora for her help and kindness, being with these three women filled a void Sadie had long felt. She knew in her heart she now had friends who would remain by her side as long as she lived. Hayden had given Sadie so much more than himself. He'd reunited her with her mother and brother, but he'd also given her this extended family. Sadie never wanted to leave.

Sadie laughed when, as one, the four of them turned their heads to the doorway of the living room. Their respective mates entered the room and moved to stand beside the women. War held out his hand, and Kerrigan stood so he could wrap his arms around her from behind. Maveryck sat on the sofa and pulled Natalia onto his lap, where she settled against his chest as though that's where she sat often. Ryker, who Hayden had described as broody, smiled at Rhi as he settled next to her on the other end of the sofa, sliding his arm over her shoulder. Kyllian, who Sadie thought was the broody one, stood off to the side, observing his brothers and their mates. Hayden sat in one of the oversized chairs and pulled Sadie down on his lap, encircling her waist and burying his face in her hair.

Ryker's daughter, Mac, and her boyfriend, Elijah, opted out of the meet and greet, promising to see them soon. Their own story was just as tragic, and Sadie understood their need to ease into meeting two more members of the family.

The younger twins with Mateo in tow ran into the room and stopped in front of Natalia.

"Tolly, Lolly, Lollipop," the three of them sang out together. The twins were already corrupting her son, and Sadie couldn't be happier.

"Yes, my little heathens?" Natalia, with her lilac hair, grinned at the boys, who all giggled, Mateo included. It was the best sound in the world next to Hayden's muttered affections in the dark. The last week had been the best of Sadie's life. She and Hayden sat Mateo down and explained how they were a family. Being so young, Mateo had taken it in stride that Hayden was taking the place of Juan.

Hayden's patience and love had won the boy over as easily as it had for Sadie.

"Who's hungry?" Rory asked from the doorway leading into the kitchen.

The twins yelled, "Me," in unison. Mateo was a little slower to respond, still getting used to not having to behave like a small adult at all times. After a loud lunch of pizza, yet again, Hayden and Sadie said their goodbyes to her new family. Hayden got Mateo buckled in his booster seat, then they headed toward her and her son's new home.

"Is this your car?" Sadie asked.

"Eh, it's more like a family vehicle. We have several SUVs we share whenever we don't want to ride our bikes. Speaking of which, did you ever ride with Dominic?"

"Yes, and just so you know, I loved it. I can't wait to ride with you."

Hayden grabbed her hand and laced their fingers. "That's good to know. I have already ordered a sidecar for Mateo. I'll just need to jazz it up a bit."

"Jazz it up?"

"Yes. It's his ride, and it needs to reflect that. For the twins' sidecar, I entitled it 'Double the Mayhem.' I have a pretty good idea of how to paint Mateo's, but I want it to be a surprise."

Sadie knew however Hayden painted it, it would be special. She'd seen the tribute bike he had done for Dominic, and Sadie had been awed at the realistic portrait of herself. He'd won awards for his artwork, and seeing his talent had shown her he deserved the title of being one of the best bike designers. Sadie was excited at the prospect of riding behind Hayden. Having their son along with them as they rode the wind. She was even more excited as they pulled in the driveway of a two-story home in a quiet neighborhood.

"Welcome home," Hayden said after shutting off the ignition.

"This is where you live?" Mateo asked, having unbuckled his harness and leaning between the seats to see the house.

"Yes. It's now where you and your mama live too. I know it's not as big as what you're used to, and it doesn't have a pool..." Hayden's voice faded as he looked out the windshield. Sadie hadn't thought to reassure Hayden she and Mateo didn't need a sprawling estate, but the insecurity was there.

"We'd turn into popsicles if we swam in this weather. Now, are we going to sit out here all day, or are you going to show us our new home?"

Hayden let out the breath he'd been holding and turned to look at Sadie. His eyes were filled with gratitude, and he leaned over and pressed their foreheads together. "Thank you," he whispered.

Once inside, Hayden showed them around. There were three bedrooms other than the master suite, one already appointed for little boys. Hayden explained he'd fixed it up for the twins, but if Mateo wanted that one for himself, he would set up a different one for them. Mateo chose the one next to the twins' room and asked when they could have a sleepover. Hayden promised they could get together that weekend.

Upon seeing the fenced-in backyard, Mateo turned to Hayden. "Can we get a puppy?"

Hayden ruffled Mateo's hair. "We sure can, but it will have to be a special one." Hayden had already explained to Sadie about smaller animals' aversion to Gryphons and how Lucy's mate was something of a dog whisperer. "What else would you like? I think we could put a play fort right over here. The twins have one at home, and I think you'd like one too. It has swings, a slide, and a climbing wall. Would you like that?"

"I don't know what that is," Mateo admitted. Hayden

pulled out his phone, typed something into the browser, then held it out for Mateo to see. "Wow. Can I, Mama? Can I have a fort?"

Sadie's heart broke for her son. He had been refused all the things a child should have access to, and she vowed to give him everything he wanted from that moment forward. "You sure can, *Mijo*. It'll be fun."

"Thank you, Mama. Thank you…" Mateo's happiness waned when he turned to Hayden.

"What's wrong, Buddy?" Hayden went to his knee so he was closer to eye level with Mateo.

"Are you my papa now?" Mateo whispered.

Hayden glanced at Sadie, and she couldn't hide the tears. She held her breath to see how Hayden responded.

"I love your mama, and I love you, Buddy. We're a family. I would be honored to be your Dad."

Mateo threw his little arms around Hayden and whispered, "Thank you, Daddy." Sadie wasn't the only one crying after that. Her larger-than-life Gryphon had tears streaming down his face. Hayden stood, lifting Mateo in his arms and holding out his free hand for Sadie. Together, they went back inside. As the three of them snuggled on the sofa watching cartoons that night, Sadie's heart was fully mended. Her life hadn't been as bad as what the other mates endured, and she had Mateo as a result of being taken. Sitting between her two men, Sadie knew she'd endure it all over again if it meant she ended up where she was.

Home.

Hayden

IT DIDN'T TAKE long for Sadie and Mateo to settle into their new environment. Hayden had been a little worried about not having a large enough house, but Sadie eased his mind, reminding him they wanted love not things. When he suggested getting a different place to live, she'd pulled a Rory and backhanded him. Then she'd kissed away the sting. Then she kissed something else. His mate sure did love giving blowjobs.

Hayden took them shopping and loaded Sadie and Mateo up with clothes more suited to the colder weather of New Troy. He encouraged Sadie to purchase anything she wanted to make the house theirs instead of his. Sadie didn't hesitate to pick out a few things which caught her eye, like picture frames. Photos of him with Sadie, Sadie with Mateo, and the three of them as a family soon hung on the walls as well as filled empty spaces around the house. Mateo had fallen in love with The Avengers, but Hulk was his favorite. His new bedroom was an array of bright colors, action figures, coloring books, and other toys depicting the large green comic book hero. That was all the prompting Hayden needed to know how to paint Mateo's side car.

Mateo had play dates with the twins, while Sadie spent time with the other mates. Sometimes the females gathered at Ryker's so they could include Mac, and other occasions were spent one-on-one. Sadie was flourishing with her newfound friendships. She also spent time with Rory, who was teaching her to cook. While his mate and son were off visiting their family, Hayden took the opportunity to work on the side car as well as painting one of his Harleys. When he stepped back and took in the finished product, he couldn't help but be proud.

As Hayden set about cleaning up the garage, Kyllian walked in.

"Hey, Dickhead."

"Dickhead? What warranted that?" Hayden looked over his shoulder at his brother. Kyllian had been moodier lately. "Not getting enough whip time with the kittens?"

Kyllian's usual smartass response was missing. Instead, he leaned against one of the tall toolboxes and crossed his arms. "The kittens are fine."

"Yeah? How's the new ink?" Hayden couldn't help but grin. Kyllian had made good on their bet and gotten the tattoo Hayden chose. He had drawn the picture himself.

Kyllian rolled his eyes and huffed before pushing off the tool chest, turning around, and raising his shirt. The black and white cartoon kitten had a small body, an overly large head, wide eyes with long lashes, and bright-pink lipstick. One outstretched paw held a whip in action, and the other held a flogger with the tails dragging the ground. The artwork was good, if Hayden did say so himself, but it was the placement he chuckled over. The ink was on Kyllian's lower back, the ink disappearing into his jeans. Hayden knew what it looked like since he'd gone with his brother to get it. Not that he didn't trust him, but he didn't trust him not to have it put somewhere other than a "tramp stamp."

"It's healing nicely," Hayden said with a straight face.

"What the fuck ever."

"Why are you so pissy? I know it's not because of that." Hayden pointed at Kyllian's back.

"I'm not fucking pissy." Kyllian scrubbed a hand down his face and sighed. "Okay, maybe a little, but I don't want to talk about it. I just came to see the bike." Hayden knew his brother wouldn't talk no matter how much Hay prodded, so he let it go. Kyllian had been absent more than he was present lately at family gatherings, so whatever was on his brother's mind might have something to do with that.

"I just finished. Go take a look." Hayden gestured to the other side of the garage. Kyllian strolled over and studied the bike.

"Damn, Havyk. I shouldn't be surprised, but fuck. That's beyond amazing." Sadie's gorgeous face adorned the sides of the gas tank. When Kyllian saw what was painted on the side car, he burst out laughing. "Oh, Zeus! That's fucking brilliant."

"Right? I can't wait for Mateo to see it. Speaking of which..." Hayden cocked his head to the side. "I think they're here."

The sound of car doors slamming had Hayden's heart beating a little faster as it always did when his little family came to the garage. Mateo was intrigued with the tools, but Hayden had given Sadie a couple different reasons to enjoy coming to visit. When she asked to see his Gryphon, he'd cleared room in the middle of the building, closed and locked the doors, and stripped down. Her eyes were hooded, and she bit her lip. Sadie's sexiness almost stopped Hayden from shifting. "None of that sexiness." He wiggled his finger at her, and she rolled her eyes. Hayden shifted first to his Lion, then his Eagle, before letting the Gryphon come forth. It stood around ten feet tall, and Sadie had scrambled backwards, her back hitting the metal garage door. Hayden returned to his human form quickly, prepared to apologize for scaring her. He didn't get the chance because his mate rushed him, grabbing him around the neck, and pulling him down for a heated kiss. "That was so hot," she murmured between kisses. Hayden might have taken her to the break room and showed her what hot was atop the table.

Sadie and Mateo had been visiting with Natalia and the twins while Hayden put the finishing touches on the bike. One of the things on his to-do list was teach Sadie how to drive and buy her a car. For the time being, she was relying on the mates' generosity in playing taxi. Today, it was Natalia's turn. She and Sadie walked into the garage side-by-side, while Mateo and the twins entered at a much faster pace.

"Hey, Hay." Major reached out for a knuckle bump. Marshall just grinned and held out his fist.

Mateo waited his turn and wrapped his little arm around Hayden's legs. Looking up, he smiled. "*Hola, Daddy.*"

"*Hola, mi precioso hijo.* Did you have fun today?"

"*Si.* Mama and Lolly took us ice skating." Sadie had been finding all kinds of new experiences for Mateo. Hayden knew she was doing her best to make up for the first five years of Mateo's life being spent in seclusion. The way their boy lit up at the end of each day meant she was succeeding.

"That's great. Did your mama skate too?"

"Uh huh. She fell down more than me."

Hayden arched an eyebrow at his mate. "Do I need to check you for booboos?"

"Later." Sadie rubbed her backside, and Hayden growled. He would definitely check out her fine ass later.

"Look! It's a side cart!" Major yelled. "Mateo, Marsh, come look!"

Hayden let the boys discover the cartoon he'd painted on the sidecar while he went to get a kiss from Sadie. "Hello, Gorgeous."

"Hello, Mate." That greeting never got old. But he figured hearing her call him husband wouldn't either. Hayden had already phoned Gloria and Dominic about his plan for a surprise Christmas wedding. He had thought about getting married in Texas, but Sadie loved New York. Loved the cold and the snow, so he asked her family to come to them.

"Mama! It's me!" Mateo was jumping up and down, clapping. "I'm the Hulk!"

Sadie narrowed her eyes at Hayden before she and

Natalia walked over to the bike. Sadie burst out laughing and clapped right along with their son. "You sure are." Hayden had combined Mateo's face with the Hulk's body, turning his son into his favorite superhero. Sadie's laughter changed into a warm smile aimed right at Hayden. Like always, her gaze warmed his heart. Well, sometimes, it warmed other parts of him, but she always got his heart pumping. Hayden had gone to Texas to deliver a tribute bike of a missing teen, and in the end, he'd found his Sadie. He had found his happiness. His forever.

The End

A NOTE FROM THE AUTHOR

Thank you for reading Havyk's story. If you have a moment, a review would be much appreciated. It doesn't have to be long, just heartfelt. This book was so much fun for me. I love Latin dancing. I even took lessons once upon a time. When Sadie came to me, I knew she was going to be so good for Hayden. He needed someone who loved him just the way he is, and Sadie fit that to a T. Thank you to Milgia Santiago for the Spanish translations. I wouldn't trust them to anyone else. Milgia, you're a star.

After writing the story, I contracted Covid and the flu. My body ached and my brain was on overload. If it weren't for those I surround myself with, I wouldn't have been able to get this book out. As always, Candy, Jen, Kerstin, and Nikki were there to hold me up. Even though they have to deal with their own lives, they never fail to offer the support I need each time to make my books shine, and this time was no different. Especially this time, when I needed so much hand holding. I'm truly blessed to have such wonderful women in my life.

Below is a "cast of characters." I haven't given names to all the Hounds yet. As their stories evolve, they will find their names.

Next up in the Hounds universe is Spyder. Someone from his past waltzes into his life, bringing back some painful memories. Preorder link is below.

Cast of Characters

Sutton Lazlo – Patriarch, former cop, former Pres of the Hounds Mc
Aurora Rose "Rory" Lazlo – Matriarch

Ryker "Ryot" Lazlo – MC Pres, Leader of Mercs
Rhiannon Spencer – Witch
McKenzie "Mac" Colins – Ryker's daughter
Elijah McLean – Mac's boyfriend

Warryck "War" Lazlo – former Professor, current Merc
Kerrigan O'Shea – Bartender
Lucy Ball – War's daughter, Computer Hacker
Tamian St. Claire – Lucy's mate, Gargoyle

Maveryck "Mayhem" Lazlo – MC Vice Pres, Merc
Tatiana Volkova/Natalia Jones – Russian Mafia Princess
Major Lazlo – Mav's son
Marshall Lazlo – Mav's son

Kyllian "Kayos" Lazlo – Merc

Hayden "Havyk" Lazlo – Bike Designer, Merc
Sadie Rodriguez – Mom
Mateo Rodriguez – Sadie's son

"The Girls"

Poppy & Holly, Aster & Laurel, Dahlia & Iris

Poppy & Daniel Ellis
Devon (son) & Nora
Theo (son)
Jericho - grandson

Holly & Alexander Carter
Aster & Dylan Roberts
Laurel & Tucker Williams
Dahlia & Linus Parks
Iris & Brooks Nelson

The Hounds

Jude "Spyder" Sterling
Zareck "The Reverend" West
Patrick "Tank" Murphy
Hawk
Sultan
King
Judge
Shadow
Ripper
Ace
Legend
Brick
Maximus
Locke

ABOUT THE AUTHOR

Multi-genre author Faith Gibson began writing in high school, and through the years, penned many stories and poems. As her dreams continued getting crazier than the one before, she decided to keep a dream journal. Many of these nighttime escapades have led to a line, a chapter, or even a complete story.

"Love is love, and there's not enough love in the world." This belief she holds strongly, and it's the prevailing theme in her works, all of which come with a happy ending.

Faith believes her purpose in life is to entertain the masses, even if it's one person at a time. Living just outside of Nashville, Tennessee, with the love of her life and her pit bull pup, when she's not hard at work writing her next adventure, she can often be found playing trivia while enjoying craft beer, listening to live music, or off on an adventure of her own.